GATEWAY

Book Five of The Hayle Coven Destinies

PATTI LARSEN

ALSO BY
PATTI LARSEN

The Hayle Coven Universe

The Hunted Series
Fiona Fleming Cozy Mysteries
The Nightshade Cases
The Clone Chronicles
The Diamond City Trilogy
Didi and the Gunslinger

and much, much more.
Find your new favorite author at
pattilarsen.com
Sign up for new releases
bit.ly/pattilarsenemail

ONE

There is no greater peace, no more amazing, soul-filling and pure joy experience than soaring on drach wings through the quiet of the veil. If I live a thousand lifetimes, I'm certain of that.

Muscles bunched and tightened, smoothed out and elongated as I swept my way against the soft current of the veil. In human form, I had no idea the depth and complexity of airflow in the vast darkness of the membrane between worlds, nor did I see so clearly just how connected the Universe truly was. But embracing my drach heritage changed all that.

What was once dim, though visible to my enhanced eyesight, now appeared crisp with firm lines and absolute clarity. Not so much seeing in the darkness as becoming part of it. The thin yet powerful barriers shimmered with the same rainbow magic as I possessed, pure, distilled energy of all magicks combined. It made me wonder what the veil in the Dark Universe looked like, if it was a mirror to ours.

Not that I'd ever have the chance to find out. But curiosity remained. I had to admit though it was a subtle thing, a soft allure where once perhaps it would have gotten me in trouble. Everything seemed ever so quiet now, gentle, soft. As though becoming drach removed the hard edges from everything but my sight.

I couldn't help the smile curving my muzzle, the fuzzy thrill I still experienced as I cut my way through the veil and soared into a new plane. The faint odor of ammonia made me sneeze, pale blue air tinted with a hint of green as I allowed the heat over the bubbling lake below to buoy me higher on a steady thermal into the eerie sky of that foreign landscape. A large pack of what looked like cows with three heads and tails shaped like they belonged on reptiles galloped over the surface of the water, huge feet splayed wide to carry them across the boiling surface. I allowed my senses to open wide, to taste the magic of this place. To seek, as I'd been seeking all these months, the familiar touch of Creator.

Nothing, not a trace. This news would have troubled the old me. As I spun on my tail and cut open the veil with a gentle slice, far more kind than the tearing jerks I used to use what seemed like a lifetime ago, my smile remained. The old me. I thought about her less and less as time passed, my drach nature a comfortable, safe and happy place.

The veil welcomed me with a gentle embrace as I slipped through, allowing the cut to seal shut behind me. How had I not felt the agony of the membrane all the time I spent as an arrogant and powerful child, possessing far more power than someone like me should have been allowed? Only when I embraced the drach inside me did I finally understand the sentience of the veil. That it was, in essence, as much Creator as the pieces of statue I sought.

So selfish, so petty and small. There were nights I woke, tears on my cheeks, old dreams of the life I left behind fading into nothing. And moments when my heart ached for those I left behind. But the quiet calm of the drach, the massive understanding I'd achieved and the sweet connection I finally had to the vastness of the Universe was the greatest thing I'd ever felt.

Peace. For the first time in my life, I knew peace. And embraced it with my entire soul.

I soared on, dipping into the next plane on my list. I'd covered a great deal of ground since I'd become drach, spending the majority of my days doing just this—searching out the parts of Creator I knew we had to find to keep our Universe safe. Grid by grid, plane by plane, with the full assistance of Max and the other drach, we slowly and carefully sought the most precious of items.

To no avail. I found it oddly amusing I was the only

one who didn't seem to find the search frustrating. Even Max—though his drach name sang in my head more often than not, old habits, and names, died hard—expressed occasional irritation at the prolonged search. But I found it comforting, the daily hunt, the quiet of the veil, the touch of Creator every time I passed through the edge and into another plane.

I couldn't bring myself to feel disappointment. Not now. Maybe not ever again.

Sydlynn. The word rang in my mind, the drach translation more authentic to me than the human spoken name. I knew Max did his best to maintain my identity through the language of the drach, but I wondered if it was for his benefit or mine.

I sang his true name back to him joyfully, because I could. *I'm almost done with my search for the day.*

As are we. I felt his companion with him soaring in his periphery. Jiao's serpentine, crimson shape shimmered with multicolored scales dominantly red and royal blue and vibrant green, long whiskers flickering in the breeze of the plane they flew over, her brightness a counterpoint to the shimmering diamond reflection of Max's hide. How had I ever thought the drach were gray? How had I missed the glittering undertone of crystalline perfection? Human sight. So lacking.

The mental image refocused to the glitter of his diamond eyes as our minds connected fully. The encompassing presence of the drach race flew with him, surrounding me with the soft song of our people, flooding my heart with such calm and peace I struggled, as always, to prevent tears from rising to the surface.

Yes, I missed my family, my children, the life I left behind. But, if they only knew how amazing this existence could be, the purity of being…

How could I ever go back?

Simple. I never would. Yes, I had a job to do, a task to fulfil. And I intended to do so. Reassembling Creator's statue, stopping Liander Belaisle from destroying our Universe by opening it to Dark Brother and the Order was my absolute priority. Saving the planes so the inhabitants of those planes could live on, be the masters of their own choices, their own destinies, that was my calling.

How simple things seemed to me now.

I exhaled into the icy air of the plane of my current search, the touch of Creator only in the membrane of the veil as I ducked through and out again, while Max's mind calmly observed.

You are content, Sydlynn? His question was familiar. Because he asked it every single day. And every day I gave the same response.

This is how things are supposed to be. The old me would have been angry by now, to be questioned so frequently, as though he didn't believe I could embrace my life. But instead I found myself laughing at him as I always did while showing him the joy in my heart.

Why did that make him sad?

We will meet you at the Stronghold, he sent, before gently releasing me.

I pondered his seeming lack of enthusiasm for my happiness as I checked the final five planes on my list. I flew gracefully and effortlessly over a dead landscape of burned out forest and dying grasslands, through a pink sunset across a patch of soaring mountains topped with orange snow. As my gaze skimmed over a wide river alive with massive, leaping fish with human eyes, I searched not only for Creator's pieces, but for any trace of regret in my heart.

It should have been there, perhaps. Was that why Max was so sad? Should I be feeling guilt, grief, loss, emptiness? I simply couldn't comprehend such emotions, not while my wings snapped against the currents of air, my long neck curving when I slipped through the veil, body spinning in absolute joy as I barrel rolled my delight over the leaping fish.

I'd let go of everything and everyone when I left the plane of my birth. Including the maji to whom I belonged, in favor of the bloodline of the drach. And, in doing so, I seemed to have erased all need to return to those I'd once clung to in desperation and longing.

How curious this lack of regret. I sighed into the quiet

darkness and winged for home. The Stronghold felt more like a place to call by that name than any house or dorm room I'd once inhabited. As I slipped through the veil and into the once dead plane, dipping over the surface of the endless, stone castle, its walls reaching far into the distance, much further than I'd ever imagined as a maji, I realized at last what troubled Max. Not that I had no regrets. But the fact I'd swung so far in the opposite direction.

Once there would have been voices to talk this conundrum over with. Three of them, one quiet, one full of fire, and a third with the delicacy of a princess. Once. Not these days, though. And maybe that should have bothered me, too.

I settled on the wall, transforming into human shape as I touched down. Instead of proceeding inside immediately, I leaned over the stone and looked down at the lush, green grass of the meadow, the happily burbling river. My actions had woken the sleeping plane many years ago, the downfall of Belaisle and the dark prophecy allowing this place to wake at last.

Max's presence during my contemplation didn't surprise me. Yes, he lived here, too. But he seemed to follow me around with a hangdog expression at times, as though anticipating some kind of breakdown on my behalf. Which meant his heavy silence was about as familiar as he joined me in looking out over the thriving plane.

You worry I've forgotten who I was. He was right. It was easy to forget, the notion I should reach out and find the voices of the girls. The reason for their silence slipped away as quickly as it had risen.

The woman you were, he sent, soft and contemplative, *shaped this Universe in ways even I could not have foreseen. And I fear her loss is our loss.*

I turned to face him, hurt waking in my quiet heart. *You begrudge me this happiness?* He, of all people, who'd lived more lifetimes than any other in all creation. Surely he understood.

Never, he sent, diamond eyes more beautiful, more vibrant, color intensity increasing with his emotional state. *But with each passing day I fear for our Universe.* He looked out again, tall and powerful and so still he appeared like a shining statue. When he spoke out loud, I jumped slightly. "You have earned happiness, Syd. But you must know the Universe isn't done with you yet."

"I am doing Creator's work." Old anger stirred, then quieted. I didn't want it anymore, the acrid tang of it in the back of my throat, the way it made my heart clench, my skin tingle.

"You are," he said. "And it was I who planted this idea in your psyche not so long ago. That your insistence on embracing the small problems of those around you interfered with your ability to do what needed to be done to save the Universe." He shook his head, looking down, hands folded before him. His vast drach form was visible to me even though he wore humanoid shape, wings spread over his back like ghostly webs. "And perhaps this transition was necessary to allow you reprieve."

"What are you saying?" Panic woke, a feeling I hadn't encountered in what felt like a lifetime.

"That we are failing, Sydlynn," he said. "And will continue to fail, I fear, without the assistance of those I drove you from."

So much hurt and guilt in his voice. The panic faded from me, replaced by bitter anger I thought I'd shed. It surged like a bucking horse into my chest, choking me even as I spoke.

"A little late now," I snapped. "I've made my choice."

He met my eyes, his sad. "So you have."

I didn't get to respond, to push past the fury I hated so much, the old anger I'd thought long gone. Max turned and left me, descending from the top of the wall down the wide stone stairs and into the Stronghold.

Only then did I notice Jiao watching. The *lóng's* quiet observation used to make me uncomfortable, nervous even. But now I knew better. Understood how deeply Jiao cared, how hard it was for her to express that caring outside the slow, steady and constant pressure of her gaze.

I approached her, embraced her. She stiffened in my

arms until my presence made her relax somewhat. Her touch opened her heart to me like nothing else had ever done. The first time I embraced her and felt the depth of her emotions was an awakening for me.

"Who would have thought," I said with a smile as I let her go, "that you would become my closest friend?"

Humor flickered in her eyes. "Says you."

I laughed and linked arms with her, leading her to the stairs. "You agree with Max?"

Jiao sighed, barely audible, more a feeling through contact with her body than a sound. "You already know how I feel," she said. "We've both walked away from the lives we knew, left behind those we loved and who loved us. My brother and sister reside still under the control of Empress Moa." As did the rest of the handful of her people who remained in existence. Max's supposition her race was the next evolution of drach did nothing to alleviate the fact that same race was almost extinct but for a few. "I think," she said, "you should do what you choose to do and to hell with duty."

Why didn't her firm words make me feel better?

We parted at the dining hall, Jiao not questioning me as I bypassed the impressive room, the large number of drach taking a meal together within. She rarely questioned me, one of the reasons we got on so well. A quick visit to the kitchen for a simple plate of stew and some fresh bread were all I needed.

I still wasn't accustomed to the open stares, the touch of drach minds, the way their subtle awe made me feel as though I belonged and, then again, didn't. My people did nothing to purposely make me uncomfortable, but their scrutiny and unabashed and genuine emotion still made my skin creep slightly.

I perched in my usual place on the window sill of my quarters and watched the sun set, enjoying the simple pleasure of the meal as my mind settled. Max was wrong. This was the right choice. How could I feel so absolutely at home, at peace with myself, if he was correct? Surely Creator wouldn't offer me this perfection of existence only to tear it away from me again?

Surely.

I set aside my plate and my worries and sank into the comfort of my bed, closing my eyes. I'd chosen. And I couldn't bring myself to change my mind.

His hazel eyes spark with green, blond hair shimmering with a hint of red as he smiles at me, full lips parting, showing off flashing white teeth. Kindness radiates from him, and sadness, though his love pours over me like a waterfall. I reach for him, unable to stop myself, fingertips almost touching, almost.

But he's falling away from me, tears on his cheeks, body impacting the ground below, disappearing under the dirt in an upward explosion of dark soil while he reaches for me, pale face full of regret and longing. I fall to my knees in the place where he disappeared, weeping now, my tears wetting the earth. The ground shudders under me, splits open, sending me back as an oak tree erupts from the depths and surges overhead, leaves shuddering in the air, sighing my name.

Sighing his.

I weep even as the ground below me splits wider, the roots of the oak tree pulling me underground, jerking me into the moist depths, smothering me with the cool pressure of earth. I smell fabric softener and feel the touch of soft cotton even as voices cry out to me, voices I know as well as my own. Who are they? The fiery one, the one of the earth with the heart of green. The cool, white one with the logical mind… they fade away as a single, crisp voice breaks through, though not the one I was expecting. Not Liam's.

Syd. *Her desperation is obvious, clear and poignant. I open my eyes and find Alison Morgan, my dead best friend, hovering before me.* Go home.

I gape at her, heart pounding. I can't. *I just can't. I've left it all behind—*

SYD. *She flies backward, voice a wail as the dark swallows her.* GO HOME.

TWO

Sheets flew sideways, my body spasming as I sat upright, panting into the cool darkness of my room. Something squeezed my right wrist, so painful in a pain free body I rubbed at it to try to make it stop. My drach senses, heightened by the form of the first race, flooded with smells and sounds I'd forgotten.

The crackle of fire, the scent of smoke.

The heavy, wet odor of fresh turned earth augmented with the whisper of a spring breeze.

And the light, crisp, yet dusty touch that tickled my nose while the glow of white light seemed to wake all around me.

What... that voice, cool but soft. I knew it, didn't I? Had just heard it in my dream. But it was only a nightmare, nothing more. While my drach heart whispered there was no such thing as "only".

Something—some*one*—stretched inside me, made me shudder, while the aroma of burning increased, the spark of flame waking even as it—she—did.

So sleepy, she whispered.

I rubbed the sides of my head, my throbbing temples, my drach soul soothing me, easing back around the stirring in my mind. But the third scent grew stronger, too, the burbling of water and the insistent, heady presence of new summer pushing back the calm and retreat I'd lived in since shedding the life I knew.

What's happened? Shaylee. Her name was Shaylee. A princess of the Sidhe, Seelie daughter of Aoilainn, queen of the realm.

With that knowledge, everything flooded back, their presence, their influence. And, as it did, the drach in me retreated with a sigh of regret that made my throat ache.

The girls. The egos I carried inside my mind. I hadn't shed them when I'd chosen this life. I'd purposely kept them with me. But in a fog that tried to return and mask my thoughts I realized again—as I had on the wall a few short hours ago—they'd been gone ever since. Only this time the understanding didn't fade, the curiosity and concern remaining.

Gone where?

We're still here. My vampire seemed confused, drowsy.

My demon snarled, uncoiled, on alert. So painful compared to the dullness, her anxiety and anger. *I'll repeat*

Shaylee's question, she sent. *What the hell happened?*

I shook my head, sat back with my shoulders pressed to the wall, drawing my knees up to my chest. *I don't know.* Tears threatened. Why was I sad? I tried to reach for the drach quiet only to feel the girls fading. They fought this time, clawed and pushed and cried out. I immediately stopped trying to retreat and shivered.

I think I understand, my vampire sent. There was sorrow in her tone, too.

An explanation would be peachy. My demon's harsh temper made me wince. Was she always this corrosive?

Yes, Shaylee sniffed.

Right, they could hear my thoughts. Though my demon didn't seem to take offense.

The drach, my vampire sent. *By accepting the power and form of the first race, you're smothering us.* Even she winced at the term while I shuddered from it. *I remember feeling elated we were leaving, a new beginning. And then... darkness.*

I fell asleep. My demon sounded puzzled. *How could I fall asleep at a time like that?*

We all did. Shaylee's mind spun inside mine, as though she looked around. *But it's more than that, isn't it?* She seemed to tug and pull at the edges of herself, power growing stronger as she did. *Not smothering*, she sent at a whisper with a hint of horror. *Absorbing.*

Oh. My. Swearword.

You mean she's eating us? My demon's fury roared in my

head, but my vampire's huffed sigh calmed her down while I rested my aching head on my knees and let her handle it, emotional overload clenching my heart in a hard, thudding ball.

Don't be ridiculous. My vampire softened. *But, if Shaylee is right—and I suspect we're thinking the same thing—if Syd hadn't experienced the nightmare, if we hadn't woken at that moment, eventually the personalities that make us up would be gone.*

Did that mean what made me was going, too?

Likely, Shaylee sent, as kindly as she'd ever spoken.

I can't go back to being the way I was before. That road led to hurt and loss and the little things.

Agreed, my vampire sent.

But no way are you swallowing me whole, my demon snapped. *We've had this fight before, Syd. I won't let you destroy who I am.*

My vampire didn't defend me this time. And I wasn't surprised. Nor did I want her to. Because I needed the girls.

Didn't I?

And yet, the last few months I'd spent as a drach... I hadn't.

Didn't find Creator's pieces, did you? My demon's snort of derision hurt, the reminder painful. *Miss I Don't Need Anyone Else.*

Smartass demon

Syd didn't do this on purpose. Shaylee's kindness held an

edge. *But now we know… what are we going to do about it?*

There must be balance, my vampire sent. *A way for Syd to remain drach and maintain the peace she's found while the three of us continue to exist.*

We all fell silent, even the black ribbon around my wrist relaxing. I looked down at it. Stroked it softly. The drach soul I'd been given, a dying gift from Andre Dumont, wasn't from our Universe. At least that's what Max seemed to think. It had latched onto me and never released its hold. I'd forgotten it, too, in my descent into drach.

Was that what being first race meant? Forgetting everything? But no, Max had his memories, painful and aching. Of the schism he caused, breaking Creator's magic into the elemental parts, causing the creation of the Dark Universe with his act. So what was really going on?

It's not like your mind is blank from your time being drach, my vampire sent. *I can access those memories. But, it's like you've been in a fog.*

I examined them myself, chest hurting. And agreed with her.

The drach in me exhaled, reached out to wrap me up in its kind peace. While the girls again struggled for their own existence. Forcing me to put a wall between them and who I'd become.

Not a perfect solution. My vampire squirmed against the barrier. *But, I suppose, the best we can do until we figure this out.*

My demon added a layer to the wall herself, Shaylee copying her. My vampire did so last, reluctantly, while I felt the perfect calm I'd existed in fading further from me.

Could I live with that? No choice. Not if it meant losing the girls. Even I wasn't that selfish.

Yes, my own personal ego whispered to me, nasty and biting. *You are. You left everyone you loved behind. Why not them, too?*

Oh, shut up.

I sat up most of the rest of the night staring out the window into the quiet darkness, watching the stars spin overhead, the silence of the black turning slowly over into daylight. I blinked into the rising sun, surprised to find my body tight and cramped where I perched still with my back to the wall, arms around my knees, muscles rigid. I rubbed endlessly at the flexing, hot circle of black, like a touchstone of calm I wished would make me feel better.

What do you want to do about the dream? My vampire's soft voice still startled, reminding me with a slap to my cheek about the thought, long gone, that crossed my mind on the Stronghold's wall just last night. And how many more times before had I remembered, only to forget in the lull that was my drach mind? She and the others I carried inside me backed my departure 100%, supporting my decision to join the drach, to cut ties and do what I had to do. I don't recall when I realized their presence disappeared, absorbed inside the vast power that was the drach side of me. But, with my vampire's renewed touch, I grasped at her with a faintly needy mental grab that shocked and chilled me.

And made me feel more human than I had in a long time.

I don't know. I whispered back to her, shivering inside. *It was just a nightmare.* So nice to talk to her again. How could I have just let her go?

Was it? My demon's mental voice had lost its anger, though she still sounded slightly sullen. *Didn't feel like just anything to me. Considering it woke us up where nothing else has... wouldn't you agree that's significant?*

Exactly. Shaylee pondered a moment. *Alison told you to go home. Could she have meant wake up? As in, wake us up and remember?*

As much as that romantic notion might appeal, my vampire sent, *I believe her command was more deliberate. And literal.*

I embraced all three of them tightly, stirring, as I did, the darkness of the sorcery inside me, the black blossom swelling and sighing at the ripples of power the girls returned to my awareness. The soft burn of the white power I shared with my sister, the strange, pale sorcery I now knew was Creator's magical intent, was the only magic to sit, calm and quiet.

Because it was part of my drach soul already. Only then did the black ribbon ease the last of its tension, an audible sigh marking the relaxation of its grip.

How interesting the newest of my powers was the first to fully integrate.

Most likely because the rest of us have had our own personality for too long. My vampire sounded sad but resigned.

I leaned my head back against the stone wall and blinked the tears away into the bright light of the rising sun. Could I just let them go, the dear voices, the strong willed women—bodiless but for me or not—the way I had everyone else? Or could I keep them with me, find a way to share who I'd become with them now we knew?

My drach form eased forward, offering love, peace, contentment. The wall between who I was and the girls faltered, sizzling as my demon's wards strained.

I had my answer.

It would seem, my vampire sent as the black flower of my sorcery folded up quietly beneath me and slumbered once more, *you can't have one without the other. More's the pity. And yet, this is the choice we all made, Syd. If you continue to be drach, if you choose to remain, eventually we will simply cease to be.*

True integration. My demon grunted, anger flaring a moment. I felt her resistance die, turn to resignation as she spun away from me, back to me, retreating. The fight gone out of her. That hurt me more than anything. We'd been together my entire life. She was my first woken ego. Could I simply let her fall into quiet and lose who she was?

Integration, Shaylee repeated. *As it is meant to be, I would imagine.* I was surprised the most emotional of all of us was the most practical and realistic in that moment. *And may eventually happen regardless.*

If I chose to be drach.

I'm sorry about this. Seemed like a weak and pathetic thing to say. But I had to say something.

Don't be. My vampire's cool spirit power brushed over me. *But now we know, are awake and aware. And we must choose together.*

Both my demon and Shaylee muttered agreement.

My heart pinched and a surge of stubborn refusal cow kicked me in the gut. *We'll figure it out*, I sent, sharp with anger so rare to me now. But hadn't I been angry twice now in less than a day when I didn't think I'd felt that emotion in weeks and weeks?

Was I willing to release my peace in order to keep the girls intact? And would doing so make my job of saving the Universe easier—or stand in my way?

There's no way of knowing, my vampire sent. *I believe we were meant to be integrated fully into you. This symbiosis, though satisfying in many ways, can't be the natural order of things.*

I don't imagine anyone else evolved the way Syd has, Shaylee sent. *Which means we have no precedent.*

You're shocked? My demon snorted a laugh. *That's us. Breaking molds, one power at a time.*

Again my eyes stung. I wiped at tears. *I missed you guys*, I whispered to them, realizing it was true. And registering the newfound ache in my heart that was the emptiness left behind by the loss of the ones I loved. The gaping wound where the family magic once lived had scabbed over, but I knew if I picked at it I could make it bleed.

The black ribbon flexed in sympathy.

Enough, my vampire sent, sharp and harsh enough to make me start. *We made our choice, all of us. There was no other to make. And I for one refuse to allow myself the pity of regret.* More murmurs, hugs from the girls, for me and for each other. *We have survived much. And we will survive this. No matter in what form.*

Together, Shaylee sent.

Just try to get rid of me, my demon growled. Paused. *For the second time.*

Should have sounded lame, but didn't. And the memory of losing her, of her capture and containment by the Chosen of the Light, only made me more convinced I'd not let them go for anything. *Wouldn't dream of it*, I sent, sniffling away the last of my tears. *Please, don't let me forget you.* Why did the idea break my heart and make me want to sob?

Their power wove around mine. *If you want us to stay, to live, to exist*, my vampire sent, *then it will be so.*

I really hoped she was right. Because I'd given up enough already, hadn't I? Shock at the resentment I felt pushed me to my feet, made me shake my head. How had I gone from loving this life to suddenly wondering what the hell I was thinking in a space of a few hours?

Stubborn, Sydlynn Hayle.

Warm water did wonders for the ache in my body, though I found myself staring in the mirror this morning like I'd never done before. At my diamond eyes, the pale gray iridescence of my drach skin. The way the soft scales played over the angles and planes of my face, my neck. I hadn't adopted the gray robe of my people, something I now knew was a simple construct of their magic, fabric woven from power, not true cloth. My legs liked jeans, my torso the softness of a t-shirt. And though Mabel had offered several times to show me how to braid my hair into the beautiful waterfall of plaits she sometimes wore to the floor, a simple ponytail sufficed for me.

So, drach, but on the other hand... still a woman of sorts. Maybe one day I'd fully shed my humanity. But doing so, I now guessed, would mean the loss of the voices in my head. There were some who might think I was nuts for wanting to preserve them.

They had no idea.

Feeling refreshed and more at ease, I had only just turned toward the door to leave my private quarters, to begin my search all over again, when something sharp stabbed deep into my heart, drawing a gasp of agony. I bent over, hands braced on my knees, panting as the beloved and desperate touch of a mind I knew better than my own reached out for me.

Gabriel. He'd been searching for me all along. This was the first time he'd broken through the drach power, the shielding I'd maintained to protect myself—and my son and family—from connecting. Maybe it was the wakening of the girls, or the dream, or just the fact he was stronger than ever before. Regardless, I felt him latch onto my mind with his own, so powerfully I had to use force to separate us again.

MOM!

I found myself on the floor, on my knees, sobbing into my hands as his presence faded, my drach power cutting him away even while the black ribbon groaned its sadness. The girls whispered comfort to me but there wasn't much they could say. For the first time since I'd left home I felt like I'd abandoned my family. The peace and ease I'd grown accustomed to shattered into shards, blades of blame and hurt slashing me over and over as I sank into guilt.

Sydlynn. My vampire's power jabbed me so sharply I gasped, shocked out of my bereavement. *Enough.*

Go to hell. I clenched my teeth, wiping at my wet cheeks with the shoulder of my t.-shirt. *What have I done?*

You don't get to fall apart, my demon sent, angry, hostile. *Not now, damn you. Get your ass up.*

UP. Shaylee shook the ground beneath me, barely a tremor, but enough to drive me to my feet. *And pull yourself together. Honestly. Such behavior.*

I almost laughed. *I'm sorry*, I sent, still choked up but successfully wrenched free from the aching agony my son's longing had created. *I'll do better.*

You bet you will, Shaylee sniffed.

What would I do without you? I hugged myself, crying again, but with less abandon and softer regret to replace the racking guilt.

Fall to pieces, clearly, my demon sent.

Sad, really, Shaylee sent in her best Sidhe princess tone of disdain.

I couldn't help it. All the emotions flooding me while I'd been so calm and without for so long made me volatile. I giggled and choked on tears while giggling some more. Snorted. Caught my breath.

Sighed.

Feel better? My vampire eased back, the girls all retreating and only then did I realize they'd been supporting me with power. Keeping me from flying apart.

I'd almost let them vanish. But I really did need them.

The dream. Shaylee hesitated a moment. *Syd, I don't think it was a dream.*

What if Gabriel was trying to tell us something? My demon rarely fretted, but she felt that way now, anxious suddenly. *Alison might know what it is.*

Alison is gone, I sent, sinking to the end of my bed. *With Sebastian and a large number of the vampires. To who knows where.* The spirit power of my home plane was all screwed up, though I discovered the focus of the damage was there, and decreased the further out I went from it. Why that was I had no idea.

Could she have managed to come back? My vampire sighed. *We have no answers. And the only way to get them—*

Is to go home. My demon sounded hesitant. So not like her.

Or, we ask Max or Mabel to find out. Shaylee's solution made sense and damn me if I wasn't cowardly enough to agree with her.

I couldn't go home, not now. Not ever, likely. Endings were meant to be forever.

Weren't they?

I'll talk to Max, I sent, rising and heading for the door, reaching for the drach inside me, asking the power I held to please, please help me find balance yet again without having to give up the connection I had to the girls. And though, as I walked into the corridor and headed for the dining hall, I felt my heart quiet, my soul calm, I knew it was a veneer this time.

I'd lost the steady stillness I'd come to adore. And I wasn't sure how I felt about that.

There is another way. My vampire's reticence made me pause. *Someone we could approach who we have no ties to, have never been tied to.*

And who might have the answers we need. My demon was nodding mentally. I waited not-so-patiently for them to get to the point.

Ameline, Shaylee sent.

That froze me in my tracks as I entered the wide entry to the Stronghold, the giant mirror that was the magical entrance shimmering on the far wall. I barely registered the drach who passed me in their slow and measured paces, nodding their greetings.

What do you mean, Ameline? What did she have to do with this?

She will know the state of things, my vampire sent. *Without having to ask Max for help.*

He would help, I sent, not sure why I felt the need to defend the drach leader.

Of course he would, she sent, familiar dry tone the same one that made me feel like she was talking slowly to a child. It used to irritate me. Yeah. Still did, turned out. *But are you prepared to tell him about the dream?*

Why shouldn't I? If it wasn't a dream, if Alison and the vampires were back...

You know how he feels about using Gabriel to find the pieces of Creator, my demon sent.

My heart snapped shut. *Never*, I shot at her, red fire flaring in my mind.

Exactly, Shaylee sent, soothing, gentle. *If you bring up a dream of your plane, he will suggest you go home and investigate. And, in doing so, open us to using Gabriel again.*

I'd sworn to myself when I left my son behind, my

daughter, my now ex-husband and everyone I loved, I'd never use them again, not ever. Me Creator was welcome to control and manipulate. But they would be left out of it.

Before we tell him anything, my vampire sent, *let's get some answers*.

Answers. Right.

Why did I have the feeling I wasn't going to like what I found?

THREE

I swept into the veil, leaping from the wall of the
Stronghold, bypassing the dining hall and Max, leaving
Jiao behind though I felt her curiosity at my departure. I
reassured her with a flashed image of the darkness, a
touch of my need to be alone. She let me go without
comment for which I was grateful.

It wasn't that I was watched or followed. Quite the
contrary. I thought being a coven leader and a witch
meant being in touch constantly with those around me. I
had no idea what true loss of privacy meant until I joined
the drach. Funny, it didn't bother me so much just
yesterday. Now, as I shifted shape and spread my wings,
soaring into the slice in the veil, I shivered at the thought
of having all those minds in mine.

And while I felt a momentary pang of loss for the
peace I'd left behind, I embraced the bits of the old me I

allowed to return, even grinning with my muzzle stretched over my sharp teeth in the perma light of the veil at the thought.

A drach with attitude. I was going to ruin everything.

I circled the edge of my plane twice before realizing I was stalling.

We could just hover here all day, my vampire sent in her dry tone.

Sounds like a hoot, my demon snarked.

Oh, honestly, Shaylee snapped. *You two. Sydlynn. Just do it*.

I drew a breath, feeling the heat inside my chest stir, the fire at my command rising in answer to my nerves. I'd only breathed flame a few times, thoroughly enjoyed the rush of excitement and exhilaration that came from the experience. Mixing power with chemical and oxygen in a blast of fiery fury from my muzzle was some of the most fun I'd ever had. For a moment, I longed to let loose and just char anything I could get my claws on, feeling a pulsing need to shout or vent or something building beneath the flames. But the pressure passed as I shifted into human form, reaching for the veil and the maji chamber beneath the vampire mansion.

For Ameline.

I quickly reinforced my shielding, shoring up any gaps or holes I might have missed as I passed out of the veil and into the stillness of the underground. The magic here stirred at my arrival, in welcome but not recognition, not any longer. This was maji power after all, and I'd given up my connection to it when I'd embraced my drach heritage.

So strange, so odd, the feeling of it welcoming me, as though afraid, hesitant, wondering what I wanted, why I was there. I soothed it as best I could, sad at the reaction, noting how much sharper everything felt, how more in tune to power I was since my change. I'd always been aware of the magic down here but never to this degree. As I stood in the quiet, breathing the faintly musty air, the magic of the maji murmured in my head, thrummed under my feet, whispered past my cheek, a living, breathing thing.

Embodied a moment later by the tall, slim form of a beautiful young woman. She hadn't aged, Ameline Benoit. Still twenty-two or so, pageboy bangs crisp over her forehead, black hair falling in silken strands, shining in the low light that glowed from the very rocks. Her expression, however, was far different than the Ameline I'd first met. Gone was the cold calculation from her icy blue eyes, replaced with kindness and worry. Her full lips pursed, her hands clenched tight before her. Ameline might not have had a physical form any longer, but she was as real to me as anyone. I'd long ago forgiven her the death of Liam, the kidnapping of Gabriel. She'd shed her ego when she'd died here, when I'd killed her. Only her soul remained behind. And as I stood there, waiting for her to speak, wondering if I'd be the one to break the silence first, I felt just how pure she'd become.

And my sorrow for her rose all over again. This life she lived, as the voice and heart of the maji chamber, wasn't much of an existence. Not once had she complained. But I could feel the hurt in her, the sorrow and the longing for freedom. Even if that meant her death, finally, fully.

I couldn't help myself. I approached her in a rush, hugged her. The power of the maji chamber was enough to give her corporeal form, as solid and real as any person. Ameline hugged me back, cheek against mine before her cool lips brushed over my face.

I was wrong. She felt more real. Pure magic.

When I pulled back from her she smiled, tears sparkling in her eyes.

"We've missed you," she said in her beautiful voice, French accent coming through faintly.

I shuddered from the truth of it. Because standing there, holding her hand still, I had to embrace the fact this visit might just break me.

"You, too," I said, managed past the lump in my throat. And stood there gaping at her, heart aching, silent and unable to muster another word.

Syd, my vampire whispered. *The dream.*

Right. Damn it. I squeezed Ameline's hand and let it

go. But, she was already talking before I could say a word.

"You look different." She cocked her head to one side. "I like the eyes. Now I'm jealous."

Another giggle, this one painful while full of the pleasure of being human again. Sort of. "Thanks," I said. "They'll do."

"Not so sure about the scales." She tapped one finger against her full lips, gaze narrowed. "They work, oddly. On you."

"Don't knock it until you try it," I said.

Ameline laughed. "I'll pass." Winked. "But I'll take your word for it."

It really wasn't that funny, but we both laughed. It felt good to laugh. To stand there with her and feel her warmth and remember she was a good person under all the horribleness that made her my enemy once upon a time.

And, at last, the final threads of anger I held against Ameline broke and fell away, leaving me refreshed.

"You're not here for skin care advice," she said. "Nor to stay, I assume."

No judging. Just fact. I nodded, swallowed.

"I had a dream last night," I said. "And you're the only one I can ask who won't pressure me to stay."

Ameline's hand reached out again, fingers slipping into mine, twining us together. "Says you," she whispered. "Tell me."

I did, halting and hurtful, remembering Liam, the oak tree's bursting growth. When I finished, Ameline shook her head, black hair rippling, eyes sad.

"There has been no word about Alison or Sebastian in the time you've been gone," she said. "Though I'm sure you know that already. The veil itself would have told you."

She was probably right. If such a surge of spirit magic had returned to my home plane I would have known about it.

"Just a dream then, I guess," I said. Sighed. A good thing though, wasn't it? That it was just a dream?

"Perhaps," Ameline said. "And perhaps not. You said she appeared to you from what felt like the burial place of Liam."

"We didn't bury Liam," I said. "We burned him."

"Exactly," she said. "So why the symbology? And why would she tell you to go home?"

Guilt? My demon chimed in.

Unlikely, my vampire sent. *Until she had the dream, Syd had no such feelings lingering.*

It was only after we woke again that her emotions came to the fore. Shaylee sounded guilty herself.

If that's the way it has to be, I sent to them all, *then so be it.*

"I'm sorry I'm unable to be of more help," Ameline said. "The only thing I can think of—if it wasn't a dream—is that somehow Alison is reaching you through the dead." She shrugged her narrow shoulders. "A stab in the dark and perhaps more morbid than is the case."

The dead. And yet, it made sense. "Spirit magic is tied to death," I said. "Interesting." But Liam was long gone, his soul free, ego passed over. It had to be nothing.

Time to say goodbye. And let this fall behind me. I had planes to patrol today and being here, so close to my old home, was beginning to wear on me. I couldn't help but hug Ameline again though. As I turned from her sad face, her forlorn expression, the air beside me suddenly flickered in shadow and two figures hurtled from formerly empty space and crashed into me.

The familiarity of being the center of a vampire sandwich almost ruined me. Sunny pressed her body to me, arms tight around my shuddering body, cheek against mine as Uncle Frank squashed me from behind, his strong grip not only engulfing me but his beautiful wife. Trapped and helpless, I sagged against them a moment, breathing in the soft scent of Sunny's shampoo from her thick, blonde hair, the warmth of their skin—they'd eaten, clearly. And feeling the subtle thrum of their spirit magic linking with the vampire inside me.

I have to go. I threw that horrified burst of desperation at the girls.

No, my vampire whispered. *You don't.*

Not yet, my demon sent, wistful and soft.

Just a moment, Shaylee begged.

35

I was going to die.

"Syd," Sunny whispered. "Oh, Syd. Thank the elements." She leaned back and I realized I was, in fact, still alive, though I wasn't sure for how much longer as my heart was about to give out on me. She blinked tears, long lashes fluttering, pale blue eyes full of grief and a splash of hope.

I turned from her, landing me right into Uncle Frank's arms. Not that I intended it. Or did I? I just couldn't trust myself anymore, it seemed. He hugged me so tight even my drach human form felt it.

"Don't leave," he murmured in my ear, over and over. "Please, don't leave." A litany.

Sunny's hand settled between my shoulder blades, made soft circles as I panted my pain into my uncle's chest. When I finally pushed away I think he knew, they both knew, this was temporary. Though if I stayed much longer I wasn't so sure.

"How?" I'd shielded against them, damn it all.

"Triggers," Sunny said, stumbling over words, hands reaching for me even as I backed away. "We've all set them, just in case you showed up. Syd, we're so glad you're here."

I shook my head, continuing my backward motion. I reached for the veil, fumbled at the edges of it, but couldn't quite manage to open a gap. It was as though my entire being rebelled against my need to flee from them, from the jabbing agony of their eagerness and love.

So much love. I could feel the bonds forming all over again, the same ones I'd destroyed, cut off on purpose. And slashed at them, freeing myself once more. It hurt this time around.

Hurt a lot.

"Thanks for the warning," I grated between clenched teeth. "I'll watch for them from now on."

Sunny's face crumpled but she refused to quit. "Syd, please, listen. We need you. The plane…" she glanced at Uncle Frank, at his grim expression, his slumped shoulders. "Everything is falling apart, Syd. We can't do this without you."

I stared at her, heart pounding. No, I couldn't get drawn in again. Couldn't.

"I, too, fear for us," Ameline said, soft and sad. "I worry about the maji, Syd."

I shook my head, a sharp gesture of denial. "Not my problem."

Is it not? My vampire sighed. *Perhaps you should let me sleep after all.*

I barely refrained from reminding her she'd been with me in my choice. She didn't have the right to back out now.

Sunny stiffened, turned half away, hands cupping her elbows. "Maybe not," she said. "But we need you, nonetheless. And I'm not above begging."

Why was she doing this to me? "I had my reasons!" I didn't mean to shout at her, at the three of them, at the voices in my head. "Don't you get it? I had to go! I had no choice." I panted after the words, realizing I'd been wanting to say them to someone for a long time. Had to get them out.

Had to find a way to believe them myself.

Uncle Frank slipped one arm around Sunny's shoulders, pulled her against him. "We know," he said. "And while we might not understand why, Syd, we all get that you only do what you have to do. That we need to trust you made the choice you did because it was your only option. We believe in you, always have." Damn him for making me feel worse and worse and worse with every word. Why wouldn't he just shut up or scream back or accuse me of something already? An attack I could handle. This?

Not this.

"Syd." Ameline's smooth voice cut me just as deep for all its reasonableness. "No one blames you."

Except me.

"We're trying," Sunny said. Wept. Head down, blonde hair hanging around her shivering body. "But I don't think we can hold things together much longer." When she looked up, her blue eyes were full of such desolation I had to clench myself rigid to keep from running to her and hugging her. "We know you can't come home. But, please. Find a way to help us."

Could I do that? Allow the little things back into my life?

Who says they are little? My demon's snarl had enough anger in it for all of us. Her, too? Traitor. *We agreed with you when we made the choice to leave. But if things have changed...*

I unclenched slightly, reached out with my completely shuttered mind. Just a peek. Just a quick glance into the world around me. Enough to decide what to do, I told myself.

Didn't make it far. Gasped. The mansion above me wasn't empty as I expected. The first thing I encountered was the presence of spirit magic. A lot of spirit magic.

The house was packed full of vampires.

FOUR

I didn't get to ask Sunny and Uncle Frank why what seemed like the entire population of their race was hunkered down in their house above. The beautiful blonde beat me to it.

"They've come looking for help," she said. Almost apologetically. As if they'd made some horrible error.

Uncle Frank didn't seem to agree with her. As his arm slid around her shoulders again, pride beamed from his handsome face when he spoke.

"Moa went into hiding shortly after you left," he said, without a trace of accusation. At least I chose to believe he didn't blame it on me. "The entire vampire race was left without their Empress."

Sunny snorted, a delicate sound. Everything she did, even something as ungraceful as snorting, seemed perfect.

Funny how the small things, the odd and quiet things about the people I'd left behind, seemed to jump out at me now. Was I so lost in what I'd been I'd failed to truly see them as they really were?

And yourself, in the bargain, my vampire sent, soft and kind.

Likely.

"The Empress," Sunny said with enough heavy sarcasm to make me grin despite myself, "might have thought herself a guiding spirit of our race, but since she ran like the rat she is we're better off." A faint tint of pink colored her cheeks, though from embarrassment at speaking that way or from the heat of her words I wasn't sure. "Not that coming here was a much better idea."

Embarrassment. But why?

"Whatever, Sunshine," Uncle Frank said, planting a kiss on the top of her head. As if she wasn't a powerful vampire queen or anything. Just his wife who he loved with all his heart. It made me choke a little on emotion. Damn it. "They came to you because they know what true leadership looks like."

Now she really was embarrassed, deprecating, a frown pulling her perfectly shaped eyebrows together. "I wouldn't say that," she said.

"Don't have to." Uncle Frank winked at me, slow smile on his full lips. Just like old times.

Would it really be this easy to slip back into my old

life?

"I'm doing my best," Sunny said.

It was Ameline's turn to speak up. "More than that," she said, thoughtful and frowning herself. "Your altered magic, I assume, has given you some edge, has it not?"

That was right. Sebastian's power had changed when I saved his life, using maji magic to revive him years ago. In doing so, I'd fundamentally rearranged his power as much as his life. Gave him back his heartbeat, for one. As for the rest, I had no idea just how far the changes had gone. Though, before he disappeared, he'd been able to walk in sunlight for years and didn't seem restricted to only spirit magic, but had access to maji—at least, a version of it—as well.

"I don't know," Sunny said. "We've been trying to figure that out." Her hands clenched together in front of her, fingers pulling at the cuffs of her cream silk blouse. "I have, as yet, to feel the pull—or whatever it is that has taken other vampires from us—decimating our race. And, a time or two, have managed to keep a few of our people from vanishing."

"Making the other vampires think you have a solution." It made perfect sense.

Indeed, my vampire sent.

"But," I said, "if Sebastian had the same ability, why is he gone?"

Sunny shrugged. "As I said, I don't know if that is the

reason, though we must assume it's the case. And, knowing Sebastian, he chose to follow the pull. Went willingly." She smiled, soft and sad. "His curiosity, like a cat's, has led him places he shouldn't go in the past. I see no reason why that wouldn't be the case now."

And Alison would have gone with him, even if it meant traveling to the end of the Universe.

"The trouble is," Sunny said, still frowning, fingers now twining over and over again around each other, though I was sure she was unaware of the gesture, "we have no idea how we're keeping vampires here. And, once one is targeted," she grimaced at the word, "even if we bring them back it's only a short time before the pull on the target vampires happens again and they are gone."

"But word got around," I said. "And now you're inundated."

"They're still coming in," Uncle Frank said. "From all around the world." He squeezed Sunny's shoulders with his arm. "Abandoning their queens for the chance of salvation."

I needed to find Moa, to figure out why she was in hiding. She had to help her people. And there was the fact Sunny seemed to be able to save the vampires temporarily. Maybe I could work out a more permanent solution—

It hit me like a five pound sledgehammer in the face. The moment I realized what I was doing. What was happening. And, in that moment, I gasped a breath and staggered backward, away from them, slamming up a wall of shielding between us.

I didn't have to say anything, though my heart trembled and my head spun. Sunny pulled free of Uncle Frank and came to me, slipping physically through my shields, pressing her cool lips to my cheek as I shook and wanted to weep.

"Go," she whispered in my ear. "Find Creator's pieces and save the Universe. And then, my darling Syd, come back to us."

She backed away, sadness in her eyes. And pride. For me.

I wanted to die right then and there.

Proud. How could she be proud? I was failing even at the promise I made to myself, weakening by the moment.

Uncle Frank watched me go, silent and sorrowful, as I tore open the veil and stepped through. Only Ameline appeared serene, thoughtful. It made me wonder if she knew something I didn't.

Not that it mattered. The moment I passed into the veil I reached for my drach form. And, for the first time in a long time, struggled to find it. Almost wept when it evaded me. Latched onto the shape and bulk of my true form the moment it became available again. Panted through my muzzle, puffs of smoke escaping as I spread my wings.

I would not succumb. I would not go to Wilding Springs, to Harvard. I would not.

Would. Not.

But, even in drach form, I finally had to admit as my wings trembled and I fought for balance with each sweep of them, I was weak.

So cruel, Shaylee whispered. *We are strong, Syd.*

All of us together. My demon's pouting tone sat heavy in my head.

Peace, my vampire murmured. *This too shall pass. And we will be better for it.*

I only hoped she was right.

My wings ached, shoulders pulling against what was once so natural. I ignored the pain as my vampire spoke again.

If the plane is in trouble, she sent, *perhaps it would be in our best interest to check in from time to time.*

I resisted immediately, almost violently, flames escaping my muzzle this time as I belched my agony into the veil.

Not to visit, my demon sent. *To observe. To aid and assist.*

Silently, Shaylee agreed. *Without them knowing.*

Impossible. I slapped them all down. *You should know that by now. Impossible for me to meddle and not become embroiled in their petty problems.*

You took Max's words, spoken I think in anger, too close to heart, my vampire sent, more aggressively than normal.

Even he recanted. And though I was with you in the beginning, I'm wondering if it was the right choice to leave entirely. You seem to insist the lives of those we care about aren't important, something I never *agreed with.*

My demon grumbled, Shaylee sighing.

Important, I sent, *yes. To me, to you three. But, vital to the protection of the Universe?*

Not one of the trio had anything to say to that.

Surprise, surprise.

I won't make what I did a mockery by returning without excellent reason, I sent. *I won't waste the time I've spent, the effort, the heartache we all endured leaving on a whim. Nothing has changed.*

How I wished that was true, even though I knew everything had. Because I could feel them again. The ones I'd severed myself from. Hints and whispers of them, of their lives. Not the tethered threads I'd cut, not that deep. But the echo of where they had been remained, growing in power and awareness.

Try as I might to reach for the calm of the drach, I was failing. And the girls were the reason.

You can't have it all, my vampire sent.

This meant I had to decide if I was willing to give up everything, after all. Even them.

My heart had never felt so heavy, a weighted lump of iron in my chest, as I winged my way to the Stronghold.

FIVE

The moment I passed through the veil at the Stronghold, I spun and retreated again. I simply couldn't bear to return feeling this way. Jiao would know, would prod and poke until I confessed my feelings. At the very least, Max would feel guilty over the choice I now faced. And he carried enough misery and regret with him for a thousand lifetimes. He didn't need more of mine to add to that.

Instead, I soared the veil, forcing myself to focus, to ignore the steady presence of the black ribbon's pressure, returning with my stress. To struggle between losing the girls and falling into quiet. Not on the pieces of Creator. Those, I feared, were lost to us without assistance. Aid I would never ask for again. At least, not from the one who had the ability to find them for me. I'd used my son that way for the last time.

No, this time my search was more personal and, despite my drach nature, fed by a need for vengeance. Even at my most acclimatized to my new form, I'd retained my animosity for Liander Belaisle and Eva Southway. And I longed for the moment I found them. In full drach form.

Breathing fire.

Those kinds of thoughts gave me happy dreams.

Bad Syd. Not very drach of me.

Couldn't bring myself to feel guilty about it, not even a scrap. The former leader of the sorcerer's Brotherhood and the traitorous Steam Union head both earned a messy and hopefully painful end by my hands. Claws. And I was more than happy to deliver.

I just had to find their slippery little butts first.

Thing was, I was certain they weren't hiding on my home plane. I'd felt far too many traces of the pair of them in the veil to assume they were anywhere near there. And, though it pained me to do so, if I allowed myself to put my own thought process in Belaisle's ugly assed shoes, it made sense for him to create a home base—or possibly multiple bases—throughout the Universe to evade my searching.

The man was nothing if not clever. And slippery. But we'd see just how smart he was when I crushed the life from his body and drank his blood from his still beating heart.

My, my, my vampire sent, clearly amused. *How bloodthirsty.*

Damned straight, my demon snarled. *Bet he's tasty.*

Doubt it, Shaylee sniffed. *Most likely his foul blood will give us a belly ache.*

I loved them. Loved them.

So much.

Could I ever give them up? Choose to release them forever, their personalities, in favor of my own happiness? And was it really happiness I'd found being a drach, or another way to hide from who I was meant to be?

I hated doubting myself.

Searching for Belaisle and Eva gave me something to do when I wasn't hunting the pieces of Creator. Because, honestly, the only reason he was out here was for the same mission. And maybe if I finally caught up with him I'd be able to retrieve the pieces he stole from me.

With Trill Zornov's help. I shook my big head, snorting more smoke into the veil as I allowed my senses to expand, my power to seek the faintest trace of the pair. I wouldn't think of my former friend or her betrayal. It didn't matter now. She wasn't my problem. Unless she got in my way again.

Then we'd have a problem.

You seem to be slipping back into old habits. My vampire

sighed. *Temper, Syd.*

I like her temper, my demon sent.

Shaylee laughed. *Of course you do.*

But my vampire's words had the opposite effect on me. *You're right,* I sent, drawing a deep breath, exhaling. My shoulders eased, the tightness in my wings falling away, making it easier to fly. *This isn't about revenge. It's about Creator.*

Revenge would be a happy byproduct.

Oh, Syd.

I spun through a few planes, from purple sky to crimson to gold, before settling on the side of a mountain in a quiet, humid world, twisting vines and towering trees seeming to move of their own accord, as though sentient. And, for all I knew, they were. Instead of investigating, frustrated by another dead end, I folded my wings and closed my eyes.

He was here. Briefly. Searching as I was searching. But, from here, the trail ran cold.

For all I knew, Belaisle was leading me on a wild sorcerer chase. Wouldn't be the first time he screwed with me nor, I imagined, the last. And I just couldn't resist taking the bait.

Tired and frustrated, knowing the futility of my search and worn at the edges from the past day's emotional turmoil—not to mention my lack of sleep the night before—I tucked my chin against my broad chest and settled onto my haunches, claws hooking securely around the pale lavender rock below me.

A nap would do me a world of good.

My vampire's soothing voice hummed in the back of my mind while Shaylee's Sidhe, pure and clear, sang me a lullaby.

He appears to me from the darkness, hands outstretched, though this time he seems grief stricken, terrified. I try to scream as I lunge, plunging into the black after him, but he is tumbling again, falling from me, swallowed by the dimness while the voices of my demon, Shaylee and vampire call for me to come back, to stay with them. No matter how hard I flap my wings, how much power I pour into my own descent, I know it's futile.

Liam is gone. Has been gone for a long, long time.

I crash suddenly from the dark onto a stone floor, thudding heavily in human form. Look up to see him standing over me, weeping. He turns and points around him before vanishing without a trace. But I know where I am. I've been here before.

The crypt under Harvard. Where my family's bones reside. While the black ribbon wraps around my neck and chokes me into darkness.

I woke with my wings already unfurled, fell into the sky in a swooping dive, the veil parting before me. I didn't think, didn't doubt. Just acted. Because Liam asked me to.

It wasn't until the veil parted and I stepped through into the dull quiet of the underground in human form I realized what I'd done. Without a second thought, I'd thrown away my promise to myself yet again, the assurance that I would remain detached from the place where I came from.

But Liam's message—if it was a message and not just my imagination running rampant—seemed so powerful I simply couldn't deny it. Which led me here. To the crypt.

Where the echoes of my family remained with their bones.

It was, not to be overly dramatic or incite a pun groan, deathly quiet in that dark and solemn place. I seemed to recall it being less creepy and more active feeling the last time I was down here. Mind you, I'd been in a state of utter shock, believing my son was alive despite proof to the contrary, and that the bones in his place were that of an imposter. And I'd been far from alone, surrounded by the living more than the dead.

This time, only those who had passed were here to attend me. And, it seemed, as I slowly turned in a circle to look around, half hoping I'd see my long lost husband's soul despite knowing it was impossible, even those who had once been a part of the Hayle bloodline were silent. Not a single echo flickered into existence, the muffled feeling of the air swallowing everything, including my breath. I had to remind myself to draw air, coughing softly on the mustiness of it, hands firmly in my back pockets as I shivered with gooseflesh.

The only echo I wished to appear was Liam's. But he wasn't a witch. And his soul was long gone, the part of him that might have lingered passed to my son through the power of the Sidhe Gate his family guarded for so long. We'd burned Liam's bones, knowing as a Sidhe he didn't have an echo.

No matter the truth, I let myself hope. Even moved forward with nervous fingers stroking the quiet ribbon around my wrist, nowhere near choking me into oblivion. I moved deeper into the crypt, reaching out for Liam as I neared the back of the space where once the body of a normal infant took the guise of Gabriel.

She appeared in a wavering image, startling me as I gasped a breath, hands lurching upward from my pockets to clutch at my chest in shock. Her echo was soft around the edges, wavering and loose, as though she struggled to form. I knew her face, the familiar bone structure of the Hayle women I was descended from. It didn't seem to matter how many generations passed, we all carried the same high cheekbones, wide jaw, full mouth, blue eyes. Her dark hair was curled elaborately, redder than mine, piled at the nape of her neck, curling over the rim of her lace collar. Her gown shimmered, pale green, hands reaching out to me.

"Please, tell me," she said in a voice so soft I had to

lean closer to hear her, "have you seen my darling Sassafras?"

I have no idea where the tears came from, how they emerged so fast, so hot, so uncontrollably. No, that's a lie. I knew. From the heartbreak of the reminder of my loss. I staggered back from her, hands covering my mouth this time, unable to stop the deep, ragged sob that tore my throat, the gushing tears, now silent, pouring down my cheeks and over my fingertips.

She didn't seem to notice, longing on her face. "I beg you," she said. "It's been so long and I miss him so much. Can you tell me of him? Is he well?"

There was only one person she could be. And even as her name, carved on the rock of her tomb, read murkily through her wavering form, came clear, I whispered her name.

"Thaddea." Of course, Thaddea. The Hayle witch who'd started it all, who'd formed our coven. Who'd rescued Sassafras from England and brought him to the family. The witch whose name I bore.

"Does he yet protect the family Hayle?" Thaddea's own tears were crystal sparkles on her echo's face. "Has he found happiness of his own?"

Damn her and her questions. A surge of anger—guilt fed and hot—tore away my distress. With a chopping motion of one hand I silenced her, pulling at the necromancy I had at my disposal. I'd done little about it since discovering it in my teens, but it remained, that unique power to call the dead. And banish them, if I so chose. Rusty, far from adept, I pushed against her, feeling her try to resist. But she was already weak, and, as I shoved her down, sent her back to the darkness from where she'd come, I felt the pain I caused her. And hesitated.

Not her fault. Syd, for the love of the elements.

I did my best to stop, to ease the passage, to soften her retreat. But it was too late, she was gone and the touch of her echo with her. I slumped, knowing I'd done her a disservice, my ancestor who only wanted to make sure her beloved Sassafras—my beloved Sassafras—was all right. And though I knew I couldn't truly hurt her echo, that her spirit was safe and the part of her remaining was simply a shadow of her ego, it still troubled me I'd reacted so badly.

Jaw clenched, refusing to be that person, I reached for Thaddea again. And tried to pull her out.

Only to run right into a wall of black, thick and cloying. It felt like the veil but not quite. Deeper and suffocating, drawing me in even as I pulled away. My mental fingers brushed over the edge of Thaddea and, without thinking, I jerked at her, trying to free her, too.

No, not Thaddea. With a gasp of shock I realized who it was I'd touched. Even as Alison Morgan's power slipped away from me.

I dove in after her again, roaring in my drach power, throwing the rainbow light of it after my old bestie. The white sorcery I'd so recently taken on flickered to life, licking at the edges of the dark, pushing it back. I strained to find her again, to touch her, while the black ribbon groaned and pulled against me.

Fought me. But it was too late. I felt her. Grasped hold. And pulled her to me with all my strength while the ribbon begged me silently to let her go.

I gasped and folded in half as she appeared, as though pulling her through opened a hole in my magic, sucking at the strength within me. Like a hole in a bucket, my energy gushed from me while Alison, her pale face afraid, gestured at me. Her mouth moved as I groaned from the loss of magic, trying to tell me something I couldn't hear.

Another moment and I was going to pass out. Alison broke the link on her end, the snap and crackle of the separation making me cry out from pain while the black ribbon slashed from ours. I fell to my knees on the stone floor, panting as my strength slowly returned, looking up at last into the eyes of Thaddea Hayle.

She wept into her hands. "Oh, Sassafras," she whispered. "Where are you?"

I gaped up at her even as her echo faded once more, vanishing. It took a moment to regain my feet, to inhale and exhale regularly, without making my lungs ache. Even as my wrist felt like it might be broken. I looked down at the writhing ribbon while my power returned to me, but it was as though I'd been in a giant battle on no sleep for a week.

What the hell was that? And what did the black ribbon have to do with it?

I leaned against the stone wall, forehead beaded with sweat, marking the tomb of one of my foremothers. Which one I didn't know. But I was grateful for her support just then. Even if only in the form of cool, solid rock.

It wasn't until I felt the tug of power, magic I knew as well as my own, I jerked upright and immediately reached for the veil. Fear coursed through me, panic so strong I was already leaping through and into the dark beyond before the woman on the other end could finish frantically screaming my name in my head.

She didn't have to, not to identify herself, at any rate.

Like I would ever forget my own mother.

SIX

Flying seemed even harder this time, though I managed to wrestle myself back under control more quickly than before. By the time I reached the Stronghold the ache across my shoulders and chest carried over into my human form. As though the drach I'd become was fighting the woman I'd been.

I wasn't enjoying the analogy or the reality.

It didn't help Max stood in his quiet and patient way, waiting for me on the stone wall of the fortress. A sharp jab of anger at the sight of him made me prickle before I exhaled heavily, fingers plucking at the ribbon I wanted to shed in a fit of pique, embracing my human form with as smooth and calm an expression as possible.

Careful, my demon snorted. *Your Syd is showing.*

Smartass.

"You are troubled." Max's lack of preamble was as

irritating as my demon's snarky remark.

I brushed past him, sneakered feet stomping on the stone. When was the last time I let my temper get the best of me? I couldn't remember. All the worse that Max's observation was correct.

Knowing I couldn't just walk away from him, that I needed to get a handle on my feelings if I was going to make this work, I pulled myself to a halt and spun, another deep breath doing little to settle my nerves. Wouldn't you know he didn't comment, just watched with that soft, patient expression of his? The one that made things worse for its lack of judgment, leaving me to judge myself where he wouldn't do the deed.

Grumble, mumble.

"I'm fine," I told him in a grating voice that assured him, even as it pierced my bubble of anger, I was anything but. My shoulders still bothered me as I shrugged and looked away from his quiet diamond eyes, over the grassy meadow below. Everything seemed particularly cheerful and peaceful today. And just added layers of annoyance to my already stirred up emotions.

Maybe feeling so little for so long was a bad idea. All of my emotions seemed heightened, as though they'd been saving themselves up for just such a weak moment as this.

Max allowed me my blatant lie. "You've been hunting?"

"Not just Creator," I said. And grasped at something I could share with him. "I think I found Alison. But I don't know where she is."

Okay, that came out wrong, but Max seemed to get it. I finally explained the dream and subsequent visit to the catacombs under Harvard where I met Thaddea. I pointedly left out my impromptu family visit with Sunny and Uncle Frank under the vampire mansion. If he sensed the omission, he didn't say. Typical Max.

"Intriguing," Max said, big hands folding in front of him, rippling the gray robe he wore. Funny, his drach form didn't seem so vibrant today. Had to be my imagination. "You were able to reach her, however. A step in the right direction." His gaze fell on my wrist, frown furrowing his brow. "You claim the drach soul saved you?"

Maybe. It felt that way now that I had time to analyze it. "It tried to warn me." I didn't mean to sound so ungrateful.

"Fortunate you had it with you."

If he said so. And like the damned thing ever left me alone. Though I had to admit it was a good thing both Alison and the ribbon acted when they did. The thought of having to go through that power drain again made me shudder. "Seems like another stone wall of nothing to me." More griping? I really was slipping.

I like you better this way, my demon whispered.

I wasn't sure if her opinion was a good thing or not.

"Your success warrants examining the process of your connection," Max said.

"Are you sure?" Standing here on the shoulders of the Stronghold, far from the trauma of my old life, it didn't seem as important as it had just a short while ago. "There's nothing we can do for the vampires, is there? Outside of finding Creator." Which led me right back to where I'd started.

Restlessness rippled through me, not the response I was expecting.

Max's brow furrowed in sadness. I hated it when he did that. It felt like he was feeling sorry for me. "Forgive me for ever implanting that idea in your head and heart," he said. "Though, I fear, it's too late for that." Max sighed himself, the breath of his drach form sweet and fresh like the wash of a summer breeze. For a moment, the giant form of his natural state loomed over me, but faded again quickly until I only saw his human shape.

"Stop apologizing," I said, sharp edged words feeling alien—and yet oh so familiar—coming from my lips. "You opened my eyes." He had. In pushing me to understand the trials and troubles of minor players in this giant game were simply distractions pulling me from the most important details, Max had freed me to act as I needed to act. To set loose those I'd cared about and commit to the task at hand. And to the fate Creator planned for me.

It seemed so much clearer only a day ago, though. I clenched my hands into fists as nagging doubt at the choice I'd made wormed its way into my heart. I slashed angrily at it as Max spoke.

"The loss of the vampires is a key, I believe, to understanding what is happening to the spirit magic of our Universe." That did make sense. A soft sense of relief I could pursue it without self-imposed guilt should have made me feel better. Instead, it just added to my own trepidation. I'd worked so hard, given up so much. The last thing I wanted was to fall back into the life I'd left behind.

Wasn't it?

"It would appear your power as a necromancer has aided you in connecting with Alison," he said. Was he aware of the thoughts spinning through my head? Drach were all connected on a deeper level even than when I'd been leader of the coven. He must have felt my stirring emotions, my loss of control, the discomfort in my heart. But, instead of prying and prodding at me, Max continued on his train of thought and this time I was grateful instead of irritated by his attitude. "A guess, mind you, though the dreams of Liam's soul and Alison's insistence you meet in the presence of the Hayle dead leads me to believe that might be the case."

"It does make sense," I said. "Spirit magic is, literally,

tied to the dead." Why hadn't I thought of that before? "But I'm not sure what else I can do. Just trying to reach her almost knocked me out."

"Whatever power holds them," he said, "must feed from you, Syd." Max's hesitation sent a jab of anxiety through me, though I didn't know what he would say next. "We must be prepared for the worst. That Alison and Sebastian—and the other vampires—are, in fact, lost to us in death and only their spirits remain."

And what, were reaching for me from wherever spirits went after people die? My heart wrenched, ached, at the thought of such a loss, startling me. As though the idea they were somewhere, out there in the Universe, still alive and well and waiting for me to find them was the last anchor I had in my life.

But my vampire didn't allow me to wallow in worry. She was already stirring with unrest.

I disagree, she sent. *Alison felt as alive as ever to me. If not more so.*

As alive as a dead girl who'd absorbed pure vampire energy could feel, my demon snarked.

Touché, my vampire murmured. *My point is, it didn't feel like death she reached out from. But more of a far distant place.*

Agreed, Shaylee sent. *I sensed earth, substance, if only peripherally. And other kinds of magic.*

I let myself touch their combined power, felt what they'd felt. And admitted it as I nodded.

"Alive," I said. And my heart soared.

I should have fought the excessive emotion that truth raised in me but I couldn't bring myself to. The relief was just far too powerful.

I cleared my throat, wiping quickly at the pair of tears that escaped my eyes while Max watched with his same level, kind expression.

When I was done, he went on as if nothing had happened. "If that is the case," he said, "then we might be one step closer to reversing what's happened to the spirit magic. And, hopefully, in restoring them and the rest of the Universe."

I wished I shared his optimism. But I had a strong feeling the only thing that would put things right was the ultimate recreation of Creator through the recovery of the pieces of her statue. Something I was failing miserably at. It struck me then how badly I'd crashed and burned up to this point. My retreat from my own plane, giving up everything and everyone I loved to pursue the big picture, had led me to a kind of monotone limbo that felt, at that moment, like as big a trap as my former life. If less obvious.

More anger, this time at my lack of success. At the complacent way I'd soared through time and space without understanding just how futile and pathetic my sacrifice had been.

Damn it. Just damn it all.

I couldn't get drawn back into the petty tininess of the lives of others. I'd fought too hard to shed that skin. But, now that I understood, maybe I could finally start making a difference for real.

"We need to step up the search for Creator's pieces," I said. "End this once and for all."

"We've been doing everything we can." His gentle tone pissed me off. "All of us, Sydlynn. I fear we've come as far as we are able without assistance."

I gaped at him. "You of all people," I snapped. "Max. I won't drag him into this." Gabriel would never be used again.

He nodded heavily. Opened his mouth, though to argue or agree I never found out.

A jab of magic jerked my head around, took all of my focus. Someone had triggered a ward I'd set on one of the planes I'd visited. My family members weren't the only ones who knew how to set trigger wards.

I had no idea who crossed the path of the power I'd left behind, but I was done with this particular conversation and the possibility of catching Belaisle or Eva Southway was just too good to pass up. Without a word to Max, I leaped into the air, transforming as I did, my drach shape effortless again. As I tore through the veil, I felt the subtle pressure of another mind, caught a glimpse of red and gold and green and, though perhaps I should have been irritated by the intrusion, I welcomed

Jiao's presence. I entered the darkness of the membrane between worlds and plunged toward the plane where my trap had been tripped.

SEVEN

Not Belaisle. I knew it the moment I entered the pale green scape, the sullen suns overhead burnt orange and deep red, casting the landscape below in a wash of crimson and harsh lines. The bare earth rippled as I settled, dust rising, to face the small, dark haired young woman who waited for me with a still, patient expression on her lovely face.

I shifted into human form with some reluctance, finding it hard to meet the warm, brown eyes of Zoe Helios. The slim, young Oracle had saved my life once, saved the entire Hayle coven, risking everything to warn me just in time before the Brotherhood came. Just early enough I was able to transport all of us to safety.

A lifetime ago. More than that, it felt like. Eons. Hang on, yesterday, wasn't it? I kept my distance, though I raised one hand in greeting as she smiled gently at me.

"Fate," I said, using her title instead of her name. She'd recently taken that role from the brother and sister duo who'd filled that place for Creator since Max shattered magic and the two Universes formed. It made me wonder how Bellanca and Thanos were doing, their physical vision restored though their far and future sight was forever lost to them. I'd forgotten my regret for them as I seemed to have forgotten everything. But, seeing Zoe now, thinking of the twins and their horror and fury at being deposed, brought everything back again.

Not to mention my worry for Zoe's boyfriend, the Steam Union's young leader and my friend, Piers Southway. The urge to ask about him was so strong I clamped my jaw shut and let her speak first.

"Syd," Zoe said, faint sadness in her voice. From my form of address or was I showing my feelings on my face again? Didn't matter. "It's time, Syd."

For what? "The next piece of Creator?" I was ready, willing and able.

But Zoe shook her head. "To go home," she said.

She might as well have punched me in the stomach.

"Screw you," I snarled. Where was she when I'd left? When I'd made the decision to go? She could have tried to stop me then, instead of this idiotic meeting in a place where I'd hoped to capture Liander Belaisle.

She didn't react with anger, though my demon wished she would. She wasn't the only one spoiling for a fight.

"Everything that has come to pass has had a reason," Zoe said. "Your departure was as necessary as your inevitable return." She shrugged, apology on her lovely face. "I'm just the messenger."

"Then you can tell Creator to screw herself," I snarled.

Zoe hesitated. "Syd," she whispered. "Gabriel is missing."

My.

Heart.

Exploded.

And suddenly there was nothing, no one, not this plane, not Jiao watching from a careful distance, not the pieces of Creator or the pain I'd buried in leaving my loved ones behind. The black ribbon was a distant irritation. There was only the distance—now closed—between Zoe and myself and the puff of smoke escaping my nostrils as I grasped the front of her leather jacket and jerked her physically off balance while I snarled in her face.

"When?"

She didn't seem afraid. She should have been terrified. Terrified.

"Go home," she said.

I pushed away from her, body snapping into full drach form as my demon roared, my vampire snarling, Shaylee shaking the very air around us through the particles of dust floating in the atmosphere. No care went into the opening of the veil, nor did I wince in sympathy at the pain I caused the place between the planes at my passing. Chuffing smoke, flame trickling from my lips, I dove into the still darkness and roared for home.

Home. My son.

And the elements and all the power of the Universe protect those who did him harm. Because I would make sure they never, ever, found their way back from the hell I was about to put them in.

GABRIEL. I thundered his name into the power of my home plane as I parted the veil and burst through. Nothing, silence, emptiness, though a thousand voices rose in protest to my appearance, then in shock, then in hope. I had nothing for them, blocked them fully, reaching, touching, searching.

And found him, at last, through Shaylee.

The Sidhe.

The Gate.

And Liam.

I burst through into the Gate cavern in such a state of shock I almost forgot to shift out of drach form. As it was, I made it to about half mass, just small enough to fit, still chuffing fire, wings half furled, Jiao's snakelike length winding around beneath me. I hit the ground hard, a roar escaping my jaws at the sight of two familiar faces.

Pale, shaking, terrified. Hortense Spaft and Sonja

O'Dane stared up at me as though the very maw of death had opened and was about to consume them. And so it had. I drew a breath to sear them both with fire, to devour them utterly, when my gaze fell on the crumpled and silent body lying in the center of the floor.

Beneath me.

Curled on his side with his pale hair spilling over the stone.

Dear face empty and still.

Eyes staring sightless and lifeless up into mine.

A giant sob tore the last of my drach from me as I collapsed forward, a woman again, almost falling onto the shell of my son. I noticed only peripherally that earth magic was used, that Sidhe power carried someone away. That the sinewy form of the crimson *lóng* was gone, too.

None of that mattered. Not while I gathered the empty body of my son in my arms. And bent my head over him to sob into the soft, sweet scent of his blond hair.

Syd. My demon's sizzling power smacked me, hard and swift. *Syd, pay attention, damn it.*

He's not dead, Syd. He's not dead. Syd! Shaylee's soft voice pierced with its intensity.

But he was dead. His lifeless eyes, his dull and pasty complexion. No heartbeat.

No heart—

Beat.

Da-dum.

There. Just there. Barely. I pushed power into him, desperate and panicked, panting over his quiet little body.

Da-dum.

I don't understand. Shaylee shivered, her own tears in her voice. *Where is he? We felt him.*

She was right. I snuffled, wiped my running nose with the shoulder of my t-shirt, and struggled to pull myself the hell together. Gabriel was alive. And I needed to keep him that way.

Desperation turned to intense focus as I scanned the cavern for evidence of what had happened. Meanwhile, the girls chattered away in my head.

He was supposed to be safe, my demon growled.

Safe from all of it, Shaylee agreed.

We left him to make sure of that, my vampire sent. *That he would never be used again.*

None of that mattered until I knew what happened.

Mom? And then he was there, his mind touching mine, and I was reaching for him with so much power he flinched back from me for a moment.

GABRIEL. I didn't mean to yell at him. I wanted to wrap him in love like a bale of cotton and smother him with it until no one could ever, ever touch him again, not with a bad look or an unkind word or anything that would ever cause him a moment of anguish.

But it came out in a collected snap of fury.

Mom. He sounded relieved though, almost cheerful as his magic embraced me. Wait a second. Not just his magic. More than his power, as immense as it was to begin with. He'd taken on the energy of the Gate when he was just a baby, everything the Sidhe left behind in the entrance to their realm.

He'd grown in power, I knew that. Was the Gateway. But this was more, much more.

Gabriel felt like the veil.

And, as I reached for him with more control and less panicked anger, I realized why his body seemed dead and his soul so free and vibrant. My son was in the veil.

No. My son *was* the veil.

Oh. My. Swearword.

I was already acting, reacting, jerking him free of the membrane's endless touch, stuffing him back into his tiny body with enough force to make him gasp. This time, the black ribbon worked with me, seeming as eager as I was to return Gabriel to his human form. I didn't thank it at the time, ignoring too my son's unhappy protest, a tiny part of me wondering if I would have been able to manage this miracle if he'd been prepared. I was strong, had access to vast amounts of energy. Edgeless, my father once said.

That was nothing, nothing. Small time.

My son felt like the Universe.

Gabriel blinked up at me, stunned by his sudden

return, green light glinting in his hazel eyes. And from that sweet, sweet face, Liam looked up at me, too. I sobbed and clenched him to my chest, feeling his little arms weave around me, the pressure on my ribs as he hugged me with his power as well as his physical form until my super strong bones groaned.

"Mom," he whispered into my hair. "I missed you so much."

I choked on a reply, unable to speak, just rocking him and weeping. It was too close to home, too familiar this feeling of loss and return. And I couldn't help but go back, sharp with agony, to the day they told me my son had died. My attempts to die, too. And his final return with the death, by my power, of Ameline.

Old hurts. Funny how fresh they seemed kneeling there in the remains of what my life could have been with his father.

It was Gabriel who finally pulled away. I drank in his little face, realizing it wasn't so young anymore. How much time had gone by? But no, he was still a boy. And while my mind tried to count the months, he spoke.

"I've been looking everywhere for you," he said. "Why wouldn't you let me find you?"

I shook my head. Couldn't answer. Guilt ate me up from the inside out. How does a mother explain to her beloved son why she had to leave him alone?

But, of anyone, Gabriel understood. I saw it in his

eyes, in his sadness, the adult way his brow furrowed as he patted my hand.

"I'm sorry, Mom," he said. "Stupid question. But you need me and you know it. Don't you?"

No. I wouldn't. Though, by leaving him, I'd put him in the most danger he'd been in since Ameline kidnapped him, hadn't I? Had I driven him to do stupid things in order to find me?

Stubborn.

There's a shocker, my demon chuckled.

I snorted a tearful laugh, unable to help myself.

Gabriel's answering grin lit up my entire world. And made me think about his sister. Longing burned an aching hole in my soul. I pulled him close again, wishing Ethie was here, too.

"You look so different," Gabriel whispered. "Like Max."

I swallowed, nodded. Cleared my throat. "Drach now," I said, hoarse. "Gabriel, what happened?" Anger swelled as I processed this whole fiasco from beginning to end. He'd been here, in a place I'd thought long gone, with two people I didn't trust with the garbage I tossed out. But he was far stronger than either Spaft or his grandmother.

He'd been here by choice.

Grave steadiness in those hazel eyes choked me up once again as Liam shone through my son's gaze. So much like his father. "They told me they could help me find you," he said. "So I came with them."

I ground my teeth together.

No use berating the boy now, my demon sent, smirking.

Berate? Shaylee's joy was contagious. *Congratulate. He's brilliant, you know. And I have no doubt always in full control.*

Not that we're biased or anything, my vampire sent, dryly delicious.

"This was incredibly dangerous," I started. Stopped. For who? I swallowed again as Gabriel smiled and kissed my cheek.

"I had to try," he said, good humor fading while tears filled his eyes. "It was my fault you left, Mom. I needed you to know it was okay, that you had to come home." He shook his head when I tried to protest. Firm. Adult. "You need me to find Creator's pieces," my son said. "And you know it."

We do know it, my vampire sent. *But convincing your mother will take some doing.*

I shouldn't have been surprised when Gabriel laughed as though the girls talked to him all the time. Maybe they used to when I wasn't paying attention.

"Mom," he said, eyes lighting up again. "You have to let me go back in."

I didn't have to ask where he meant. He still felt vast and wild, like the Universe itself lived in his little chest.

"Coming here to the Gate cavern might not have

been risky," I admitted, "but you could have died, Gabriel." I hugged him. "Your body, sweets."

Gabriel shrugged against me. "It was amazing," he breathed into my hair before pushing me back, eyes wide. "And necessary. Mom," he said, before I could say another word. "I could see everything. Everything." His voice dropped with faint reverence, awe even. "All of it, the entire Universe, all around me. And I felt the other one." No adverse reaction, no shudder of disgust as he mentioned the Dark Universe. "The edge of it. But more than that." He grasped my hands, green growing in intensity in his gaze. "Mom, I felt spirit magic." He grinned. "I know where the vampires are."

EIGHT

The air shuddered beside me, Jiao returning with a frustrated expression flickering over her young face. It smoothed as quickly as it came, though I knew with one glance she'd pursued—and lost—Spaft and Sonja.

It didn't matter right now. She stood in silence, listening as I gently gripped my son's upper arms in my hands and squeezed.

"Where?"

He bounced slightly, excitement bubbling to the surface of his power, sizzling over mine, drawing me into his happy mood. There was such purity and energy to my son, a pull so overwhelming and welcoming I couldn't resist it.

"In the place between the veil," he said.

And, suddenly, everything made sense. While raising a million questions at the same time.

"The void," I said, while the black ribbon sighed as though relieved I finally figured it out. Could have said something. I thought of my sister, of her battle with the Planeless cult, how we'd almost lost Mabel in that utterly black, endless hole of limbo that existed between the veil and, well… everything. Now the sucking pull on my power made sense, as did the inability we'd had to locate Alison and Sebastian. The void.

While I was relieved to finally understand, it was a crushing kind of understanding as the truth sank in.

"They are lost, then," I said. Resigning myself to that fact might take time.

Who was I kidding? It damned near broke my heart.

But Gabriel seemed more hopeful. "We'll see," he said. Too cryptic for a boy with all the power of the Universe shining in his eyes. Or just cryptic enough.

I loved him so much in that moment I could have just burst.

"Gabriel." Jiao's interruption drew out a hiss of irritation from my lips, but his gentle hand squeezed mine while he smiled gently up at her. "Do you know what the two who brought you here were after?"

Damned good question. And one I should have asked myself.

Might want to cut yourself some slack, my demon sent. *Or not. Up to you.*

Shaylee sniggered.

Asshats.

Even so, I grinned in response.

"I don't know, honestly," Gabriel shrugged. "Didn't really care." He grinned back at me. "I knew they were after something besides helping me find you. But when they mentioned this place, I had the idea to search for you through the Gate itself." His cheeks pinked. "Seems to have worked."

"Too well," I said. Just the thought of him being lost forever in the veil made me want to throw up.

"Anyway," he said, "I'm pretty sure whatever they were after, it backfired. The second I felt the Gate, I reached out to it and it drew me in. I could hear them arguing just before you arrived, Mom." He rolled his eyes. "I didn't even get much of a chance to explore before you pulled me back." Gabriel sounded pouty a moment. "Just lucky I found the vampires before you made me return."

I looked away from him at last, gazing over and up at the looming Gate of the Sidhe. Thought of Liam even as irritation crept in. "We closed this place down," I said, shocked to be pissed at the wooden portal as if it were responsible. A tiny thread of green power zipped up one side and down the other, like a guilty hiccup.

"It just went dormant, Mom," he said. "Or so it told me." Now he was talking to the Gate. Lovely. Well, no one ever accused me of being normal and ordinary despite my hopes to the contrary so long ago. Why should my kid be any different? "He said we could never actually destroy it. It's part of the veil."

"He?" Jiao's soft query reminded me she was there. I already knew who "he" was, but Gabriel filled the *lóng* in.

"Cian," he said. "The Gate builder. He left fractions of his soul in each of the Gates he created. And though I took most of the power with me when Mom brought me here to close the way, enough of him remained to seal it and keep it in stasis."

"Until now." Which meant we'd have to deal with the yearly knock once again, did it?

Wait a minute. We?

Sigh.

How was I going to tell my son I had to go?

Maybe he already understood that. Because his face fell, even as he looked around, too. But, when he spoke, it wasn't sorrow for me, after all. "This is where my father lived."

Oh, hell. He had to say that, in that exact tone of voice, didn't he? The waterworks burst open and, with a silent sob I couldn't control, I bent forward, both hands covering my face while my son gently rubbed a constant circle between my shoulder blades.

My mind flashed back.

To this very spot on the stone floor.

Blood soaking into my jeans.

Liam before me, life fading, leaving me, gone before I

could save him.

My chest ached, breath almost impossible a moment, until I forced a deep inhale into my lungs when sparks began to dance in my vision.

Breathe, Syd. Just breathe.

They were there, my alter egos, holding me, supporting me. Without them I wouldn't have survived the return of such agony. Wouldn't have made it the first time either.

And I'd contemplated giving them up? Giving my son up for the second time?

When I lifted my head and found him watching me, my soul shriveled in my body and tried to hide from his steady gaze, his unwavering love, his refusal to judge me.

Who needed him to? I was doing a great job all on my own.

"I want to keep this place open again," he said.

He might as well have told me he planned to stab me over and over with a knife. Of course I'd let him.

He was my son.

But there were others who would have to deal with it. I had to go.

It was Jiao who spoke up before any of my egos could do so. Her voice penetrated the fog of anguish in my head, slapping me firmly with her cold logic. And, finally, her judgment.

At least someone had the guts to tell me what they

thought of me.

This is wrong, she sent. *Your family needs you.*

I gaped at her. *We both made our choice*, I sent.

No, she snarled, chopping one hand through the air. *I had no choice. And, perhaps, at the time you didn't either. But you are here now. And we have done all we can with what we have to finish our tasks. To no avail.* She gestured at Gabriel who watched with intent eyes. *Creator gave us the powers we have for a reason. And not even you, Sydlynn Hayle, can keep the Universe from getting what it wants. What it needs.* She grimaced, shining black hair swinging as she shook her head. *Who are you to make that decision for Fate?*

My jaw was unhinged, obviously. As was my mind. Fighting to comprehend what she was saying.

Jiao was more than happy to clarify.

Stop being so arrogant, she snapped in her crisp and cold mental voice, the dragon in her crackling with command. *Your needs?* She scoffed. *What are your needs compared to that of the Universe?*

I'm trying to do what Creator wants, I sent, stunned, hurt. *To save the Universe.*

By refusing to use the tools she made for exactly that purpose. Jiao snorted out loud. *Foolish child.*

It had been a long time since anyone called me a child. Least of all a child herself.

Jiao finally softened. "While I honor Max and his long and endless battle to protect the Universe, to follow Fate to the end, I see more clearly with the eyes of one who has had to look out for herself." Black glittered under thick lashes. "While we may wish it otherwise, while we might choose to throw everything away to protect the ones we love, we have no right to stop the turning of the wheel. To tell Creator we know better than she." She pointed at Gabriel who gained his feet, offered me his hand to help me to mine. I stood as she went on. "The Gateway must be allowed to make his own choices. For better or worse, as Creator intended."

I looked down at my son, so young, so grim and grown up. "You agree with her?"

He nodded. "I've been feeling the call of Creator since I can remember," he said. "Please don't stop me again, Mom. I don't want to have to go against you." Real sorrow. And, at last, for me, final clarity.

Gabriel was my son. But he was also a child of the Universe, made by Creator to fill a role. I'd known it all along. Hadn't I lived it? Defended that position to others before? And had allowed their fears to convince me otherwise.

He was just so young.

So are you, in the grand scheme of things, my vampire sent.

My heart hurt. "I can't stay," I whispered to my son.

He nodded. "I know, Mom," he said. "And that's okay. As long as you take me with you when I can help." He ducked his head a moment. "They're looking for me."

Guilt in his tone, soft and hurt. When Gabriel met my eyes, I hated the regret there. "They're really worried."

Frantic, he meant. Mom would be losing her crap all over the place.

Quaid.

Breathe, Syd.

I could have let him go alone. Maybe I should have. But if I was going to allow myself to trust Creator, to use my son as I swore I would never again, to accept the fact he was as necessary in the healing of the Universe as I was—more so if truth be told—I had to be willing to face those who would fight to protect him from me and that choice.

I turned to Jiao who was smiling at last. "I'll inform Max of what happened here," she said before disappearing through the veil, leaving us alone. I couldn't resist another long, hard hug for my son.

Then, with a heavy heart but his sweet little hand in mine, I reached for the veil and took Gabriel home to Hong Kong.

NINE

I meant to return to the main lobby at the World Paranormal Council headquarters, to discreetly warn those I was about to encounter of the return of my son— and myself. Instead, as though my heart ruled my actions and not my spinning head, I stepped out of the veil in the middle of Quaid's living room.

My ex-husband's quarters had a gorgeous view of the Hong Kong harbor, the delightful mix of old and new world vessels over a crescent of blue water and equally blue sky. The high rise towered over the city, always giving me a sense of detachment, much as flying in drach form did.

That feeling didn't follow me here. Not when a honey blonde woman looked up, gasped. Stood from the long, narrow table at the far end of the room near the pristine white kitchen. Her gravid body showed in clear relief, engorged breasts popping over her neckline, the strain of life pushing out her bellybutton against the inside of her cotton dress.

Payten stared at me with her wide eyes, hands cupping her round stomach with a look of protectiveness crossing her face. Fear. Sudden fear.

I was so stunned by the sight of her pregnant it took me a long moment of quiet and incomprehension to finally order my thoughts into some semblance of understanding.

And suddenly I knew who the father was. Of course.

Who else?

And the last faint and distant love I carried for Quaid died in a sigh of despair.

Payten's mouth gaped, neither of us able to speak, it seemed. But when one of the doors crashed open and a tiny girl with long, black curls and blue eyes burst into the living area, we both turned from each other. With relief?

Hell yeah.

"GABRIEL!" My daughter threw herself at her brother, almost knocking him over as her slim form crashed into him, arms twining around his neck and choking him. I wanted to kneel, to hug them both, heart pounding at the sight of Ethie and Gabriel, love swelling, swallowing the deadness brought on by Payten's condition. But I stood too long, hesitated as I stared.

And felt the fuzzy warmth of our reunion shatter like

a living thing as my daughter looked up at me with fury in her eyes.

"You're not my mother anymore," she snarled before bursting into tears and running from the room once more.

I deserved that, didn't I? For leaving her behind. One glance down at my pale, gray hands, the fine edges of scales visible just under the skin, and I saw through my child's experience what I must look like to her.

And she was right. Her mother was gone. And only I remained.

Gabriel grabbed my hand, squeezed it in his. I met his gaze, seeing the depth of his own wisdom, knowing just how much of his father he carried within him as I failed to utter a sound in either anger or grief.

Almost missed Payten's whisper of magic, but not the result as blue flame erupted between her and me, filling the space with a wash of heat as Quaid appeared in a rush of Enforcer power.

His chocolate eyes flashed wide, jaw jumping a moment as he studied me just before he held out his hands to Gabriel. "You're okay." His voice shook, the only weakness Quaid was going to show my son, I guess. His hands trembled too, words thick and heavy with the last of his fear. "Where were you?"

"It's a long story." Gabriel waved him off, as though the trauma he caused Quaid was of no mention and made zero effort to go to my ex-husband despite Quaid's continuing open armed stance. Finally, the tall Enforcer I'd once loved dropped his hands to his sides, gaze rising to meet mine again.

Grim. Dark. Angry. At me?

Just try it. My demon snarled.

Hush, I whispered. *They have the right to be angry.*

"Payten," Quaid said, voice calm and soft despite his emotions bubbling under the surface. I knew him too well to miss his imminent overflow of whatever it was he was feeling. "Please take Gabriel to his room. Syd and I have to talk."

She hesitated, eyes flickering to me. More fear. Was I that scary? Her hands closed convulsively over her stomach again. But she did as she was told, didn't she, after a moment? Came forward, one hand held out to my son, staying behind Quaid.

I wanted to think her a coward, to shout horrible names at her. Hate her. But couldn't muster it.

Just couldn't.

Gabriel looked up at me. "Mom."

I nodded. "Go with her," I said.

He sighed. And went. Though I noted he refused to hold her hand, to which she blushed. And ignored his own door, retreating through the one his sister had slammed her exit.

Alone at last. I held very still, not sure I was capable

of much more than that as my mind spun on empty.

"Thank you for finding him." Quaid's voice broke. He cleared his throat. "We've been panicked looking for him. All of us."

Maybe I should have been offended. He was my son. But all I could say was, "You're welcome."

Syd. Seriously.

He stared at me a long moment in silence before drawing a breath. It was so still in the room I could almost feel the air stir from his intake. "You look… different." And winced. "Sorry, stupid thing to say."

Captain Obvious. I shrugged. "I do." Kicked myself. Quaid wasn't the enemy. But there were enemies out there stalking my kid. "Gabriel was with Spaft and Sonja," I said, telling him in as few, terse words as possible the state I found my son in. My son.

Not ours.

Mine.

Possessive much? My demon's sarcasm seemed aimed at him, not me, despite her words.

He is ours, Shaylee sent.

Indeed. Even my vampire seemed disinclined to give Quaid any credit.

Sigh.

"I'll have them tracked and brought in," he said.

I almost commented. About trusting him to take care of things. And didn't. Because, well. I wasn't there to do it, was I? Someone had to try. Might as well be him. I had chosen to step back. And he needed to step up.

"Syd." Quaid stopped, glanced ever so slightly toward the doors leading to the bedrooms.

My throat closed over. Please don't bring it up. Don't talk about it. I can't.

I just can't.

"It's twins." How could he sound equally defensive and proud at the same time?

"Okay," I said. It was the only word I could muster.

Quaid's hands clenched at his sides. "She's six months."

That meant nothing to me. Or did it?

"Okay," I said.

"You've been gone six months." Was that hard for him to admit? No harder than for me to count backward and realize he was right.

"Okay," I said.

He huffed a frustrated breath. "Stop saying that," he said. "It's not okay. Is it?"

I couldn't even shake my head in denial. "No," I whispered. "But I gave up the right to be angry with you when I left, Quaid. So, okay."

He looked like he wanted to shout at me. Or have me shout at him. "I didn't mean for this to happen." Discomfort, awkward and apologetic. I should have been mollified, comforted.

I just felt raw.

My daughter's bedroom door slammed open one more time. Her tiny face covered in tears, she pushed past Payten, past her brother, and stomped up to me. Fists on her hips, she thrust her jaw out and glared.

"I thought I was clear," she snarled. "Payten's my mother now. You can go."

She waited, tapping one tiny shoe on the floor. While I crumbled the rest of the way inside. Of course she hated me.

"Did you hear me?" Ethie hissed like a furious cat. "I never, ever want to see you again."

"Ethpeal." Quaid's halfhearted attempt to rein her in wasn't helping any. Neither was the united front he and Payten made as the pregnant witch joined him, his arm tucking protectively around her waist, one big hand on her distended tummy.

He used to hold me like that. When I was pregnant.

The veil parted quickly as though in sympathy to my feelings. I suddenly wished I didn't have them, that the drach in me would soothe the hurt, the gaping emptiness I knew was about to erupt into ugly crying and personal damage of the worst self-punishment. As I turned to enter the tear, Gabriel's power reached for me.

I'll be back, I sent as I stepped through and left him there. *I promise. I just need to leave for a little while.*

Mom. I'm sorry, Mom. I should have warned you about

Payten. Too much hurt for him to carry.

My power hugged him and let him go. *Not your fault, sweets*, I sent. And left.

And he let me go.

TEN

There was nothing I wanted more than to retreat into the veil, to fly on drach wings away, far away, from the pain I'd just endured. Though, as I returned to the quiet of the rubbery membrane between the planes, my heart settled, soul softening.

I'd done what I had to do. And I would pay the price for my actions. My kids were safe and Quaid was happy. I couldn't begrudge them that. Besides, falling apart now would serve no purpose.

There would be time for beating myself black and blue later. I had music to face and more people to track down so they could yell at me.

Her office was exactly as I remembered it, the faint scent of pine cleaner, the warmth of the wood, her massive desk and leather padded chair. I stood in a sunbeam heavy with dust motes, absorbing the heat while

I just breathed and prepared myself for what was about to come.

And opened myself to her power, letting her know I was there.

Mom burst through her office door from the sitting room, blue eyes full of tears. She lunged for me but I was faster, backing away, one hand up, keeping our distance.

I couldn't let her hug me. I'd fall utterly and completely apart after all.

"Gabriel is safe," I said, pushing the drach in me forward, the song of my people echoing in my voice. Mom's hand covered her mouth, shaking as she drew in my appearance, absorbed the sound. The truth.

"Syd," she whispered. "What have you done?"

Anger snapped and sizzled. She always knew how to push my buttons, even now, damn her.

"What needed to be done," I snarled, the drach song falling away, leaving only me behind. "What all of you freaking pushed me to do, damn it, Mom. You wanted me to save you, right? What the hell is it you think I'm doing?" I was shaking now, with rage, with loss, and she just stood there and listened, watched, waited. "I gave up EVERYTHING. To save all of YOU." I half turned from her. "So don't you dare judge me."

"Sweetheart," she said. "I never wanted this for you."

I almost laughed in her face. Held it together long enough not to. Ignored what just passed between us.

"Gabriel is back with Quaid and Payten." I bit off her name like it left a nasty taste in my mouth.

Mom said something, garbled with sorrow. "I'm sorry," she finally said.

I shrugged, stared out the window. I couldn't show Quaid my hurt, but Mom? Mom and I had a lifetime of pain between us. It seemed easier—and harder—to let her see just how much it cut me. Just how deep.

"I don't want to talk about it," I said.

Mom nodded, the gesture short and small, caught out of the corner of my eye. She wavered as though considering trying to come to my side again. And didn't.

I almost wept, wishing she had.

"We've been so worried." She paused, swallowed. "That wasn't a judgment."

Damn her.

"Are you... are you back?" Mom sounded so young, so frail and afraid. Enough I turned to face her again, surprised to find her hugging herself, bottom lip turning white from the pressure of her teeth against it.

"Nothing's changed," I said.

Liar, my vampire whispered.

Oh, shut up, I snapped back.

Mom leaned against her desk, brushing one hand over her face. Deep circles darkened the skin under her eyes, the bones and tendons of her fingers showing in sharp lines under her skin. So did her cheekbones, her clavicle.

Only then did I realize how much weight Mom had lost, how pale and sick she seemed. My magic reached for her, found her in perfect health if weary.

I wanted to ask her what was wrong but could guess. Though it wasn't like her to fall apart, not when others needed her. Not over me.

Was it?

"We're a mess, Syd," she said, sighing out a shaking breath while she sagged onto the desk top. "Our North American Council is a disaster, the integration of all covens into the voting body creating far more issues than it solved. I almost have things in hand, it seems, and then we are hit with problems from outside our borders." I'd never heard Mom whine before, and this wasn't exactly the case, either. But it wasn't like her to be weak. All the more reason I had to leave.

Had left. And would again.

Cold, Syd, my demon sent, angry with me from the snapping of her fire.

And yet, practical and the very reason we cut everyone loose, my vampire sent.

Mom had no idea I was carrying on a conversation in my head, that the black ribbon around my wrist had tightened once again. A punishment? She was still talking.

"If the other councils would just stop trying to bully us." She shook her head, threads of white in her long, black hair reminding me my mother wasn't getting any younger. And, unlike me, wasn't immortal. "They firmly disagree with our change in format," she said, bitterness coming out in a bark-like laugh of frustration. "And have made sure Femke and the WPC see things their way."

I wanted to help. I wanted more than anything to cross to my mother and hug her before barreling off with my power blazing to beat the living snot out of anyone who would dare stand in her way. In the way of the progress she was fighting to make. And that included my old friend, Femke Svennson, the leader of the WPC.

Wanted to.

Couldn't.

The door squeaked softly as someone slipped through. I caught the shock on Dad's face as he spotted me, the sudden concern as he rushed to Mom. She allowed him to support her while he stared at me.

"It's good to see you, cupcake," he said. Simple, straight forward, to the point. With understanding and grief in his eyes. Of all people he understood, didn't he? He'd left us behind once, gave up what he loved to rule Demonicon. He had to get it.

Didn't make the sadness on his face any easier. The blame he showed, not for me, but for himself.

"I'm sorry," I said, in my best drach voice. "What I'm doing takes priority. You're going to have to resolve your issues on your own from now on." I'd made that damned clear, hadn't I?

Dad's brows pulled together, hands clasping Mom to him tightening as she turned her face and pressed it into his shoulder. "You don't have to tell me," he said, a faint growl in his voice. "I get it, Syd." I knew he would. "But no matter what you think, you're doing it wrong." He shrugged almost violently, as if trying to shed something he didn't like from his broad shoulders. "You learned nothing from my mistakes, I take it."

He would not do this to me.

"Like it or not," he said, doing it anyway, "we need you." Mom nodded into his chest. "We're facing disaster after disaster thanks to your departure." How was that my problem? "Most of which we've managed. But the witching world is falling apart, Syd. The councils, Femke, all of it."

I didn't want to know. But my mouth and mind had a miscommunication and I found myself speaking anyway. "What's wrong with Femke?" The last time I'd seen her we hadn't had the best meeting. In fact, I'd pretty much told her to go to hell and take the rest of the world with her. She'd just come through a rough kidnapping by the Russian mafia, controlled and blocked magically by a Black Souls sorcerer I'd defeated to save her. Only to be betrayed by her when it came to Liander Belaisle. Who she and her precious Enforcers had allowed to escape.

Just like them to blame me for his emancipation. Leading, in part, to my six month hiatus and total eradication of any connection to the people I loved.

Mom answered while I stewed over the past. She seemed to have regained some of her old poise, though she still looked world weary. "She's not herself, Syd. And hasn't been since you left. No," she shook her head. "Since you brought her back from Russia."

"Something happened to her," Dad said. "She's been impossible to communicate with. Aggressive, power hungry, standoffish."

That definitely didn't sound like Femke.

"We have more immediate problems," Dad said softly while Mom muttered something to him. Sounded like a denial. But Dad spoke up anyway. "Tallah Hensley has declared emancipation for herself and her coven, severing her territory from the North American Council."

"That's even possible?" I suppose if she wanted it bad enough. Hadn't I done so with the Hayle coven when we found out Erica Plower, the then leader of the old council, had sold us out to the Brotherhood? Still, I'd had a ton of power behind me and an excellent reason to become outcast. Tallah, on the other hand… her act would leave her family weak and without support.

Not that the Hensley leader had been acting all that rationally either. Since the Brotherhood attack on our territory, and the loss of a large number of her members to the sorcerers, she'd been bitter and distant, angry. And had poached her sister, Sashenka, from my side when I was still coven leader. My former second had run back to California and abandoned me.

I didn't want to think about her final words to me when I'd confronted her at last as to her real reason for leaving. But the echo of the truth lingered and was the second reason I chose to leave.

I got tired of trying to support someone who has tools in place of people she cares about.

Mom spoke again, interrupting the memory.

"She's claimed the majority of California and has started recruiting covens," she said.

She what? Okay, totally different from what I did. I wanted to protect my family when I parted ways with the council. Not create an organization of my own.

I drew a breath. Not. My. Problem.

"What are you doing about it?" Stupid mouth/brain issues.

Mom shrugged. "Nothing," she said, making my teeth grind together. "Watching and waiting. The last thing I want is an internal war, Syd." Defensive. Which meant she knew she was cornered and without choices.

But she was right.

"Our only real allies are the Steam Union," Dad said. "The vampire consolidation here in our territory is a good thing, but they are so wrapped up in trying to save themselves they've been of no help."

"And Femke has refused to allow Charlotte and the

werewolves to interact with us, citing some foolish law she's come up with that contains paranormals to the continental territories of their origin without specific permission from the Council." Now Mom sounded angry.

As she should. And I was pretty sure my werequeen friend was probably ready to tear Femke a new one for tying her hands like that.

"Piers and the Steam Union have their own issues," Mom said. "The continued defection of their people to the Brotherhood has placed a massive strain on them."

I knew it was a piece of Creator making that defection possible. That somehow whoever was using the piece was altering the foundation power of the sorcerers in the Steam Union and forcing them to become Brotherhood. But until I found the piece and retrieved it there was no way of reversing the effects.

That we know of, my vampire sent. *We didn't look that hard, did we?*

I didn't even bother to tell her to shut up this time.

There was more, I could see it on my mother's face, in Dad's angry eyes. But I was done.

So done.

"Syd," Mom said suddenly, as though only then remembering. "What were you doing in the Hayle crypt?"

Wrong question. No way was I going to tell them I was looking into the vampires. That could only lead to further pressure to help them. And that would end up in a whole world—quite literally—of trouble I just couldn't deal with right now.

Instead of answering her, I tore open the veil. "Quaid is hunting Spaft and Sonja," I said. "If you spot them in your territory, tell him. He'll deal with them."

Neither said a word as I left but they didn't have to. The pressure of their stares and their outpouring of mixed emotions hit me between the shoulder blades like a blow as I fled.

ELEVEN

I didn't want to think about why it was so hard to fly yet again, why I struggled, ungainly and out of sequence, my wings desperately flapping to keep time with my need to run away. I blamed the uncomfortably tight black ribbon that clung to me, but only so I wouldn't have to acknowledge the horrible fear in my heart I'd done irreparable damage to the drach in me by building a wall between that soul and the egos inside me. Turning the tide back toward the woman I had been.

I wouldn't think about it right now. I had important things to focus on.

I crashed through the veil at last, unable to remain aloft and still a fair distance from the Stronghold plane, frustration forcing a massive bellow from my throat. Mountain peaks beckoned, pulling me down toward them. I could spiral, at least, clawed feet extending toward a familiar flat expanse at the top of one jutting spire.

I'd been here before, had met Max here, officially, for the first time. Why I'd ended up on Demonicon I couldn't say. But it seemed an appropriate place to lose my crap in private.

The moment my feet touched down I let my body transform, the woman's shape taking over far more easily than it should have, as though pushing away the drach form with aggressive rejection. I fought a sob in the back of my throat. No. Freaking. Fair. I'd come so far, given up so much. Only to feel myself falling apart all over again.

Our fault, I fear, my vampire whispered, her power trying to fall free of the wall holding back my drach, her sorrow making my chest ache in sympathy.

I tried to muster denial. But she was right, wasn't she? From the misery in both my demon and Shaylee, they knew it, too. I drew panting breaths while I stared out over the amber tinted landscape, wind buffeting me at the top of the mountain, fresh, heated by the multiple suns overhead. Tried to pull in calm with each inhale even as the drach in me slipped further away despite the failing wall of power holding her at bay. I focused on the distant horizon, the barest view of a towering city in the distance.

Refused to think about my sister.

Damn it.

So what are we going to do about it? My demon's gruffness

did nothing to hide her worry.

What were we going to do?

Can we go on this way? Shaylee's tentative question broke my heart. Made me crumble further inside. I'd let them slip from me for the last six months.

And didn't really miss us, did you? Not an accusation from my demon, but it might as well have been.

No, I whispered. *You were still there.*

But sleeping, silent, my vampire sent. *Perhaps as things are truly meant to be.*

I shuddered from that possibility.

This isn't working, Syd, my demon sent. *We've only been active less than twenty-four hours and you're already a mess.*

Thanks a lot, I sent. But she was right.

Can't we find a happy medium? Shaylee's sorrow was the worst.

In the end, my vampire sent, calm, soft, gentle, *I doubt we can.*

Okay, I was wrong. That was the worst. The worst ever.

Not so bad, my demon sent, deflating inside me, her fires dampening. *I recall being content. Sleepy. Distant.*

Indeed, my vampire sent. *More whole than a part of one. Does that make sense?*

Agreed, Shaylee sent, not quite so sad anymore. Trying hard, bless her heart. *Peaceful, like we were all together in a quiet place.*

Was that a better solution than this? Than being able to talk to them, to hear their voices, to share my life with them? I barely remembered a time when I didn't have an extra ego hanging around, badgering or influencing me.

Hey, my demon sent.

I caught myself grinning into the first of the sunsets in the distance, despite the sadness of the moment.

Though we won't be available to you this way, my vampire sent, *we will always be with you, Syd.*

I choked on a reply, unable to say a thing.

Saved as the veil overhead opened and a drach sailed through. I knew it was Mabel long before she landed with a backwash of air from her wings, my drach power automatically grounding me, surrounding me with a thin shield to protect me from the force of her landing. She shifted into human form and strode toward me, graceful but with purpose, shaking me out of my lonely—despite the voices in my head—decision making.

"I'm surprised to find you here," she said without even a nod of welcome.

That stung. "Because my sister is here?" I didn't mean to sound so angry, but Mabel had caught me at about the worst time imaginable.

She shrugged, ignoring my mood. "I know how attached you have been to your family," she said. "I would think it painful to be here and not have contact with Meira."

Like I needed the reminder. "You were looking for me?" See if that ended the conversation.

"I have felt the disturbance in your power," she said. Leave it to Mabel to get right to the point and punch me where it hurt. Not that she meant to damage me, I knew it in my heart. She was my ultimate grandmother. Her blood in my lineage allowed me to claim the drach form, to shed everything and everyone and gave me wings. For that I would always be grateful. But, like all drach, she had a more pragmatic view of the Universe than my humanity had taught me originally. Her bluntness was just a symptom of it.

Not that the knowledge made it hurt any less.

I shook my head, backed away from her, feeling a soft thrill of vertigo as I looked over the edge of the flat topped mountain. Damn it, that, too? I'd pretty much lost my fear of heights—a fear triggered on this very plane, years ago, by a near fatal fall from the top of the Seat. Flying with Max and then taking my own drach form seemed to have cured me. Only, as I stared once more into the distance, I felt it returning.

Just like everything else I'd thought I'd shed was returning.

Failure, my ego whispered to me. An older voice even than my demon's.

"I thought I had this all figured out." I didn't mean to speak but frustration opened my mouth, forced the words out. "It's not fair. I worked so hard."

Mabel nodded, surprising me. "You have done more than anyone," she said, "more than even the Universe should expect from one heart, Sydlynn."

I hadn't expected sympathy. "I refuse to fail," I said.

She shrugged again, long, shining black hair a loose braid over one shoulder, the end of it brushing the ground, the tips of her gray toes at the hem of her robe. "Then don't," she said.

There was drach logic for you.

"Your time with us has been soothing to your soul," Mabel said. "And necessary. I have observed you the last few years, Sydlynn. Despite your strength there have been times I have feared for you."

Really? I rubbed my arms with both hands, at the goosebumps raised there.

"But, I fear, the quiet you have earned must come to an end." She took two steps closer, large hands rising to settle on my shoulders. I realized then I'd not taken the full height of the drach this time. That I was small, frail in appearance. That I was Syd the coven leader in body and size.

Another back slide.

"I, however, believe no matter what you've done, no matter what you have left to do, the Universe owes you." A sharp edge cut through her words. Wait, was Mabel pissed off? For me? I'd never seen her angry. "And, unfortunately, at the same time, owns you." Well, that was a kick in the ass, wasn't it? Mabel's hands fell away, sorrow in her eyes replacing the kick of temper. "Those of us who have spent our lives in service to Creator and the Universe must learn our hearts don't matter. What we want, who we love, all of it must come second to our destiny." I'd never heard Mabel talk this way before, found myself held rapt by her speech as she looked away from me, gaze distant. I knew Max had been through a lot over the seemingly endless centuries. But I'd never given thought to what Mabel and the other drach had to endure in that same time period.

What had my ancestress given up to stand here with me in this place?

Mabel looked back again, wisdom and years and stillness settling around her and, in turn, around me. The girls listened with the same intensity I did when she spoke again.

"It's time, Sydlynn," Mabel said, her words like a geas on my heart. "Time to embrace your destiny fully. To accept things will never be perfect. That you will suffer and love and live while others do not." Shudder. Did she know things I didn't? "And to let go of your need to protect those who can help fulfill the destiny of the Universe." She was talking about Gabriel. And others?

Likely, my vampire whispered.

"I don't know if I can," I said to Mabel, to the girls

inside me. "That's the reason I left. To make sure the ones I loved were safe."

"How arrogant," Mabel said, mild and with a hint of amusement, "to think only your actions can protect them. One way or another."

Youch. I flinched from her words even as my vampire sighed.

Therein lies the rub, she sent while my demon chuffed her unhappiness and Shaylee bristled. *I fear she's right*.

Double youch.

"So," I snapped, unwilling to accept it just yet despite the softening of my alter egos to the idea, "you're telling me everything I've done has been a waste of freaking time?"

Mabel's soft smile took the edge off her words. Or, maybe, was meant to.

"You needed to rest," she said. "But nap time is over, little pet. Time to get back to work."

Condescending, gray skinned, soulless—

Syd.

Sigh.

"I fear for you," Mabel said, bowing her head, turning away from me. "That it is your very humanity that will be your downfall in the end." She sighed deeply. "Your inability to embrace logic and act. But, please, consider Creator would not have made you this way without a reason. Without knowledge and purpose." Again a soft smile, but at the horizon. "There's only one way to find out."

"Could you just put everyone you love at risk and say to hell with caution?" I flinched as I realized what I'd just asked, and of whom.

Mabel just nodded, as though sensing I understood how stupid that question was.

She'd already done it, hadn't she? A lifetime of it.

Suck it up and get back on track, Hayle.

"If you're ready to act," Mabel said, tilting her head so the sunlight caught her diamond eyes, "we have a task at hand."

Something to focus on? Okay then. Though I held off making any kind of decisions about moving forward. Because, yeah. Procrastination.

"Where are we going?" I reached for my drach shape as Mabel began to shift, leaping into the air after her, finding my flight a little more stable than it had been. Bonus.

"To speak to the one person who can help us with the conundrum of spirit magic and the place the vampires dwell," Mabel said, voice carrying back to me on the wind. "To your sister."

Oh, *hell* no. And yet my wings kept beating, carrying me toward Ostrogotho and the emotional beating waiting for me at Ruler's Seat.

Meira was going to kick my ass.

TWELVE

I ducked my head as Mabel and I stepped down through the large window into my sister's office, partially to avoid looking into Meira's eyes a few moments longer. To shut out the shock and then rage roaring from her, hitting my shields like a blow.

Meira might have been my younger sister but we were both adults now. I still thought of her as my little Meems, couldn't help it. Except for moments like these when she stepped fully into her role as Ruler and let loose all the power of Demonicon to show her displeasure.

Swearing I could handle. Flaming amber power crashing into my shields, no problem. But the hurt under her rage? The accusation, the guilt she harbored for who knew what reason coloring her outburst of fury?

That I would have taken from her if I could.

I looked up, forcing myself to face my sister, met her

blazing amber gaze. The magic of the plane swirled around her in a tightly contained tornado, ruffling the papers on her desk despite the magnitude of her magic, so firmly did she hold it to her. I just stood there, not sure what else to do, as she wound her way through every curse word she could come up with, even making a few out of nothing, I was sure.

Mabel waited too, hands folded in front of her, face still and calm. When Meira finally broke for a breath of air, the drach raised one arm, index finger waving before her.

"If you're done," she said, mild tone a shock after the crackling, snapping fury of Meira's emotions, "we have work to do."

My sister sputtered out and fell silent, red tinted face deep crimson as she fought for control. "Like hell," she snarled, jabbing her own upraised finger at me. "Like bloody hell."

"I understand you're upset with your sister," Mabel said as though Meira and I had only had a falling out over a minor transgression. Talk about drach understatements. "But the Universe has waited long enough."

"And whose fault is that?" My sister planted both fists on her hips, glaring at me like I was the culprit.

Well, my vampire sent, *you really are*.

Oh, shut up.

Oh dear, Shaylee whispered. *How embarrassing*.

The Sidhe princess had no idea just how embarrassing. And shameful. As the full realization sank in and I drew a shaking breath past the giant jab of understanding, my sister relented in an exhale of her own.

"Whatever," she grumbled, turning away from me, Demonicon's power falling to a muttering grumble. "Just tell me what you want and get it over with."

I'd finally done it. Ruined my relationship with Meira once and for all by leaving without saying goodbye, cutting her off without full explanation, though at the time it seemed my only option. And I'd never forgive myself for it.

Use it, my vampire sent. *To make you stronger.*

I wasn't sure how. But, oddly, her comment was comforting.

"Sydlynn was contacted by the vampire spirit, Alison Morgan." Max must have filled Mabel in on what happened. "Through the echo of one of your ancestors."

Meira seemed interested at least, though she refused to look at me, focusing on Mabel. "Which one?"

I almost sighed. Like it mattered. "Thaddea," I said.

Again she didn't look my way, just nodded, frowning. "And what was the result?"

"It felt odd," I said. "As though all of my magic was being pulled out of me."

That got a reaction. Meira's gaze finally flickered to mine, frown tightening. "That sounds familiar," she said.

I nodded. "Gabriel confirmed it."

My sister flinched as though I'd hit her, sorrow flashing over her face so fast I wasn't sure it even happened. "He's okay?" Her hand half lifted toward me, falling to her side.

Damn it, I should have told her right away. Mom must have been in touch to alert her to be on the lookout for him.

"He's fine," I said. "I found him in the old Sidhe Gate room in Wilding Springs." It felt like years ago now. And I so very much wanted to hug him suddenly. To cross the distance to my sister and hug her. But I held my ground and ached instead.

She nodded brusquely, looked away. "It's hard being here sometimes," she said, soft and distant. "Knowing there's nothing I can do to help."

Was that a jab at me? Probably. Then again, if it was, I deserved it, didn't I?

"He sent his spirit into the veil," I said, clearing my throat so I could speak, shocked my voice didn't shake. Again she turned toward me, focusing. Maybe I didn't ruin things completely after all. "Said he could see everything." I shivered as I finally absorbed what he said. I hadn't really had the time—or the inclination—to process his words. Until now. I felt my gaze widen as my eyes locked on my sister. Breathed out the next words as best I could. "He was the veil, Meems. The whole

Universe."

She swallowed, nodded. "But he's back?"

I clenched my hands at my sides to keep from shaking. My body begged me to allow it to shake itself to pieces but I held myself rigid instead. "I was so scared I dragged him back and stuffed him into his body again."

She snorted. Cleared her throat. "Bet he was happy about that."

I shrugged. "Not so much."

A long moment passed where we just looked at each other. And my heart began to soften.

"He confirmed what I felt," I said. "He said he saw the vampires. In the void between the edges of the veil."

Meira sighed, sank to the edge of her desk. Her anger at me seemed diminished to a pale flame. "I was afraid you'd say that," she said. Looked up again. "What do you want from me?"

"You rescued me from that place," Mabel said. I almost jumped when she spoke, having totally forgotten she was there. Lost in my sister and our conversation. "It is my hope you can be Syd's anchor and guide when she attempts for the second time to reach the vampires."

Meira nodded. "Of course," she said.

Just like that. Really made me feel like a slacker these last six months.

We've been hard at work, my demon protested.

Have we really? My vampire prodded me. *Try it now.*

I reached out my hand to my sister who stared at it in silence before standing and crossing to me. Her skin was warm, large fingers gripping mine without any semblance of familiarity. Just a touch of necessity. She'd gone back to avoiding my eyes, too.

Lovely.

She didn't give me warning, just opened the place to the void, her white magic battering its way through the membrane of the veil and plunging us into the darkness beyond. The black ribbon gasped, tugged at me while Meira forced me onward. I could feel her tether herself to Demonicon even as I fell, as though descending into a tunnel of emptiness, sucking away at the power in my possession, draining me. The lasso of the drach soul hauled backward, fought the gaping emptiness, but even it wasn't strong enough to save me from plunging deeper into the abyss.

I panted into utter silence, unable to stop my fall, feeling Meira's desperation as she tried to hold me back, the joined power of Mabel linking with her. Not enough.

Never enough.

Her touch slipped, a thread remaining as I fell headlong into the dark.

A fingertip of contact. Almost severed.

And then, a push. From below, beneath, shoving me back. And a whispered voice in my head.

Not this way, Sebastian sent, his power my power, my

old magic, but morphed and changed into something bright, shining, beautiful. *Only through the dead.* With a massive heave, he tossed me upward, toward my sister and the drach woman whose blood we shared, out and clear of the void.

I collapsed on the floor next to Meira as Mabel heaved her own massive breaths. My sister's fingers held tight to mine, my right hand where the black ribbon sagged, her shoulder pressed to me for mutual support as the two of us panted for air.

I looked over at Meira, caught a moment of pain in her gaze before she pulled her hand free and stood. Turned her back to me while I staggered to my feet beside Mabel. "That message was pretty clear," she said, as though I hadn't almost been lost.

It hurt. A lot.

"Indeed," Mabel said. "Though, I believe you are still the key, Meira."

My sister didn't comment only because the door to her office opened and two familiar demons entered. The first looked at me with shock, stopping on the top step, his handsome face alight with happiness. But the second didn't hesitate, hurtling herself toward me, giant grin on her face as my niece threw herself into my arms with a squeal so loud my ears hurt.

"Aunt Syd!" Zuza hugged me tight around my neck, the nub of her horn digging into my ear. Not like I cared even a little. For the first time I allowed myself to embrace who I'd been through the small demon in my arms, cradling her against me while she squeezed her enthusiastic welcome.

"Hey, munchkin," I whispered into her curly black hair, throat tight. "You're getting so big."

She leaned back, bouncing in my arms. "My horns are growing, see?" She stroked one of them with happy fingers.

"They're beautiful," I said, smiling though I wanted to cry. Meira was already moving forward, hands outstretched. It was with great sorrow I returned her daughter to her. Zuza seemed to sense the tension, looking back and forth between her mother and me, smile gone, brow furrowed.

"Mom?" She poked her mother in the cheek with one finger. "What's wrong?"

Meira didn't comment as Ram joined us. His soft kiss for my cheek only made my sister's distance all the more intense. As did his instant forgiveness for my absence and choice to leave.

"So good to see you," he said. "Like the new colors. They suit you."

Right. Gray skin, diamond eyes.

I couldn't do this any longer. And turned to go. Meira's voice spun me around while Mabel paused on the lip of the window sill.

"Running away again?"

There was nothing I could say to that. Though I wept into the hot Demonicon evening as Mabel and I flew out of the city and into the veil.

Thankfully my ancestress didn't comment. Because I just wasn't in the mood.

THIRTEEN

I stood under Harvard, in the tomb of my ancestors with a heavy heart, the drach leader and the *lóng* I now called friend standing behind me, allowing me to take the lead. While I'd already seen my mother, I wasn't looking forward to a second visit so soon after the first, not with the way I'd left things this time. Though I wasn't sure warding myself against her would do much good, I built shields between the catacombs under Harvard and the power of the North American council leader. Telling myself it was about privacy, that Mom didn't need to be part of this experiment.

Knowing I was just being a coward.

At least I had Max and Jiao with me to act as buffers if Mom did make an appearance. Mabel I'd left back at the Stronghold, though "left" might have been too strong a word. She'd let me go without her, silently, after waiting and watching as I filled Max in on what happened on Demonicon. At least with my sister. The conversation between Mabel and me, that I kept to myself.

If she judged me for that, she didn't show it.

Didn't matter now. I had to focus. Drew a breath and braced myself for visitations while cupping the black ribbon in the palm of my free hand, circling my wrist. It felt tired, almost sad. Because of its recent activities or the location we found ourselves in? Bit of both. It had tried to save me several times now, enough I trusted its judgment no matter the fact Max believed it had come from the Dark Universe.

Save me once, awesome. Save me twice, I owe you.

Places like this tended to overflow with echoes thanks to the bones of the witches buried here. But even after I let my power out, called to them, not a single one made an appearance.

I tried not to take it personally while as I despaired even the dead were pissed at me for leaving.

It wasn't until Max made a soft sound of distress and I looked up to see him frowning I realized it wasn't just me.

Arrogance again? Mabel was right.

"The spirit magic of this place is badly damaged," he said, striding forward, laying his hands on the stone slabs behind which the bones of my family rested. "Even more than I've felt in other places."

I didn't expect the sorrow that rose in my chest. They were all dead, after all, long gone. People I'd never met before and knew only through stories and legends. So why did their inability to rise hurt so much?

"Without the souls of the dead, I fear your friend's attempt to reach you is lost." The big drach turned toward me, bowing his head.

"Do we need them?" Jiao was always blunt, something I'd grown used to. But in this moment her lack of caring seemed especially hurtful.

"I think we do," Max said, gentle as always while I choked on nasty words I really would rather not say out loud. "There is a reason the vampires are gone, that the spirit magic of the Universe is vanishing." His diamond eyes met mine. "And that this particular plane seems to contain the most—and be hit the hardest of all."

That was news. "What do you mean?"

"I have always been aware your plane was unique," he said, returning to my side. I shivered in the cool damp of the place as he went on, as though someone walked over my grave. "The truth is, no other exists like it. It's as though when I severed sorcery into the elemental magicks this plane became the center of the schism."

"That does make sense," Jiao said. "As it was this plane where my people ended up."

Interesting, my vampire sent. *Was it here you created the other magicks, Max?*

He paused, head tilted to one side. "So much time has passed," he said, voice low and vibrating with the song of his people. *Our people*, my brain whispered. "But now that you mention it, that does seem to be the most likely explanation."

So my home plane was the center of Max's rebellion against Creator? No wonder we were screwed up.

"Regardless," he said, "there is a reason the vampires are gone. And a reason they are attempting to reach us. Both of those I believe to be important."

"Which means we have to find a way to talk to them through the dead." I shivered again. "Dead who aren't here to rise."

"They are here." Max half turned, nodding. "Just unable to speak."

I reached out, felt the faint touch of echoes. But they seemed locked behind walls, weak and quiet. There was a time I had used necromancy to speak to the dead, a family gift passed down from Gram—

—don't think about Gram, don't do it—

But I didn't seem to have access to it right now.

It could have been lost when you gave up the family magic, my vampire sent.

Another thought to avoid at all costs.

"We need assistance," Max said, voice sad. Did he know what he was asking? There were only two people I could think of with necromancy powers. One of them was in a no fly zone for now. I just couldn't face her. And the other… well, the other had lost his mind.

Though the possibility Pender Tremere, the former North American Enforcer leader, had recovered from his mental break caused by the Brotherhood was a distinct possibility. And if he was hale and whole, that would mean I wouldn't have to face Gram.

What was I going to do if I had to face Gram?

And the furry, silver ball of fury who would never forgive me?

Pender it was.

Max didn't comment as I opened the veil and stepped inside, keeping my human form. Jiao followed in silence, our constant shadow, once reviled, now welcome. More welcome even than ever. The realization I'd traded one group of loved ones for another wasn't lost to me.

Damn it.

I stepped out of the veil into a lush, green park, my power tentatively prodding the edge of the coven's territory. Karyn Barrett felt shocked at first, but welcomed me immediately, the coven's wards opening and inviting me inside. There was a time I wouldn't have even knocked, but a lot had changed.

Including Karyn. She looked older, more mature, though in a good way, as though her power and position had finally caught up with her. The young woman I'd met not so long ago, whose eagerness and intensity led me to agree to be the leader of the Shadow Council, looked more put together and in control than I ever felt. Made me a bit jealous, really, even as she waited for me in her living room when we stepped the brief distance through the veil to her presence.

Only the tiny widening of her hazel eyes and the bob of her dark ponytail told me she was shocked by my change of appearance. She'd dyed her bangs back to the shock of blonde, lightening her face, making her look younger and lifting the tired corners of her eyes. Karyn was young, only in her mid-twenties, but she, like all the other new coven leaders, had been forced to take on a large burden since the attack of the Brotherhood, far before her time. The warmth in her greeting as she impulsively reached for my hands and pulled me to her tightened my chest and made me want to hug her hard. As it was, I embraced her with as much distance as I could, if only to keep from tears.

She didn't seem to take offense from my lack of enthusiasm, just smiled at me, then at Max and Jiao in greeting.

"You have no idea how good it is to see you," she said.

I gently touched the edge of her power, felt the swell of her family's magic, the stability and contentment there. "Your family thrives under your leadership," I said, the formal words falling from my lips, my drach soul taking over at last. How odd. I felt the girls retreat. Was this they're doing, to protect me?

Karyn beamed, nodded. "Thank you for your kind words," she said. "I'm doing my best. And things seem to be going well, at least for us." Her lips softened, a tiny frown forming between her brows. It felt odd to be standing in her living room, the full cushions of her sofa beckoning. Just six short months ago I might have sunk into the microfiber softness, had a cup of coffee, chatted. Instead, I stood stiff and quiet in this foreign feeling place, the curiosity of the Barrett coven barely contained as it sniffed around me.

"I'm glad to hear it." At least she wasn't in trouble. "I know that's not the case for everyone."

Karyn grimaced. "There have been some difficulties." She laughed. "Listen to me. It's been crappy ass awful, Syd." And just like that the wall between us broke and I sagged out of the drach and into the woman I was. The scent of something baking in the kitchen—was that chocolate chip cookies?—made me want to cry. "But we're managing." She glanced at Max and Jiao again, slight awe in her voice. "I can only imagine how hard things have been for you." Sympathy. Please, not sympathy. I didn't deserve it. "Thank you so much for checking in." And gratitude.

She was killing me.

"The other covens?" I had to change the subject. To

escape her understanding, her caring.

"When your grandmother refused to take over as Shadow Council leader," Karyn said with a faint blush on her cheeks, "they bullied me into it." And now, apology. A seeking of my approval.

I was honestly going to die.

"I'm surprised you've maintained the Shadow Council, considering the new laws." That was better. Drach, do your thing.

Karyn shrugged. "Your mother's decision to open the council to all covens was a brilliant one," she said. "But theory and practice are two different things." Rueful smile, dimples. "Infighting and old school against us newfangled," she laughed without humor, "means we still have to be careful."

Neither Mom nor myself believed making the council open to all covens would be the end all of fixing centuries of issues, at least not right away. But, from the sound of things, it was a bigger mess than either of us expected.

My fault.

Stop that, my vampire sent, crisp with anger.

Yes, ma'am.

And, remember this when you speak to Miriam next, my vampire sent. *That Karyn Barrett should be her successor.*

Ah. How brilliant. And I almost missed it.

"Have you spoken to Tallah?" I was surprised how much it irked me suddenly, the thought of my former friend, Tallah Hensley, sticking it to my mother the way she did even after Mom did everything she could to put the entirety of North American witches on even footing. But Tallah had been struggling with issues of her own— issues maybe I never fully understood—from the moment the Brotherhood attacked, decimating her coven. In her shoes, would I have acted as she did and decided to do my own thing?

Sigh. No brainer. I was the queen of doing my own thing.

"She's cut all of us off," Karyn said, true sadness in her face. "All but a few she's recruited to her new territory. But only local covens. Though, I fear, she'll start drawing in others as time goes on."

"Power hungry?" It was a possibility. Almost losing her family could have driven her to the brink of possessiveness.

"I don't know," Karyn said. "I truly wish I did." She hesitated. "What I do know of her... it's doubtful she'd act without her own agenda."

Surprise, surprise. Well, Tallah's little plans could wait.

Max shifted behind me, enough of a subtle prod I knew he wanted me to get on with it. "I'm not just here to say hello," I said, weak and pathetic, really.

Karyn started, nodded. "Of course," she said, another glance to the pair behind me widening her eyes. "Forgive me. You must have important business." Jeez, seriously? Oh, yeah. I guess we did, though, right? "Whatever the Barrett coven can do for you, Syd, just ask."

I swallowed, wondering if I'd have to take her up on that. If what Mabel said was a foretelling of something to come. And if I'd be able to ask when the time came.

Or not.

"Pender," I said. "I need to see Pender." While Mom and I had taken Pender home to Wilding Springs—not home, Syd, not anymore—for treatment when he'd been initially recovered, Karyn and the Barrett family had kindly asked to care for him when it was apparent he wouldn't recover from the damage done to him by the Brotherhood. Hard to let him go, but I hadn't had the time to focus on him back then and Karyn seemed a perfect choice to watch over the broken Enforcer leader.

Karyn's face fell a little, but not in disappointment. In sorrow. "He's still... not himself."

I nodded, sighing. Of course he wasn't. Hoping he'd come back was just too big a leap. It had taken Demetrius Strong, Gram's husband, a major battle and the assistance of a massive amount of magic to help him heal his mind and heart. And even then I was sure he still had residual issues—

—stop thinking about her RIGHT NOW—

Pender's recovery was a long shot. Still.

"I need to see him," I said.

Karyn led me without complaint down the hall, away from the large kitchen where the delicious cookie smells emerged, through the silent house, past dust mote laden sunbeams emerging from bedroom doors to a closed entry at the end of the corridor. She paused with one hand on the knob as though about to speak before sighing and opening it.

He sat on the floor with a large pile of wooden blocks in front of him on the pale blue carpet, long, thin legs folded before him. He didn't notice me at first, slim hands turning the blocks, finding numbers and letters he assembled into shapes and collections, the meaning of which were lost on me.

"He's like this most of the time," Karyn said, a gentle smile on her face. "Peaceful." Sounded like a blessing. "But he can get worked up."

A warning? More a request, I guessed. "I'm sorry," I said, hardening my heart. Mabel's words bounced around in my head as I crossed to the tall, skinny man, thinning hair showing shining skin through the sparseness, his head bent over his work. I stood there, looking down at him, at the hole he'd worn in the knee of his jeans, the veins standing out on the back of his brown spotted hands. And wished there was a way to make things right.

"Pender." I folded my legs under me, sitting next to him. He didn't look up, still humming, lower lip caught between his yellow stained teeth. He'd aged and yet looked so young somehow. As though in taking his mind the Brotherhood dragged him finally into old age while freeing his mind to be a child's. When he bent forward, his button up shirt seemed to cave in toward his thin chest. While he'd never been all that robust, he looked like a scarecrow of a man to me, his power subtle and distant even as I reached for it and spoke his name again.

It wasn't until I touched the back of his hand with my fingertips he looked up. Pale eyes seemed to stare through me, past me, two blocks held in his suddenly silent hands, hovering over the stacks before him.

"He's like this sometimes," Karyn said, apology in her words. "No one can reach him. It takes effort just to make him eat."

I squeezed his hand with my fingertips, gently. "Pender," I said, with my voice and my power. "Pender, do you know who I am?"

For a long moment he stared, lips slack, a faint line of drool forming a drop that trembled and threatened to fall. And then, in a flash of something deep inside him, he inhaled.

"Syd," he whispered.

I had to clear my throat to speak again. "Hi, Pender," I said.

The blocks fell from his hands, arms going around me. I let him hug me, felt his body shudder as he sobbed on my shoulder. Wished there was something I could do.

We will make this right somehow, my demon growled.

I hoped she knew what she was talking about.

He pulled away, blinking through tears, wiping at his running nose with his sleeve. "They're coming, Syd," he whispered. "With their armor and sorcery and all the darkness, they're coming."

Max drew a breath behind me, spoke. "The Order?"

Pender bobbed a nod, but his eyes never left mine. "Coming to get you, Syd," he said.

Let them try. If only I felt as confident as those words sounded my head. I was already terrified of the soldiers of Dark Brother, trapped in the other Universe. Had tried to convince myself not to be afraid, that there was no way they could cross over. I was safe, we were all safe from the immense power of the Order.

Pender might have been cracked into a million shards but there was enough sanity in his gaze in that moment, I believed him.

"How do you know?" Maybe he wasn't as broken as I thought. He might be able to help me find Belaisle, to track the rest of the pieces of Creator the former Brotherhood leader had stolen from me. But the moment I asked I saw the man inside him fade away, the shattered remains of Pender Tremere rising to the surface yet again.

He pulled his hands from mine, turning back to his blocks. I looked down at them as he lifted the last two and placed them.

And froze while the black ribbon shivered in response. The left grouping was a jumble of numbers that made no sense, of shapes mixed in with digits I was certain had zero meaning. But the right hand pile, the stack of eleven blocks, ended in the top with a large, red "D".

Doombringer.

FOURTEEN

I left Pender to his blocks with a chill in my gut. Karyn didn't say anything until we were all back in the living room, chatter of other witches now coming from her kitchen.

"That's the most lucid I've seen him," she said, hands wringing before her. "Should we be preparing for something new?" She had her coven leader hat on, clearly. But what did I have to tell her, what comfort to offer when my very soul shook at the thought of the marching, endless seeming army of Dark Brother coming to get me?

Boogeymen, maybe. But I'd felt their power. And my own weakness in the face of their massive touch. I had no doubt if the Order did somehow make it across the place between Universes we would have zero chance against them. Even the might of the drach seemed equal to their power, in a deadlock match I was certain they weren't used to outside the might of the maji. And the numbers of the Order eclipsed that of the first race of this Universe by multiples of ten.

What should I tell her? I sent the desperate question to Max.

Who sighed mentally. *Only that we are doing what we can to keep this Universe safe*, he sent. *What more can you tell her?*

I mumbled something that sounded vaguely promising to Karyn. She accepted my reassurance at face value. Even as I shriveled with guilt inside.

"I know you'll keep us appraised," she said, sounding much more confident than she should. "I'm sorry Pender couldn't be more help."

"It's good of you to take him in like this," I said. Her family had found him, homeless and raving, on the streets of their city.

Karyn smiled. "He's a good man who worked hard for our people. It's an honor to care for him."

A dark head poked out from the kitchen door, brown eyes flickering over me as the young woman did her best not to stare.

"Do we have dinner guests?" Had to be Karyn's second, though I didn't recognize her.

The coven leader turned to me clearly with the intention to ask but I was already shaking my head with real regret. Maybe when this was over. Maybe.

"We have to go." I stepped back from Karyn, heart heavy, knowing I now had no choice. Even as blue fire lit the air beside the sad faced coven leader. She spun at the sight of the tall, lean woman who emerged from the flames, her wrinkled face creased in a scowl, iron gray hair clipped close to her scalp. Two thick brows came together at the sight of me, thin lips pursed while Varity Rhodes pointed one thin index finger at my chest.

"You," she snapped. "Get your ass home right now, young lady."

It was a testament to the sheer physical presence of the Enforcer leader I almost did as she told me without thinking. Almost. Made me smile, too. Varity's lips curved just a little, thin shoulders bowing slightly under the weight of her black robe.

"I mean it," she snapped, eyes sparking with joy. "Ethpeal's been a bitch for six months. I can't stand her." She blew a raspberry. "Your fault, you ungrateful brat."

Her words should have hurt, they were so true. Or so I'd discovered. But all I could do was grin at her. At least she wasn't yelling at me.

"Oh, shut up, you bossy old bat," I said. "I'll go when I'm good and ready."

Varity barked a laugh and lunged for me, pulling me against her chest. She felt as strong as ever, old wire under hardened leather. But there was a frailty to her I'd never encountered before, a thinning to her physical body that left me worried. Still, her power pulsed with familiar contact and, as she pulled away again, tears sparkling in her eyes, she pinched the end of my nose with two fingers.

"Thank the elements you're here," she breathed. "We need you now more than any of us were willing to admit."

For the first time I didn't feel guilty. Just responsible. And, with new resolve, nodded.

"If you don't mind," I said, throwing sarcasm in as thick as I could, "I'm a bit busy."

She huffed. "Get lost then, pest." She waved one thin hand in my face. Grinned. "Wish I could be a fly on the wall when she sees you." Varity laughed. "Go on, then. Give your grandmother a heart attack."

I didn't have to ask Max and Jiao to stay behind, feeling them part with me the moment we entered the veil. This reunion I had to do alone. Most of all, this one would take the greatest toll.

My heart was already breaking even as it soared.

The fact the excitement far outweighed my fear told me it was the right thing to do. Needing Gram's help or not—I could think about her now without wincing, without a wave of guilt. Much more than her assistance, I needed *her*. The strength she always brought me, her calculated and snarky remarks. Her love.

Had needed her all along. The sister of my soul,

owner of the magic I carried for seventeen years, who knew me better than I knew myself. Who'd come through her own tragedy, through madness and loss of her power for the second time. Power I returned to her when I forced her into the role of witch once again, thrusting on her the magic of the Hayle coven before I fled.

Dread mixed with anxiety danced with joy as I drew a breath and, well shielded, stepped through the rubber membrane of the veil and into the achingly familiar dimness of the basement in Wilding Springs.

Even the veil seemed to sigh its happiness, though there was enough trepidation in my heart I had a hard time embracing the pure giddy pleasure I took in going home. I stood for a long moment in the quiet, breathing in beloved scents. Funny how I never noticed Mom's lilac perfume lingered here, nor the deeper scent of earth despite the concrete walls. I longed to reach for the family magic, to embrace it, but hesitated, taking in the pentagram etched in the floor at my feet, the single bulb overhead dark at the moment. My eyes traveled the well-known space, to the stairs leading upward.

I felt them, heard them moving above me. Allowed a moment more of lingering happiness, choking on tears begging to be shed. Pretended I had only been gone a little while, that none of what passed happened, that I still belonged. Until my vampire sighed.

And broke the spell.

As much as we'd all like to enjoy this little fantasy for a while longer, she sent, *doing so serves no one. We must move forward.*

Thanks for ruining the moment, my demon grumbled.

Shaylee jabbed her. *It was lovely*, she sent. *But it's time.*

Time to face the music.

As my feet carried me to the steps, I felt the oddness at last, accepted how weird it was to be here and not feel the full weight of the family magic as part of my power. That slice of me was gone forever and had been hard to shed. It wanted to stay with me, something I simply couldn't allow. The coven needed to be safe and that meant severing my connection. And making Gram take over the role she'd handed to me for a life with Demetrius.

That alone made me worry she'd not forgive me.

I stopped at the top of the stairs, feet silent in my sneakers, careful on the way up to avoid the one creaking step that could have given me away. Pressed my ear to the door. Heard their voices, chatting, the clink of cutlery on plates. Smelled the scent of casserole and coffee.

Felt the heat of daylight on the other side of the door. It might as well have been miles away I was so detached from it. Regardless, as I raised one hand and gently pushed the door open, it was as though the very house embraced me.

I revealed myself to them as gently as I could, opening my shields a tiny fraction at a time as I crossed the threshold and onto the sun warmed kitchen tiles. Even so, all activity froze, three faces turning toward me, slack lipped, eyes wide. A dollop of food fell from Gram's fork to her plate with a soft plop as I hesitated before waving.

"Hey," I said.

Demetrius rose first, coming to my side, a huge smile on his cherub face. His white curls tickled my cheek when he embraced me, hugging me tight. His sorcery slipped over mine, welcoming me home even before he spoke.

"Syd," he said, choked up, cleared his throat. "Syd, my dear. You look…"

I shrugged. "Yeah, sorry," I said. "Takes a bit to get used to." I rubbed my gray hands together. Glanced over his shoulder.

At Gram's furious face.

Oh, hell.

A ball of silver fur hit the floor with a heavy thud, Sass's portly body disappearing down the hall and out of sight. Tears burned my eyes at his rejection, but I'd been expecting it. And didn't blame him. He'd begged me at the end, tried so hard to stop me. And I'd ignored him, left him behind without even a goodbye.

Why did I ever think it was a good idea going the way I did?

They would have stopped us otherwise, my vampire sent softly. *We had to leave that way or we wouldn't have left.*

Okay, fair enough. Still. I hated having regrets, especially now.

Gram slowly stood, shaking all over, blue eyes flaring with witch fire. She felt real to me, more than she had when she was a sorcerer, her witch power gone from her. Not like the woman I knew, loved, cherished. Here was the woman who I'd shared magic with for so long. I'd missed her more than I ever would have admitted when she was still a sorcerer.

"Sydlynn. Thaddea. Hayle." Her voice shook, power rippling over her as the coven's magic hiccuped its joy, held tight against her even as it tried to come to me, to snuffle and hug me. "What have you done to yourself?"

I looked down at my hands, up into her eyes. "Just a few modifications," I said, fighting to keep my voice steady.

"Modifications." She set her fist on one hip, the other beating against her thigh. "You little fool."

I stood there as still as I could, waiting for the explosion. There would be one, I had no doubt. Some kind of screaming, hurtful awfulness I clearly deserved.

That never came. Of course not. My fear of her rejection had nothing to do with the soul of Ethpeal Hayle. Instead, she gasped a breath, sobbed once, collapsed in on herself, both hands covering her face. And, in a rush of emotion, I went to her. Wrapped my arms around her shoulders and let her cry against me even as my own tears flowed.

"Syd," she whispered. "Girl, why did you leave me?" I choked on an answer, wishing she could understand. Until she spoke again. "Stupid question," she said. "But don't you ever do that again." Her strong hands gripped my upper arms and she shook me. "Ever, Sydlynn. Or I will never, ever forgive you."

I kissed her cheek. Wished I could promise her. Not sure even if I did, if I meant it now, the future wouldn't hold some new truth that would make me break such a promise.

Did she know what I was thinking? Maybe. Or not. Regardless, she hugged me suddenly, crushingly, rocking me as she did, whispering my name into my ear.

She finally let me go, wiping at her cheeks with both hands. Demetrius handed us both tissues. Gram blew her nose with gusto before waving at the back hall, eyes bright with new tears.

"Just go get him," she said. "He's been hell to live with since you left. You think *I'm* mad at you."

I couldn't speak, could barely breathe. Turned without argument for the hall. Feet heavy and growing heavier by the step, I made my way past the stairs, looking up at the landing, to the bedroom door where once I'd slept with Quaid, conceived my daughter. To the back door and the empty yard, the ghostly images of the rise of The Wild and Gram's recovery, Sunny's shower, my marriage to Liam, so many moments in time flickering through my mind as I stepped out into the lush grass.

And reached for him.

He tried to block me but I would know his power anywhere, the warmth of it, the multilayered flavor. So many witches had given him a portion of their magic over the years, the demon power he held inside him as beloved as my own. My heart light but my body deep in dread, I crossed to the edge of the yard and over the property line to the next lawn. Into the trees where a dilapidated treehouse still remained, hidden in the branches of an oak.

Which reminded me of Liam, suddenly, poignant moment made all the more so as I climbed the rough wooden ladder to the platform, vision adjusting to the dappling of the leaves over the dark floor.

Empty. But for an old, blue blanket tucked into the corner. And a shaking ball of silver fur, huddled tight and closed.

When I was a girl, I used to wonder where Sassafras would disappear to. There were times he would vanish and my young mind would conjure remarkable stories and mysteries around his absence. It wasn't until Sass became human, trying to help my father return to Demonicon, I discovered this place. His secret hiding place, away from us. Not an adventure or anything remarkable. Just an abandoned treehouse in the neighbor's yard.

That discovery had roused pity in my heart. No more than now. My favorite blue blanket, now ratty and threadbare, was his only comfort in this cold and barren place. I had no idea he still used it. And perhaps he didn't, except for times like this.

Times when his heart was breaking. Or broken.

And I'd driven him back here.

"Sass." I reached out to him but he didn't say anything. Just shivered and ignored me, nose tucked under his tail. I stroked his soft fur, bent to smell the delicious scent of him. Tried to gather him in my hands. But his power prevented me, blocked me. And while I could have easily broken through his wards, I left him his dignity if nothing else. Sighed and turned to the entrance. "I'm sorry, Sass," I said. And began to climb down.

My stomach clenched in fear as I took the first step. Damned vertigo. Then in pain as he spoke, stopping me on the rung.

"You said you still needed me." Had anyone ever spoken words laden with so much misery?

This time when I approached, he cried, tearing sounds, shaking his entire cat body. When I tried to lift him, he went limp, wards falling away, a shuddering, agony riddled bundle of silver fluff in my lap.

I wept with him, hands stroking his fur over and over again, trying to soothe him with my touch, to soften away the pain I'd caused through physical contact. He did still somewhat, his wracking sobs easing, but there was no release of his agony, no lessening of the misery in his magic.

"Syd," he whispered. "Promise me. When you go again you take me with you."

I honestly never felt such shock. Sass? Leave the coven? He *was* the coven, a hundred and fifty years' worth.

"What about the family?" He was the one who, no matter what happened with me, stressed endlessly the importance of family.

He looked up into my eyes, his amber ones dull and sad. "I'm not here for the coven anymore," he said. "Syd, don't you get it? Because I finally do." He sighed out some of his hurt, ears sideways, whiskers drooping into my lap. "I've been waiting for you all this time."

Damn him. He had to make me cry all over again. I hugged him against my chest, nuzzled his fur with my nose. "Silly cat," I said.

I rocked him as Gram had rocked me, my feet dangling out the opening of the treehouse, vertigo forgotten, faint breeze carrying the sound of traffic from the next street over, the squeal of playing children from the park on the other side of the yard, scent of wild roses and fresh air. But, despite the outside world's attempt to intrude, there was just the rustle of the oak leaves, the soft warmth of the sunlight and Sassafras in my arms.

This promise I would have to keep.

"Sass," I said. "I can't help it. I'll be going again."

He nodded against my chest.

"And you're coming with me."

FIFTEEN

We sat there in the tree's foliage until the sun started to set, just me and Sass, Sass and me. When I finally set him down beside me, my hands sweating from holding him so tight, he shifted slowly, growing in size and form, until his human shape perched next to me, amber eyes still sorrowful and worried but more himself than when I'd first appeared again.

"Nice," I said, smiling. "You've come a long way in controlling the shift."

He shrugged, dark hair shaggy over his brow, pointed chin tucking down toward the top of his button up shirt. Dark jeans ended in black and white sneakers, swinging in the open air. I gulped and looked back up, hating the return of my height fears.

But embracing them at the same time. Proof I was still human. Why that mattered to me in that moment I wasn't sure. Except maybe the sad eyes meeting mine needed me to be the girl he remembered, if just for a little while.

"I know why you left." He ran one hand through his hair, teenaged face serious, far too serious. I longed to hear him laugh. "I do understand, Syd. Me, of everyone. I get it." He sighed out some of his pain, shoulders sagging. "If anyone instilled in you the pressure to do what was right for others and not yourself, it was me."

I slipped my arm around him, leaned my head on his shoulder. "Don't be an asshat," I said.

Sass snorted. "Better than an arrogant brat."

"Smartass cat." I grinned into the growing dark.

"Ungrateful child." He sighed. "I missed you so much."

"Me too." I hadn't, though. Not in the state I'd been in where I'd forgotten everyone and everything. But now? Now, I missed him even though he was sitting next to me. As though remembering all at once six months of absence.

"We need you, Syd," he said, "even though the Universe calls you away from us."

I wouldn't have listened to anyone but him. And felt myself being pulled, at last, back into this world. For good or ill, with a soft sigh, I embraced the small things and let him go on without protest.

"How much do you know?" He waited for me to

shrug against him before shifting into a more comfortable position. "About Quaid and Payten?" I nodded. "Your mother and the council?"

"I know about Tallah," I said. "And the fact the other councils are giving Mom a hard time." I'd have to do something about that.

My demon cheered softly in the back of my head. Made me grin. And remember this had been fun once.

Oh, dear.

"The Steam Union?" Sass paused, continued when I was silent. "Piers is furious with you, you know."

What else was new? Everyone I cared about was out for my throat.

"Femke." Sass's hand squeezed mine in my lap. "You really need to talk to her, Syd. Something's terribly wrong."

"So I heard." I sat up, looked into his eyes. "Any idea what's up with her?"

"Not a clue," he said. "I've been kind of out of touch lately." Was that guilt? He'd better not feel guilty. This wasn't his fault. This horrible thing I'd done to him. He swallowed as I remembered the echo of Thaddea Hayle in the catacombs, how broken hearted she'd sounded, asking about her darling Sassafras. Kept it to myself.

There was only so much pain I was willing to load on him.

"I guess I have people to see and places to go." I

leaned forward, hands braced on the wood beneath me, fear of heights gone as suddenly as it returned.

He shrank next to me, furry body shuddering as he completed his transformation into Persian perfection. Magic surrounded him while he descended the rungs on padded feet, effortless, amber fire staircase bringing him to the ground. I suppose I could have floated down or sprouted small wings, but instead I climbed, enjoying the feel of the wood under my hands, the pressure of the planks under my sneakers.

When I touched down on the ground he stood on his hind legs, front paws on my knee. I scooped him without thought, cuddling him to me, carrying his furred body into the yard, to the back door while he sighed soft joy at our closeness.

I felt his magic link to mine, the moment of joining. It tripped me up, made me stumble over the threshold of the house. I stood for a moment in the dark of the back hall, still holding him, heart pounding. The tie I'd severed reunited as if it had never been broken, stronger even than ever before.

"Never leave me," he said, soft and trembling. "You promised."

I fed the link power and sealed it against all destruction. For better or worse, Sass and I would never be apart again.

Another sigh from him, this time contentment. I was

so wrapped up in what I'd just done my feet carried me into the kitchen before I realized Gram and Demetrius were still there.

And they weren't alone.

She glared at me with icy eyes, blonde hair loose around her shoulders. Her red leather jacket—her favorite color—hugged her curves, her broad shoulders, as a wolf's gaze flashed over her blue eyes a moment.

I set Sassafras on the table and opened my arms. And Charlotte came to me and embraced me like I'd never left. And, in that one hug, granted her forgiveness and understanding.

I let her go at last, kissing her cheek on the way out. Charlotte touched the spot with her fingertips, shook her head.

"About time," she said, voice gruff. "Now sit and tell us everything."

I did. Took a chair with a coffee before me and Sass in my lap and filled them in on the last six months. Realized just how uneventful it had been, days and weeks of flying through the veil, of exploring planes. Saw the wonderment and shock on their faces. And grimaced.

"And accomplished little," I said. "Despite my best intentions."

Until, my vampire sent.

"Until," I said. And told them of the dream of Liam. Of Alison. And all I'd learned since.

Gram listened with her fingers steepled before her, eyes narrowed as she watched me. She nodded a time or two then sat back as I finished, tapping those same fingertips on the table before her. So lovely to feel the family magic within her, around her. To feel the witch in her again. And the sorcerer, too.

She'd earned both.

"I've been to see Pender a few times," she said. "I wish there was more we could do for him."

Demetrius nodded, clearly saddened by the man's state. And utterly familiar from the haunted look in his eyes. "Perhaps someday we'll have a cure for what the Brotherhood has done," he said.

The implication was huge. When we finally brought them to their knees.

When I did.

"So you need a necromancer." Gram nodded. "You forget, of course, Varity is one, too."

I had. On purpose?

"With the two of us, we should be able to arrange something. Enough power, hopefully, to draw out what you need." Gram glanced at Demetrius who looked anxious. "I'll be fine, dear."

He smiled instantly, the sun rising over all of us. "I know," he said. "I still worry, though. I hope that's okay."

She laughed, deep and rich, leaning forward to cup his face in her hands. "Have I told you lately I love you?"

He sighed happily. "Never often enough," he said.

Too. Much. Cute.

"I realize tracking down and communicating with Sebastian and Alison is important," Charlotte said.

But.

I nodded for her to go on.

Her wolf appeared in her eyes again and I was strongly reminded she wasn't just my friend, but werequeen. "Femke," she said.

Again with Femke. "You want me to talk to her before we try this?"

Charlotte shifted in her seat. "I would never ask you to do anything against what you feel is necessary," she said.

Again with the pregnant but.

"Miriam has held the North American council safe from Femke," Gram said. "Pulled us from the WPC." I didn't know that. "The only council free, as a matter of fact." Mom was nothing if not brave. Now I really felt guilty. I needed to talk to her, too. If I was going to stay.

If. Even for a little while.

Yes, I'd be leaving again. I had no doubt of that. But I had a chance to make things right here with the people I loved. To salve the wounds I'd made by cutting myself off from them, make amends and apologies I really did mean. And I had every intention of doing so.

I patted Charlotte's hand, feeling her tension through

her flesh. "This can wait a bit," I said. "If I'm going to fall headlong into the problems of this plane again, I might as well make as much noise as I can. Right?"

Charlotte's relief was palpable. "I suppose," she said. Grinned. "I'll be coming with you, naturally."

"And me." Sass's claws dug into my jeans.

"And, I think, me." Gram stood up, face stern but eyes bright. "For a bit of an adventure. I've missed adventures."

Charlotte joined her, Sass still in my arms. The werequeen paused, tilting her head to one side.

"A word of warning," she said. "Femke's ear has been claimed by the Sidhe lord Everonus. And she listens to none other these days."

She might as well have punched me in the stomach. "Sidhe?" I immediately thought of Spaft and Sonja O'Dane. And my son. It was highly unlikely he was unconnected to their luring of Gabriel to the Gate chamber. Considering the last time I'd seen them together they'd been talking in Hong Kong. "What if he's behind Femke's issues?"

Charlotte frowned. "It's possible," she said, "though the WPC leader has been odd since her rescue from the Russian mafia."

Maybe Everonus was exploiting my friend, then. Regardless, I'd find out the truth. And if he was tampering with Femke, he'd learn that was a bad idea.

A very bad idea indeed.

Never mind I'd cut myself off from her as much as I had everyone else. Fences would be mended. I was back to do what needed to be done I inhaled and embraced the happy feeling that thought brought with it.

And to hell with the big stuff for now. It would be there until I figured out how to deal with it or the Universe collapsed in on itself.

The small stuff needed me.

SIXTEEN

I'd been in Hong Kong already, but this was different. Official. I clenched my gray hands together, feeling the scales rise to prominence on the surface as I collected my power and expected the worst. Stepped out of the veil with my three loved ones around me.

Waited for the fireworks as the tall, slim blonde with the ice blue eyes looked up from her desk with shock and stared.

And stared.

No explosion. Just a slow, quiet pain, a dull descent from surprise to joy to grief to anger. But none of it had weight aside from the initial joy. As though Femke lived behind a wall of something that wouldn't allow her to fully embrace what she felt.

I prodded for the source but found nothing of magical origin even as she straightened, her back rigid, hands tight at her sides.

"Sydlynn Hayle," she said. "Welcome back."

It could have been worse. She could have ordered me arrested or something. Still, it hurt, the coldness. And though I wished I was stronger than that, I answered in kind.

"Council Leader Svennson," I said. "I understand you could use some help around here."

That was quite possibly the most insulting and worst thing I could have said in that moment. Nice to know the old Syd was still alive and kicking and able to stick her foot so far in her mouth she choked.

Femke's gasp and eye widening told the tale. While I winced inwardly at my social awkwardness and wished I could take it back.

"Council Leader." I knew his voice, didn't turn as the Sidhe lord Everonus entered, ignored him completely while he crossed the room and joined Femke at her desk. His long, black hair hung to the floor over his elaborate robes, pale skin and silver eyes Sidhe perfection. He gave me the creeps.

"My lord Everonus." Did Femke sound relieved to see him? She certainly seemed to bend toward him, almost as though he were the leader and she the subordinate. Which instantly made me both suspect and despise him.

But my prodding to his power gave me nothing, no

bond or control over Femke, even when Shaylee firmly grasped his magic in hers and shook him slightly. He seemed shocked by the assault, though, to my surprise, he didn't comment on it.

I'd just roughed him up publicly and he was letting it slide? Now I knew something was going on with this Sidhe.

Time to poke the dragon. Wait, bad analogy.

"Nice try with the kidnapping thing," I said, throwing it at him like a weapon. "Turns out my son is much more powerful—and clever—than your two flunkies. You can let Hortense and Sonja know when I catch them they'll take a long time to die."

Someone else entered the room as I was speaking, the familiar touch of Quaid's power alerting me to his arrival. A warning?

Femke seemed to shift into a different person the moment he appeared. Her face twisted, a mask of rage, one shaking hand pointing at me. Like a switch had been flipped. Gram and I exchanged a startled glance while her voice boomed through the office.

"Enforcer Leader Tinder," she shouted. "Arrest Sydlynn Hayle for aiding the escape of Brotherhood Leader Liander Belaisle."

Oh, *hell* no. She wasn't pulling out that sad, old news. Not when it had been her fault in the first place.

Syd, my vampire snapped in my head. *This isn't*

important. Pay attention.

Grumble, mumble. My self-righteousness had to take a back seat, I knew it. Still, my emotions were fresh enough it was hard to put aside the knee jerk reaction to the accusation.

"In case you've forgotten," Charlotte spoke up, the weight of the werenation's power in her voice, "the escape of Liander Belaisle was your fault, Council Leader."

Yeah, things were going to go downhill quickly at this rate.

Femke began to shake, spittle forming on her lips, eyes huge and staring. Even Everonus appeared nervous of her reaction. Blue power crackled around her as she seemed to snap.

"ARREST THEM ALL!" She staggered forward, one hand pressed to the top of the desk to keep her from falling over. For a moment I was really worried she'd attack us, my shields snapping into place to protect Gram, Charlotte and Sass. But, in the instant it took me to do so, Femke seemed to sag, all the strength running out of her. The council's power died out in a sizzling pop but her rage didn't diminish. Tears poured down her cheeks while she sobbed her rage. "ARREST THEM NOW, ENFORCER TINDER."

Everonus supported her when she staggered to one side, falling into a chair. Femke thrashed against his hands, still sobbing. "Obey me! Obey me!" And then she buried her face in her hands and wailed.

Oh. My. Freaking. Swearword.

What. The. Hell?

Syd. Quaid's mind touched mine, a whip lash of power, angry and upset. But not with me. *Please, just go.*

I can't, Quaid, I sent. *I can't just leave her here like this.* I watched him go to her, kneel next to her, pat her knee. Everonus stood back, glaring at me like this was my fault. *How long has she been this way?*

A while now, Quaid sent. *I've done my best to keep it quiet, but...*

You idiot, Gram sent in a crackle of power. *She's in no shape to lead the council.*

He spun with fury on his face. *Like any of you care,* he sent in return, the power of the Enforcers flaring around him. *She's all that's holding the WPC together. And you three aren't helping.* He snarled at Sass who hissed back. *You either, furball.*

Quaid. I did my best to regain my calm, horrified and terrified at the same time as my ex-husband helped Femke stand, led her to her desk. Handed her a glass of water. She was calmer, even smiling, sipped from the glass. *Let me help.*

You can't, he shot back. *Just go. We'll talk about this later.* His chocolate eyes were full of fury. *If you're around, that is.*

Asshole.

I should have stayed, done something, anything. Demanded answers. Instead, I tore open the veil and stepped through, dragging Charlotte, Gram and Sass with me while Everonus watched us go.

But I didn't go home—when did I start thinking of Wilding Springs as home again? Sigh. This was too big, way bigger than I expected. And I thought saving the Universe was my priority? While my friend was a basket case of slowly disintegrating madness?

I stepped out into Mom's office at Harvard, glad to find her at her desk. She surged to her feet, face crumpling at the sight of me with my posse. And my guilt returned. I'd rejected her the last time I was here. So unfair.

I'd called Quaid the name in Hong Kong, but I really was the asshole.

Mom wrapped her arms around me, held me tight. I breathed in lilac perfume and soaked up her strength, willingly offered while sharing my own. "Mom," I whispered into her hair. "I'm sorry."

She let me go, blinking away tears. "Oh, Syd," she said. "So am I."

A few moments later, after hugging my dad equally as hard, reveling in him calling me cupcake and feeling relief at last at the sight of the renewed joy in his eyes, I sat down with the lot of them and began asking questions for real.

Though they filled in more technical details, they couldn't offer any new information.

"Everonus has to be part of the problem," I said at last, Sass firmly ensconced in my lap. "Which leads me to believe someone else has an agenda." Damn her. Shaylee sighed, shrugged.

I wouldn't put it past her, she sent. *But I have no idea what my mother might wish to accomplish by tampering with Femke at this juncture.*

Who knows why Aiolainn does what she does? My demon's snarl burned with amber fire.

Regardless her motives, my vampire sent, *it's apparent there's only one way to get to the bottom of his interference. We go to the source.*

A trip to the Sidhe realm? Okay, then.

They all protested when I tried to go alone, Sass loudest of all. But this was a trip I had to take on my own.

"I promised," I said, kissing his nose, stroking his fur as he shook in my arms, "and I won't break that promise." He seemed to relax a little. Trusting me? I hoped so. I had every intention of keeping my word, though I had no idea what he'd do in the Stronghold without the coven to badger, pester and boss around. The flickering image of him doing the same to the drach almost made me giggle. "I'll be back." Well, for now, anyway. How was I going to tell them what Sass already knew, that I had no intention of staying? I'd find a way to say it later. Way to put off the hurty stuff, Syd. "I just need to go smack Aoilainn around a little."

"I'd pay to see that," Gram said, eyes shining.

I just bet she would. Charlotte looked like she was going to jump me and make me take her with me no matter what.

"You're not my bodywere anymore," I said to my blonde friend. "You have an entire werenation to care for. And you." I jabbed a finger at Gram. "You have the coven to think of."

"Thanks to you," she groused.

"Just let me take care of this," I said. "You asked for my help, right?"

They all nodded, glum.

"I'll meet you in Wilding Springs." I set Sass in Gram's arms, opening the veil. Found myself choking up as I looked back at their sad faces. "Oh, stop it," I said. "You're killing me here."

Mom laughed, waved me off, despite the tears in her eyes. "Have fun, sweetheart," she said.

SEVENTEEN

I grinned my way across the veil, the short distance between this plane and the realm of the Sidhe. Green grass, an impossibly blue sky, the smell of summer, wrapped me in the glamour of the plane. I strolled my way toward the trees in the distance, covering ground at a rapid pace. More magic. Aoilainn was playing games, as usual.

I was therefore unsurprised, as I crossed over and began my walk toward the Seelie court, to find a familiar face waiting for me on the other side of the silver bridge, his white horse's long mane blowing in the breeze.

"Prince Thalion," I said, not sure if I should be happy to see him or not. We'd parted last as sort of friends. But I had no idea if Aoilainn's alleged tampering on my plane—I was willing to give her a tiny benefit of the doubt—had changed that.

"Sydlynn Hayle." His smile seemed genuine as he slipped down from the saddle to kiss my hand. The faint frown that pulled at his perfect mouth and smooth, ageless brow almost made my eyes roll. "Your appearance has altered."

Smart boy. "I'm here to talk to Aoilainn," I said. "What kind of mood is she in?"

Thalion laughed and gestured for me to go ahead of him. He led his horse at my side instead of riding, as though strolling with a friend. I'd take it.

"Methinks she will be most disconcerted by your new appearance," he said.

And winked.

Still my Thalion, then. Even more relaxed, actually, than usual. Made me go hmmm.

"You seem remarkably chipper," I said. Yes, I was prodding for info. Now I'd decided to start paying attention to what was going on around me, I felt like I was starved for information.

Thalion actually blushed. Pinked at his collarbone, the high points of his cheeks and ears. Turned his beautiful face away from me and smiled down at the bright, green grass. "I've found love again," he said.

Shaylee sighed relief. *Finally*, she sent.

"That's awesome," I said out loud, firmly reprimanding her as she giggled in my mind. "Congratulations."

He met my gaze, soft hope there. "You'll meet her? I'm certain you'll adore her."

I wasn't sure how appropriate it would be for his former love to meet his new one, but if that was the Sidhe way, whatever.

"Sounds great," I said, while Shaylee snarked.

About as great as chewing glass, she sent. *Idiot.*

Be nice, my vampire sent.

"You'll be delighted to know," he said. "She's Unseelie."

That was enough of a shocker even Shaylee fell silent. "Unseelie?" What happened to the Seelie and Unseelie hating each other?

Oh, yeah. I'd made them tear down the wall between their kingdoms. I guessed some big changes happened after that I hadn't known about.

See what happens when you don't pay attention? My vampire actually sounded smug.

"I take it things are working out between the combined kingdoms, then?" Nice to know something turned out the way it was supposed to.

Thalion nodded eagerly, with a youthfulness I'd never seen in him before. Shaylee sighed again, this time with a hint of regret. My demon poked her with a muttered, *no second thoughts, Princess Greenie*, while Thalion spoke.

"We still have a few bumps to smooth out," he said. "But for the first time our historical animosity has been set aside for the common good." He seemed so happy I almost hated to stir the pot. And it made me wonder—if the realm was in such good shape, what the hell was Aoilainn up to?

I didn't have long to find out. The realm's glamour carried us in the space it took us to have our conversation from one side of the vast valley to the entrance to the glade where the Seelie queen kept her court. I passed over the narrow bridge inside the forest, keeping pace with Thalion as he left his horse behind and swept into the glade. It looked as familiar as ever, though now the center pavilion was longer, accommodating not only the Seelie queen and her consort but the Unseelie rulers as well. I nodded amiably to King Ohdran and Queen Niamh, the Goth appearing Unseelie grinning and waving in return. They seemed happy enough. Even Aoilainn didn't come across as upset by my visit, not the least bit guilty.

If so, had I misjudged Everonus?

"Sydlynn Hayle." I hadn't heard my full name used so much in my whole life as I had in the last twenty-four hours. Aoilainn spoke up for all of them, I supposed. "Welcome back to the realm."

"Thanks," I said. "Good to see everyone playing nice."

Niamh snorted a laugh. "For the most part," she said.

"You look well, Syd," Ohdran said. "If different."

Even I was beginning to feel weird about the gray

skin and scales. My diamond eyes couldn't have been much less disarming. "I'll take that as a compliment."

He waved royally, still smiling. "You do that."

"I take it there is a pressing reason for your visit?" Leave it to Aoilainn to try to control the conversation. And to piss me off. Just with her attitude and tone of voice.

Shaylee sighed. *Temper, Syd*, she sent. *She's probably bored with all this getting along and is looking to play.*

Well I wasn't in the mood.

"I have a problem with one of your Sidhe lords," I said. "Everonus. And I'd really like to think he's not acting on your orders, Aoilainn. That would be... distressing."

My demon chortled.

Anger flashed in Aoilainn's eyes, but I sensed more than that. Pleasure. Damn it, Shaylee was right. The Seelie queen wasn't going to give me anything easily.

"I have no idea what you're talking about," she said, all airy fairy.

You know what? Any other time, even just a day ago, I would have taken such a response much more calmly. Probably tried further diplomacy.

But today?

Yeah, not today.

I didn't give her a chance to have more fun at my expense. Time was short and so was my fuse. She might have been having a blast, but so was I. It had been too long since I let my temper out to play.

It took about half a second for me to shift from human to drach. My roar made the entire glade shake, tearing at her carefully coiffed hair, sending minions tumbling as my wings downswept a vast rush of air over the pavilion. Niamh giggled into her hands, though even she was wide eyed as I puffed out a bit of smoke, lowering my giant head until my nose was on level with the Seelie Queen.

One of my claws crushed the stage-like front of the construction with a snapping sound akin to bone breaking.

"You were saying?"

Aoilainn's nostrils flared. "There was a Sidhe lord of that name once," she said. "But he was lost to us long ago, when the realm was formed."

Well now. Wasn't that interesting?

"How many of these lords and ladies did you lose track of, Your Majesty?" Because I just couldn't resist a further dig.

More snorting from Niamh. She was going to ruin her hardcore serious Goth girl reputation if she wasn't careful.

Aoilainn glared until I let some more smoke out. Right in her face.

Coughing ensued as she waved it away.

"A few," she said. I huffed while I turned my head sideways and set fire to a tree. My diamond eye cast back her reflection as she swallowed. "Four."

I turned to Ohdran who shrugged. "None," he said.

Which meant Aoilainn left her peeps behind on purpose. And while I could have further enjoyed myself, it was apparent from her frustration it was killing her she knew nothing of what I was talking about. Her power pulsed with the need to ask questions. Which meant she had nothing to do with my present issues.

Let her stew then. But let her worry, too.

"We'll have a further chat about this at another time," I said to the Seelie queen. "When it's convenient for me."

She huffed at me.

Snort.

I rose into the air, straight up, my wings answering without effort again. Maybe I was adjusting to being me after all, drach and woman and witch and demon and… well. All of me.

That would be amazing, honestly.

As the veil opened and I left the realm in as flashy a show as possible—because why not, right?—Thalion's mind touched mine.

Caution, he sent. *Those you seek she expelled for criminal behavior.*

I had my answer after all.

EIGHTEEN

I called for Max as I wove my way through the veil, feeling him answer immediately. He and Jiao joined me moments later where I hovered, considering how to proceed.

Troubling, he sent, *that the Seelie queen allowed four criminals to remain behind on your plane.*

Not just that, I sent. *Remember what Moa said?* Jiao was nodding, her serpentine neck bending and swaying, long feelers wavering in the stillness. *About the old council? How it was formed by the magic races of the time?*

Including Sidhe, Max sent. *You now believe these four were among the founders of the old council.*

Makes sense, doesn't it? It did to me, and to the three egos inside me.

Only one way to find out, Jiao sent. She sounded eager, not like her at all.

I wasn't about to argue with her. If Moa was still meddling, I'd have her scrawny head.

The Empress's palace in Nepal seemed smaller in my drach form, less towering and imposing, though even in human shape I wasn't impressed, really. We landed together in the courtyard, taking our smaller forms as we touched down, Jiao striding with what could only be described as a strut of absolute confidence. Not that she ever appeared anything but. And yet, I wasn't about to forget Max freed her from Moa's clutches, finally telling Jiao who and what she was—the evolution of the drach. It had to be satisfying for her to return here let loose of Moa's brainwashing, in full control of her power and ready for anything.

Or thinking she was. I'd been in enough altercations over the years I was confident, yes, but suspicious as well. Things were never exactly as they seemed and no amount of power would solve problems like working out the cause did.

How grown up of you, my vampire sent.

I'm learning, I sent back.

Perhaps in a few thousand years, she sniffed.

This was what I wanted to continue living with? Really?

She snorted.

It wasn't lost on me the palace seemed empty, quiet, cold. Gone were the ranks of vampires who usually tended to the Empress, missing were the vampire queens gathered around to gain her favor. Gone away, either lost to the void already or fled across the world, to Wilding Springs. To Sunny and their last hope.

That had to hurt.

Moa didn't seem surprised to see us as we showed ourselves into her chambers where she sat, alone and silent, on the throne-like chair next to her canopied bed. Her shrunken and withered shape hid her true strength, I knew, hers the oldest of the vampire souls, the very first to be turned by the power inside me.

Black eyes burned in the deep pits of her sockets, her small, wrinkled hands gripping the arms of her seat, nails like claws digging into the wood as she watched us approach. Two men in black uniforms, much as I'd first seen Jiao wear, flanked her, as deadly, I was sure, as their female counterpart. For surely these two were of my friend's race, the *lóng*.

Jiao ignored them, came to stand with haughty grace at the foot of Moa's seat.

"My dear," the Empress said in a soft and aching voice, its youthful timbre always a surprise from her withered mouth. "I have missed you so."

Jiao tossed her head. "I'm sure you did," she said. "Your slaves are valuable to you."

Moa rocked back slightly, eyes lifting to Max. "What have you done?" A whisper, hurt and angry.

"Only what she deserved," he said. "What her race deserves."

"Her race was dying," Moa snapped. "Only I saved them from total destruction."

The two men glared at Jiao, their similar almond shaped and slanted eyes her eyes, their dark hair shining like hers. Cheekbones, jawlines. They had to be family.

The black ribbon shuddered. What was that about?

"So you believe," Max said, soft and kind. "But you are wrong, Moa. The *lóng* must be free." The dark circle of drach soul around my wrist seemed to agree.

She shook her head even as Jiao saluted rudely. I had no idea she knew how to use her middle finger like that. And departed the room at a trot, face alight. Only then did I realize she hadn't come here for me, for Moa, for Max. But for her family.

That motivation I understood.

So she wasn't eager about Moa or their meeting. Her brother and sister, then? Most likely. I let her go, hoping she had a happy reunion, focusing on the slightly petulant Empress on her throne.

"Your empire is crumbling around you, Moa," I said. "Surely you can see that."

She thumped both small fists down on the arms of the chair, sitting forward. "A fine speech from one who abandoned her family for her own pursuits."

I spluttered but didn't have to counter. Max took care

of that for me.

"When you are tasked with saving the entire Universe," he said, still mild but with a hint of his drach steel beneath, "you will be allowed to speak to Sydlynn in such a manner."

Well now.

Don't get cocky, my demon sent.

Thanks a lot.

"We're here about the old council," I said.

Moa shrugged, turning half around in her throne, draping her skinny legs over one arm like a child. "What of it?"

"Do not test me today, Moa," Max said. This time there was no music in his voice. Only the faint echo of a roar that could be heard with just a little more effort.

She spun her head around, snarling at him. "Why should I tell you anything? Why should I trust either of you with the knowledge I've guarded my entire existence? Just so you can ignore everything we've attempted to accomplish, like bad mannered bulls destroying everything in your wake?"

"We've accomplished more in Sydlynn's short adulthood," Max said, "than you have in centuries, Moa. And that worries you most."

She pondered a moment, toying with the hem of her simple white gown, jaw working, emaciated face reminding me of a recently unwrapped mummy. "So much to do," she whispered at last. "And, in the end, so little time to accomplish it."

"Alone, perhaps," Max said. "But with help?"

Moa barked out a laugh. "Your kind of help, drach?" She jabbed a finger at me. "And hers?"

He didn't comment and I stayed quiet. A miracle, I know.

Well, mostly quiet.

"The Sidhe lord Everonus," I said when the silence stretched too thin. "He's yours, isn't he?"

She turned her head, glittering eyes staring at me from their corners, the edge of her mouth lifting into a secret smile. "How's little Gabriel?"

The bitch. I snarled, my drach form threatening, but Max took firm hold of me and held me still.

She's baiting you, he sent.

Well, duh.

How shallow and beneath you, my first child, my vampire sent, scorn burning a path between Moa and me.

The Empress flinched. "Time hasn't been kind," she said.

Clearly, my vampire sent. *If you would put your own hide ahead of the protection of the Universe. You who claim to have the safety and good of all at heart.*

Moa shifted, visibly uncomfortable. "How can I trust? After all the centuries of betrayal? Of having to fight for every single victory only to face even more devastation?"

She knows nothing of those disasters, my vampire sent. *Of the degradation of the vampire race. It is not her fault. It is mine. For choosing the wrong host. For becoming lost when I should have led you to the place you were meant to go.*

"Which is where?" I said it out loud, not on purpose, but because it felt right.

My vampire paused, Moa too. The Empress shook her head and looked away while my vampire spoke.

I don't know that, Syd, she sent. *Only that I am certain the race I created has a different destiny. Is, like the* lóng, *an evolution of something but paused in its change. Meant for something more.*

You never said so before. I was a bit hurt, I had to admit.

Only because I have no real proof, she sent in return. *Except for the feeling of incompleteness that plagues me. That, I fear, was the source of my initial madness. My lack of evolution led to the vampire race's lack. Making it my fault.*

Couldn't fight her logic even though I wanted to. So convoluted. And she was a master debater.

Moa observed our exchange, finally sitting back again. This time she appeared deflated, tired. "I will do what I can to introduce you to the council," she said. "Though I doubt they will be open to conversation. They are old and set in their ways."

"And you are not," Max said with a hint of humor.

She stuck her tongue out at him, such a childlike, human gesture I almost laughed. "I am the picture of youth and vigor," she said.

"Indeed," Max said.

The repartee seemed to perk her up again. Moa left her throne, coming down the flight of steps, waving off the two *lóng* who watched her descent with concern. She crossed to Max and me, looking up at us. While I knew she was small, it shocked me just how tiny she really was. No taller than my son, her bones showing through her thin, wrinkled skin, she reminded me of a possessed, ancient doll with her sharp, shining black eyes and mop of black hair.

"It will take some time to bring them together," she said. "But I will try. And if and when I succeed I will summon you both."

That would have to do. Though if she didn't trust me, well, I wasn't going to trust her either, was I?

Moa turned to me, one hand reaching for mine. She ran a sharp nail over the skin and, when her eyes met mine, they were full of hunger.

"Tell me what it's like," she said. "To be drach. To fly."

Okay, that wasn't creepy or anything. I pulled my hand back, tucking it behind me.

"Awesome," I said. "Too bad you'll never know."

Yeah, mean, sorry. Bad Syd.

Moa looked away, head bowing. Max's disapproval of my reaction was just enough to make it worse.

Perfect.

Jiao saved me by returning, her cheeks bright, eyes alight. She joined us, almost bouncing on her toes, mind reaching for mine.

They are well and healthy, she sent. Flashed me images of a young man and a girl. So, I'd been right.

Are we taking them with us? Rescue mission, check.

But Jiao was already pushing denial at me. *They aren't ready*, she sent. *And they are safe with Moa for now.*

I got the impression that would be changing shortly. But I let Jiao have her happiness.

Time for us to go.

NINETEEN

Charlotte was gone when we returned to Harvard, though Sass and Gram remained. Varity sat in casual languor, long legs crossed, foot bouncing on the end of her bobbing knee, a grin on her face.

"Hear you need some help raising the dead," she said.

"Something like that." Dread washed over me at the thought of returning to the cavern below, though I didn't know why. Maybe I'd had enough of death, thanks. Regardless, if we were going to talk to the vampires this seemed like the only way to accomplish it.

Mom and Dad joined us as we descended the elevator deep below Massachusetts Hall and emerged into the dank, dark corridor. So quiet here where once many voices whispered in the black, wanting me to pay attention to the lives they'd lived.

"It feels as though all the spirit magic has been

drained from this place," Max said, rumbling voice making me jump.

Varity cocked her head to one side, old eyes tight with concentration. "I never noticed before," she said. "But you're right, dragon man."

I hid my grin behind my hand while Max smiled kindly down on the old Enforcer leader.

Sass walked beside me in cat form, his body brushing against my ankles and calves as though trying to keep constant contact. I'd offered to carry him but he'd rejected the gesture, choosing to pad along on his own.

I missed the feel of his furry body and wished he'd change his mind.

We entered the Hayle vault, Mom shivering as we did, rubbing at her arms with both hands. Dad slipped his arm around her shoulders, the two tucking themselves into a corner while Gram and Varity strode ahead toward the end of the vault where the most recent bones lay.

"I don't know about this, Syd," Gram said, frowning in tandem with Varity as the pair looked around, clearly confused. "Usually this place is a hotbed of chatter." So she'd noticed it, too? "But I can't feel much of anything."

"Just do your best," Max said.

Gram snorted at him. "Naturally," she snapped. "I'm just saying."

Varity offered her one hand which Gram took firmly in her own. "Give us a minute," the Enforcer leader gruffed before lowering her head close to my grandmother's. I opened my power to them, to offer what support I could, but had to retreat when the family magic tried to slip free of Gram and return to me. Sneaky. Gram glared, lips twisting in irritation.

"If you want it back that badly," she said, "just take it."

I shook my head. "Sorry, I was trying to help."

"Then stay out of it," Gram said. And closed her eyes.

I shielded my power carefully from them, though was able to monitor their progress through the touch of my vampire. It didn't take long for disappointment to settle in. Even Max sighed as the two struggled to find what just wasn't there anymore.

When the pair finally opened their eyes, they both seemed sad.

"I'm sorry, girl," Gram said, shaking her head, dropping Varity's hand. "Whatever is going on, the echoes have left."

"Or have been drawn away," Varity said. "There's just nothing to reach for anymore."

Well that sucked. Not only that my family's echoes were gone—the legacy of the Hayle coven—but that, it seemed, our ability to reach Alison and Sebastian was gone with them.

"Thanks for trying," I said, doing my best to hide my

disappointment.

"The spirit magic is suffering," Max said. "More than I realized."

"Could it interfere with Gabriel's ability to find the other pieces?" If the loss of spirit magic was screwing around with the vampires, sending them to the void, it had to be having an impact on all of us.

Which made me do a quick internal check as Max sighed and shrugged, a rather noncommittal response I wasn't expecting.

"Who knows?" Not like the drach leader to seem so lost. "Even after all these centuries there are still mysteries of Creator's Universe that surprise and confound me."

Lovely. And not what I wanted to hear.

We parted ways, Mom hugging me extra tight a moment before letting me go. Max and Jiao returned to the Stronghold without a word to me, as though knowing I needed to be alone. And while I wished I could just stay in Wilding Springs with Gram, Demetrius and Sass, forget everything for a little while and pretend I was just Syd again, the puzzles of my life were piling up and up and up, just like they used to before I left. One thing I'd learned along the way, though. Trying to tackle multiple things at a time could make my brain melt down. Pick one, sort it out as far is it would go, then move on.

So Creator would wait a few more hours while I

hashed out this particular puzzle, the mystery of the disappearing undead and their spirit magic. And I only knew one person who might be able to help me find a way around the problem.

The same person who only a short while ago swore her head off at me. Maybe Meira had better control of her temper now.

Sass let me go, to my surprise. "You two need to work things out," he said. "I've had my moment. Go let her yell at you some more. Then come home, Syd."

I kissed his furry brow before returning to the basement. It felt like forever since I'd done something so formal as to knock on the veil between our planes, opening a small window from Wilding Springs to Demonicon. But it seemed like the right thing to do.

Meira sat at her desk, looking up at the interruption. A frown pinched her brow but she didn't seem as angry this time. "What's up?"

Not exactly a warm greeting but neither was it unwelcoming. "I need to talk to you." And not just about the failure to reach echoes on my plane. I discovered as I stood there, biting my lower lip in worry she'd reject me, I really, really needed to talk to my sister. To have her understand. To beg her to forgive me.

She finally nodded, standing from her desk. "I have a few minutes," she said.

So cold. I could hardly be angry with her for that.

I stepped through and into her plane, feeling the warmth of Demonicon replace the chill of the basement. I purposely kept my human size and shape, wanting her to feel my vulnerability. The last thing I needed right now was a confrontation.

Meira sat on the front of her desk, arms crossed over her chest. It never failed to amaze me just how stunningly beautiful she was in her demon form. Tall, lean body curved in all the right places sheathed in a shining black cat suit, long, curly black hair hanging around her like a cloak. Polished horns winding away from her smooth, red tinted brow. And those piercing, amber eyes that cut through me. She'd grown so much, though there were times it was still hard not to picture her as the tiny, happy girl she'd been.

So much had changed. For both of us.

"What did you want to talk about?" She raised one eyebrow. "Or did you just want to stand there and stare at me for a while?"

I flushed, cleared my throat. "The echoes are gone," I said. "Gram and Varity couldn't find any to use to reach Alison."

Meira sighed, nodded. "I've been doing some investigating here on Demonicon," she said. "The spirit power here seems greatly diminished as well. What little there was in the first place. At least it's not affecting the Node." That was good to hear. We'd already gone through a giant mess twice with the core of power holding the planes of Demonicon together. A third time would suck.

"I wasn't sure what else to do," I said. "Thought maybe the two of us could come up with something."

She didn't comment for a long time, glowing eyes slitted. "Come," she said at last, gesturing for me to join her as she stood and circled her desk. "Sit down a minute, would you?"

Um, okay. I took the low, deep chair next to hers, sinking into the soft cushioning. Was this Ram's seat?

"You're not here to talk about the vampires," Meira said.

When did she grow so wise?

"I guess not," I said.

"You want me to tell you I understand why you did what you did," my sister said, expressionless, voice flat. "That I forgive you and love you and am happy to see you."

I had a feeling none of that was forthcoming. It hurt but I had to be prepared for it.

"Of course to all the above," Meira said. "Of course, Syd."

I burst into tears. Covered my face with both hands. Leaned forward over my knees and let myself cry a moment. When I looked up, breathing deeply to pull myself under control, her expression hadn't changed. No softness, no caring. Just intensity.

"But we need to get one thing straight," she said. "Utter honesty, sister mine."

I gulped back more sorrow and nodded.

"You didn't leave for the greater good," Meira said. "You ran away."

She might as well have slapped me. Even the girls rebelled, all of us speaking at the same time. That wasn't true! I—

"Syd," my sister said, amber eyes flaring with fire. "You ran away, Syd."

I—

I.

It sank in. Her words, the truth. The girls went silent, contemplating, their quiet only making things worse. But no, I left to protect everyone, to keep them safe—

"Syd." One of her hands twitched toward me, settled. "Stop it." She leaned closer, the power of Demonicon swirling around us both. "Stop lying to yourself. Or this has been for nothing."

Did I run away?

Oh, my darling Syd, my vampire sent. *Of course you did.*

We all did, my demon sent, equally quiet, hurt.

We had to, Shaylee sent, tears in her voice.

Or we wouldn't have survived, my vampire sent.

Something hot dripped continually on my hand. I looked down to see I was still crying, a river of tears falling into my lap, wetting my gray skin.

Oh. My. Swearword.

"I had to go," I said. "To focus on my purpose."

Meira glared. "Right," she said. "So tell me. In the last six months, how much exactly have you accomplished?"

My mind tried to respond. But my heart knew what my brain refused to admit.

"Let me get this straight," my sister said, sarcasm so thick it pressed down on me like a physical weight. "You spent six months playing drach, soaring around the Universe. Found squat and did squat. And you call that a purpose?"

No, it wasn't like that. "I had to protect you. All of you."

"Wow," she said. "You did a great job. Considering everything at home is falling apart and all."

She... that wasn't... wait...

Choke.

"I ran away," I whispered. "Meems, how could I be so selfish?"

How could I? The black ribbon flexed in sympathy before falling silent.

Meira sighed deeply, smiled at last, the intensity gone from her face. My sister shone through, the old, sweet girl I knew, not Ruler any longer. "What the hell is wrong with being selfish?"

I gaped at her, tried to answer. Finally managed it. "I

cut everyone off," I cried, a wail in my voice. Hateful wail. "I left everything behind." Panic tore through me like an avenging angel, jerking me off balance, forcing the air from my lungs. I could feel myself beginning to hyperventilate, unable to get my breath, half rising from the chair in an effort to escape the truth—

Meira's power slammed into me, shoved me down into the chair. Grasped me firmly in her grip and made me look.

Right. At. The. Truth.

I sobbed again, this time in utter anguish that felt worse than anything I'd ever endured. Worse than losing Liam, than thinking I'd lost Gabriel. I relived, in those few moments of time, all the pain I'd run from six months ago. And fresh agony, Payten's swollen belly added to the insult and injury.

I sobbed until I didn't have tears left. Hiccupped my way into silence while my sister held me in her power and watched without a word.

"You done?" She handed me a handkerchief from her desk. I snuffled, wiping my face and blowing my nose.

Nodded.

My sister sat back, hands folding over her flat stomach, face finally sad. "I'm sorry, Syd," she said. "But you had to get it."

Here I'd thought she had to understand. "When did you become the older sister?"

She grinned at me, winked. "I had a good teacher."

"I wish." My body sagged, exhausted from the emotional turmoil. And I cringed as I sank into regret and, in all honesty, embarrassment so acute it hurt.

"You realize," Meira said, wry and full of humor, "we've all been there, done that. I bought the t-shirt. Wore it until it had holes in it." She wrinkled her nose. "Pit stains." I snorted a small laugh, couldn't help myself. "Used it as a rag for a while." She shook her head. "Six months to my four years, sis. I'm rather jealous."

"What do I tell everyone?" They'd hate me for sure, now. I'd never survive the shame.

"Nothing," Meira said. "Why tell them anything? Syd." She finally leaned forward and took my hands in hers. The warmth of her skin, the connection to her power, formed an instant bond, reattaching the link between us much as the one with Sass and me. "You needed to go. You had to. I'm surprised it took you that long." Meira's face, softened by kindness, hardened again. "But you only get one shot at running away. Your vacation is over. We need you. The Universe needs you."

I nodded, a soft feeling of relief rising inside me. Okay, then.

"Done?" Meira stood, pulled me up with her.

"I guess," I said. Tried to hand her the soiled hanky. "Unless you have more of these."

"You can keep it," she said. "Now go save everyone,

for the element's sake. I've got things to do."

I hugged her, laughed shakily, knees like rubber. "I love you, Meems."

"I love you, too." She let me go, smiling. Before I could leave, though, the veil open before me, she snorted, a wicked gleam in her eyes. "Did I ever tell you I had a nickname for you when we were young? That I called you in my head when I was mad at you?"

I shook my head, shocked. We'd had our moments but I thought she adored me. Imagine the arrogance of that.

"Syd the Squid," she said, wrinkling her nose, voice going nasal and lispy. "Thid the Thquid." She giggled. Held up her hands and wriggled her fingers at the floor right under her chin.

I laughed. I couldn't help it. Pictured her drawing me like that, with tentacles coming out of the bottom of my head. "Nice."

She shrugged, dropped her hands to her sides. "Helped when I was pissed at my perfect sister." Meira paused. "I know better now. And love you more for being flawed like me."

She had no idea.

I left her but didn't go home—when did I start thinking of Wilding Springs as home again? Instead, I stepped out of the veil on the flat mountain top and sat on the edge, firmly wrapped in magic to keep me safe, and stared out over the expanse of Demonicon.

Breathed. Accepted. Bowed my head at the shame I still felt.

Six months and a whole lifetime of pain.

You all knew, I sent.

Not at the time, my demon sent. *But when we woke… I guessed.*

And I, my vampire sent.

Shaylee just shrugged.

Why didn't you say something? They could have warned me I'd been an asshole.

You didn't need the pressure, my vampire sent.

The whole point of those six months was to heal, Shaylee agreed.

I thought about it a moment more, the weight of my flight finally leaving me as I embraced my weakness. And sighed out my hurt.

That, my vampire sent, soft and kind, *is the reason you succeed, Sydlynn Hayle. You are flawed, yes, as your sister says. But you are willing, always, to accept what you can't change, to allow yourself to live with the consequences and move forward no matter what.*

I almost didn't this time, I sent. *What if I hadn't woken up?*

I don't think the Universe would have given you a choice, my demon sent.

Right. The dream. Liam. And Alison.

You think it was time? That's why Alison appeared to me?

Made sense, I guess.

Perhaps Creator herself understood enough time had passed for you to move ahead again. And, who knows the perfect timing of the Universe? My vampire fell quiet while I turned that over. Perfect timing. Good enough explanation as any.

So, I sent, *if I woke at this moment for a reason, what was it?*

To talk to the vampires, my demon sent, almost automatic in her reply.

But without the echoes of the dead to do so, I sent, *how?*

It was Shaylee who gasped, who put the puzzle together first. *Syd,* she sent. *What if it's not the echoes of your family? But a specific echo.*

I frowned. And felt the gut punch of my own understanding. *Liam,* I sent.

They all sighed sadly.

But that can't be right, I sent. *Liam is gone.* I gulped through the fresh pain of that. *He was Sidhe. He didn't have an echo, remember?*

No, Shaylee sent, *but he was also human.*

And humans did have echoes.

I leaped to my feet. *You think he might still be waiting for me? But where?*

Oh, Syd. Of course.

The veil parted for me with a sense of its own excitement as I leaped on pure impulse, into its dark embrace.

And the only place Liam's heart could be waiting.

TWENTY

The Gate room felt empty, quiet, without Gabriel's soul in the veil. Without Liam and the power that fed him through the Sidhe portal. I'd thought this place long gone like my poor, dead love.

Could there be hope where once none existed? I wasn't foolish enough to think Liam could somehow come back from the dead. Okay, mostly not so foolish. But the chance to see him after all this time was almost as painful as losing him all over again.

I didn't dare go looking for him myself. Not without an anchor to keep me from falling apart. Instead, forcing my lungs to function, ordering my heart to keep beating, I reached for Gram.

Girl. She sounded nervous. *Are you all right?*

I must have felt off to her, frantic maybe. I was doing my best to contain my excitement but it was hard. So hard.

Can you come to me? I let her feel where I was. Her surprise fed into concern.

I thought—

I know. Just come, okay?

She didn't hesitate further. And when she appeared, nor was she alone. Sassafras sashayed his fat cat body out of her licking blue flame, looking around with narrowed, amber eyes.

"This place—"

Sigh. "Just get over it," I said.

"Don't have to be so huffy." He sank to his butt, licking one front paw with the casual care of a cat.

I missed him, I really did. But there were times.

Gram looked around, turning in a slow circle before meeting my eyes. "I take it you've had an epiphany of some sort?"

I wasn't about to tell her everything Meira and I discussed. In fact I was pretty sure I'd never, ever admit a word of it to anyone. The core of embarrassment was still too raw. Instead I gestured at the Gate, the room at large, stone ceiling arching overhead, and the thrum of faint Sidhe power under my feet. This place felt like home all over again.

"When I first dreamed of Alison," I said, "it was through Liam."

Gram's brow furrowed, arms crossing over her chest,

a slow tap of one toe showing her skepticism loud and clear. "He wasn't a witch, Syd. He was Sidhe."

"No echo," Sass said.

I'd have to remember I'd been through all of this already in my own head and not lose my patience at them stating the obvious or I was going to snap before we got to the good part.

Didn't help my demon was giggling like a madwoman.

"According to Shaylee," I said, "because he was human there might be something left after all." And if he was going to leave anything behind it would be here.

Had to be here. The one place I failed to look because I never expected any part of him to survive.

Gram nodded, dropped her arms to her sides as she relented her suspicious attitude. "There's no echo here, Syd," she said. Then paused. "No, not an echo." Was that a faint thrill of excitement in her voice? My throat hitched, eyes stinging as hope burned inside me. "Dear elements," she breathed, blue eyes widening, shining bright. "Syd. How did we miss it?"

He was here. I hugged myself abruptly, weeping in joy I didn't know I needed, laughed in soft hysterics. Liam.

Liam was here.

Gram's concern returned. "Syd."

I waved her off, shook my head at Sass's abrupt attention. "I'm okay," I said, smiling through my tears.

"It's true, isn't it? He's been here all along."

Waiting. For me to figure it out.

She nodded slowly. "I can feel him," she said. "But it's his soul, Syd. Or, a piece of it. He actually left a portion of his soul behind." Breathless, those words, sorrowful. Regretful? She'd been the strongest opposition to me marrying Liam. Did she understand now just how amazing he was? Just how much he was willing to sacrifice for me?

To leave a part of his soul behind meant the spirit that filled him was broken. And would never be whole again. How much tragedy could one young man endure? Even though I had to believe it was his choice. When did he make it? In the moment of his death, while I held him and tried to save him? Or was he able to do so after, some part of him clinging to the Sidhe Gate his family guarded for so long?

I suppose it didn't matter. Nothing did. Not while Liam lingered, waiting.

Gram wiped at one cheek, a single tear escaping. "This won't be like other times," she said. "Because it's not his echo. Syd, he'll know you, clearly know you. Might have some inkling of what's happened between then and now."

I pressed both hands to my heart. "I'm ready," I said.

Liar. But I just couldn't stand to wait any longer.

Gram closed her eyes a moment, tilted her head to

the side. A frown appeared before smoothing out. Her lips lifted in a soft half smile and she nodded to no one I could see.

"Yes," she said. "It's time. Thanks for waiting."

And then he appeared beside her. Tall, broad shouldered, blond hair with a hint of strawberry. Hazel eyes so kind, sparks of green glowing deep inside. His easy smile, one big hand running through his hair. Not the wavering, thin echo I expected.

Liam was there.

I couldn't breathe, my despondency choking me, my joy smothering my lungs. He smiled, held out his hands. And I ran to him.

Solid. Real. My Liam. My dear, dear Liam.

I couldn't bear it, not while his broad chest felt so warm, the scent of fresh earth and fabric softener washing over me, drowning me.

"Liam," I whispered.

He didn't speak, his hands pressing me against him before gently pushing me back. I felt him fading, the contact slipping and passionately tried to hang onto it. But he was already turning me around, hands on my shoulders, his touch thinning out as a second figure formed, wavered.

Appeared.

Alison's strained expression told me she was fighting hard to reach me. I threw white sorcery at her on impulse, felt Liam firm up again, heard it as my childhood bestie drew a breath.

And spoke.

"Syd," she said, voice a faint echo as if from a far distance. "Don't talk." My mouth snapped shut, automatic reaction to ask her a million questions. "Just listen. We don't have much time."

Liam's hands were fading again. I held still, back pressed to his chest, and nodded.

"We are safe, at least for now." Alison looked to her left, I assumed at Sebastian, though I couldn't see him. "We came by choice when the dark pulled at us, but had no idea we wouldn't be able to escape." She tsked at the emptiness beside her. "I'm getting to that." Returned her attention to me. "This may sound cryptic but we're waiting for the End of Days. When the two Universes become one." Her nose wrinkled. "I hope that makes sense to you."

My stomach quivered in fear. I had to talk to Max.

"There's more." Alison batted at the pestering vampire beside her. "There are others here, powerful others in strange armor." That rocked me back on my heels. "They call themselves the Order." Dear elements. "They've tried to fight us but nothing seems to work where we are, not like it used to." She shivered. "We've mostly been keeping to ourselves, the vampires. But this place, it's full of people, Syd. All layered over each other.

They can't seem to see each other, though. As if there's a bunch of planes in one place. But without power they are oblivious."

At least we now had confirmation where the planes and their people were disappearing to.

"Sebastian says it feels like a well, a holding place." She shrugged then, face lined and weary. Only then did I notice Liam's touch had faded to the point I could barely feel him. "We can cross over into the other planes, as can the Order. But no one else seems to realize anything is wrong." She wavered suddenly, transparent before recovering. "I'm almost out of time," she gasped. "You must find the rest of Creator, Syd. And end this soon. Or there will be no Universe. Do you understand?" Her voice shook with more than just weakness. "Everything will fall into the void with no future unless one or the other of the two Universes is made dominant." She opened her mouth to speak again but, as though a rubber band snapped, she vanished.

I spun to find Gram sagging, head down. Looked up into Liam's eyes. He was almost gone, too, lingering one last moment, sorrow on his face. And love in his gaze, so much love.

"We have a son," I whispered. "Gabriel."

Liam's smile was the last thing to survive before he, too, disappeared.

I grabbed Gram, eased her to the floor and hugged

her while she shivered. When she met my eyes, she was weeping.

"Thank you," I said. "I'm sorry this was so hard for you." I, on the other hand, felt elated. Not only did I have answers—odd, creepy and frustrating answers mind you—I knew now Liam was safe, and here.

I could see him again.

But something in Gram's expression made me pause.

"Syd," she said. Gasped, really. "Girl, I'm so sorry."

My heart froze. Because any kind of happiness wasn't in my cards, was it?

"He's gone again." That was it, wasn't it?

She choked on a sob, nodded. "More than gone," she whispered. "He burned up his spirit to let us speak to Alison." Her hands covered her face, shoulders slumping while I died inside all over again. "Liam sacrificed the last of himself to give us what we needed."

Of course he did. Because that was him, wasn't it? His last gift to me, destined, as though he knew I'd need him again.

Oh, my love.

I expected to be more of a mess. But instead I found myself taking charge as I faced the gathering I'd invited to Mom's office for this meeting. Maybe the six months away had been necessary. Or I was still numb from losing Liam all over again.

Regardless, I felt calm and centered so I'd take it.

Mom held Dad's hand, Gram and Varity bisected by a patiently waiting Demetrius. Sass perched on Gram's knee, attentive, silent, while Max and Jiao watched from the doorway.

I told them what Alison told me, left out Liam's loss. They didn't need to feel new hurt, too. I'd keep that tucked away for my own private agony later. When I was done, I bowed my head a moment before meeting Mom's eyes.

"We need Gabriel," I said.

She nodded. "Did you want me to go get him?"

Tempting. Quaid wasn't going to let my son go without an argument. And after seeing Liam, being with him even in that small way, I wasn't in the mood to fight with my ex-husband. Still. I owed it to my son to be the one to come for him. Something I'd sworn to myself I'd never do again.

Mabel was right, I guess. Time to accept I was a tool of the Universe and act accordingly.

I didn't get a chance to act on my decision, at least not then and there. Not when an ancient mind touched mine, her smooth voice interrupting with a subtle knock at my consciousness before speaking.

Moa had manners, I'd give her that.

The council has assembled, she sent. *And are willing to meet with you.* She sounded faintly surprised. *Eager, in fact.*

I didn't have time for politics right now and was about to tell her so when I was cut off. I didn't realize she'd tied Max into the conversation until he spoke.

We've waited this long, he sent so tightly it had to be private. *And I wonder if they have information that might be of use to us.*

Now that I'd decided to act my temper rose in a prickly rejection of delay. But, when his soft insistence pressed down on me, I relented.

Fine, I sent to Moa, lacking anything resembling graciousness. *We're on our way.*

I cut her off. Rude? Hell, yeah.

"Something came up," I said with a grimace. "We'll be right back." I gestured to Max who joined me, shaking my head at Jiao. But Sass was already hopping down off Gram's knee, both front paws on my sneakers.

"Wherever you go," he said, "I'm coming with you."

Jiao arched one eyebrow at me as I bent and lifted the cat into my arms. Kissed the end of his wet nose. And handed him to Mom.

Trust me, I sent. *I won't leave you behind.*

You're still planning to leave, he sent, the feeling of accusation in his voice making me flinch. *If you go without me, Syd, don't ever come back.*

I wished I could reassure him. Should probably just have let him come with me. But left him behind this time, reaching for the veil while still focused on Moa and her location.

They're trying to mask their location from us so they can lead us in. My vampire was actually smirking.

Silly, silly fools, Shaylee chortled.

Let's show them how we party, my demon snarled.

Sass's anxiety forgotten, I fought a grin. Okay, this was fun again. Elements help me but it was.

I stepped through the veil, followed the thread. Felt the soft panic of the council as I easily tracked them, Max's magic tied to mine. He felt amused, a bit anxious. Even more so when we emerged into a dark, high ceilinged chamber somewhere underground from the weight of earth magic around us.

I looked down at the rough carved floor so harsh under my thin soled sneakers. Caught sight of my own hands and realized with a start they weren't gray and scaled anymore, my right hand pink under the circle of black drach soul. Softly tanned, lined with chewed nails. My human hands.

I pressed my sorrow into Max and felt his power answer with a flood of support.

What's happening to me? Now of all times. I couldn't afford to lose my confidence, not in the face of the group waiting for us at the far end of the chamber.

Only your true nature reasserting itself, the drach leader sent with so much calm it helped to ease my fear. *As it should be.*

But no. I was drach. Wasn't I? Still, he seemed at peace with it. I'd just have to trust him this wasn't a total disaster.

Holding onto his steady strength, knowing it wouldn't be the last time, I drew a breath, squared my shoulders and stepped forward, the tall, imposing drach leader at my side and three alter egos in my head. Black ribbon on my wrist.

Quite the team I had here. Wouldn't trade them for anything.

TWENTY-ONE

By the time we came to a halt at the foot of the long, narrow dais, my questing mind had discovered our location—far beneath the great pyramids at Giza in Egypt. I resisted an eye roll at the cliché, unimpressed.

As I was by the shadows hiding the faces of those above me. Could they be any more Hollywood B movie? Film noir tactics would do nothing to keep me from asking the hard questions. And getting the answers I wanted.

"I'm here for Everonus," I said, watching the second from the center flinch ever so slightly. Whatever power they used to mask themselves individually did nothing to keep them from hearing me. Or from giving themselves away.

I focused on the culprit as he leaned reluctantly forward, a frown on his perfect Fey face.

"Sydlynn Hayle," he said. "When you left this plane I thought you gone forever."

"Sorry to disappoint," I said. "I'm sure Aoilainn thought the same of you when she left you behind with your three closest crime buddies."

Another faint flinch. And a deeper frown this time. If I had him off balance, good on me. But I wasn't about to underestimate him.

He waved off my comment as though unimportant despite giving away his unhappiness with my information. "The Seelie queen is of no consequence here," he said.

She'd love to hear that, wouldn't she? I barely held in my grin as Shaylee giggled.

Poor Mother, she sent. *No respect.*

"I'm sure this little parlor game of cat and mouse pleases all of you," I said out loud, gathering my power and inserting it carefully into the edge of the magic keeping them shielded and in the dark. Unsurprised to find sorcery at its core though impressed enough by the weaving of their common magicks, something no one else I knew—besides myself at times—had succeeded in doing. "But I'm in a bit of a hurry. Saving the Universe and all that." With an errant flip of my hand I tore down the barrier and revealed the seven people who did their best to hide from me.

Everonus, of course. And Moa, hardly a shock there. A few faces I didn't know. And one I did, very well. One that stirred an old anger in me and more than a little hurt she'd kept her role a secret.

Not that Nona Zornov had ever really been forthcoming. The maji blood grandmother of Trill, Owen and Apollo Zornov nodded her head to me in solemn greeting, wrinkled mouth puckered as she turned to Moa who sat beside her. It was the ancient vampire who spoke.

"Welcome to the Elder Council, Sydlynn Hayle, Max of the Drach." I was certain she could have managed singing his drach name but chose the more ordinary one I'd saddled him with. An insult? I really had to stop reading too much into things that didn't matter.

"Howdy," I said, crisp, showing my temper, my magic searching each of them. Touched on an old woman, the sorcerer of their number, her thick, white hair braided on either side of her head, cheeks puffy with a little too much weight. Still, she smiled at me, a sweet expression that put me off guard. Beside her sat an older man, face bristling with a beard. No, not a beard. With hair, lots of hair. It seemed his whole body was covered in it. And when I explored his power I realized what he was.

"Werewolf," I said. But the Black Souls created the werenation. He felt old, much older even than Charlotte's race. Where did he come from?

"You assumed the dark order of sorcerers created my race," he said, voice deep, scratchy, like he rarely used it.

"But they got the idea from somewhere, didn't they?" He shook his head, mane of hair swinging. "The true race of werewolves died out thanks to their tampering and eradication program. Only a hand full of us remains."

Sounded familiar. Like the *lóng*. Was their near extinction the result of outside tampering, too?

On the far side of Nona, a tall, blocky woman sat, almost statue like in her silence. A witch from the elemental magic she bore. But like no witch I'd ever felt before.

She nodded to me, too, as I drank in her great age. How had she survived so long? The witches I knew had normal, mortal lifespans. And yet she felt almost as old as the werewolf, centuries.

"We have deliberated long and carefully over this reveal," Moa said. Spokeswoman? Likely from her central seating location. As was Everonus, then, since he had the chair beside her. I shifted from one sneaker to the other, grumbling to myself they could at least offer us a seat, while the line of self-styled elders peered down at us from their dais. My eyes traveled over them, over the pictographs etched and painted behind them, images of war and death, magic and elemental upheaval. A history of their council?

Their unease came through despite their attempts to hide it. Fear. Of me?

"We are honored by such an invitation," Max said. I

scowled at him, tossed my ponytail.

"Says you," I said.

Syd, he sent, a warning in my name.

No freaking way. I pushed back against his need to go cautiously and turned my glare at the rest of them. "Let me get this straight," I said. "Y'all have been watching us struggle for the last decade or so against the Brotherhood and Fate. Let North America be almost overrun, allowed Liander Belaisle to possess pieces of Creator's statue," yeah, I'm looking at you, Nona Zornov. "All while hiding away in your little cave down here under the ground. And doing nothing." I slashed a hand through the air. "Not a freaking, bloody, useful thing. Is that about how it is?"

Moa scowled, the others muttering angrily, but it was Everonus who answered.

"You may see things that way," he said, all haughty and crap. "But we have long guarded over this plane. We are the true power here. And though the petty lives of those who have been lost may affect you, we only see the big picture."

Oh, no, he did *not*. I felt Max reach for me with his magic, trying to smother my anger, but he was too late. Way, way too late. And Everonus, know it or not, had just pushed the buttons on his own self-destruct.

Shaylee took a firm grasp of the ground under our feet and applied a liberal amount of earth magic, fed by the fury of my demon, the cold rage of my vampire, the depth of the bottomless blossom that was my sorcery, the spinning vortex of my elemental magic.

And, as if an afterthought, the hiccupping interest of the white sorcery that seemed curious as to what we were doing.

The underground cavern shook so hard I began to worry the pyramids might fall to pieces if I wasn't careful. Still, the aggressiveness of my displeasure had the desired effect. Seven staring faces, only Moa appearing the least surprised, even Nona—who, I thought, knew me well enough to expect such a reaction—gaping like stranded fish.

Feel better? Max's sarcasm wasn't lost on me.

Not yet, I snapped back. *But I will very shortly.*

Gently, Syd, he sent. *They get the message.*

I wasn't so sure they did. But I had far more in my arsenal than a mere tremor to share if they still needed a few lessons. *You were the one who said me reverting to my old self was a good thing, remember?*

He just sighed.

"Enough." Moa leaned forward, snapping her fingers. "Such petty arguing will do nothing to solve our mutual issues."

Like we had anything in common. I was about to say so, still feeling belligerent and not the least bit interested in actually finding out what they really wanted, when a door ground open, rock sliding over rock, and two men entered. The *lóng* from her chamber. And between them a face I hadn't thought I'd ever see again.

Not alive, anyway. It was my turn to be stunned as the smiling, vampire lush Batsheva Moromond waved at me with evil glee.

"Syd, darling," she said. "How lovely to see you." Her lips moued downward into a fake frown. "So sad to hear about Quaid."

OH.

MY.

SWEARWORD.

I would rip her head from her neck and drink her blood. Strip her flesh from her bones and grind them between my teeth. TEAR HER HEART FROM HER CHEST AND GRIND IT UNDER MY FEET—

Ahem, my vampire sent.

I choked on her calm. So much so my mental freak out stopped abruptly, in time to hear Moa speak.

"The former Wilhelm Queen, Batsheva, has been healed of her madness." The Empress didn't sound all that impressed by the decision, though Everonus seemed pleased with the results of the reveal. "For a purpose," Moa said. She scowled at my old enemy who curtsied, her full ball gown of dark blue velvet rustling, white lace frothing over her full chest and at her wrists. "You will explain yourself."

Batsheva turned to me, sly and as clever as ever I

could only guess. The last time I saw her she was a molding mummy left to rot in the darkest corner of my basement at Wilding Springs, drained of all her blood, still alive and kicking in there somewhere. It seemed the perfect punishment for the woman who murdered Quaid's parents and used him as a power source for years, who tried to kill my mother, kill me. I should have put her in the sun a long time ago and just been done with it.

Instead, here she stood, the picture of vampire good health. Damn it.

"I have a message for you," Batsheva said. "From Dark Brother."

My initial reaction was to scoff. There was no way she was in league with the other Universe, with Creator's brother on the other side. And yet the fear rolling off the elder council seemed real enough. And I had the impression they thought enough of themselves it took a lot to stir their anxiety.

Batsheva batted her eyelashes at Max, swung her skirt like a coquettish young woman looking at a suitor. "The Brotherhood took me from your hellhole of a house," she said, sweet and bright. "Liander himself brought me to health, fed me the blood of a dozen young witches before letting me watch him burn them at the stake." She laughed, gay, delighted while my stomach churned.

I lashed Moa with my furious gaze. The ancient vampire shrugged.

"We healed what we could," she said. "I suppose she's always been crazy."

No shocker there.

Batsheva hissed at her Empress before settling down. "He told me many things," she said, moving toward me, skirt whispering over the rough stone floor. My skin crawled at the thought of her coming any closer but I would not show weakness here. "About Dark Brother. About you, Doombringer." The black ribbon didn't like her, hissing and spiraling around my wrist. "I was his princess." She laughed again, a tinkling sound. Then, lighting quick, she slapped me, just a bare finger swipe over my cheek before backing away with a scowl before I could react. "And then you screwed everything up, just like you always do!" Gone was the fake, syrupy sweetness. The screech of a banshee, more like. "He left me, abandoned me." Big, ugly tears burst from her eyes, nose running, pale skin blotching from her overflow of emotion. And then, just like that, she switched again. Reminded me suddenly of Pender Tremere. It sank in she was as damaged as the old Enforcer leader, if in a different way, as Batsheva went on. "They have a way across, you know." She spun in a circle, skirt swinging.

"Who does, Batsheva?" Max's kind voice startled me. I refused to pity her, would never have been able to muster that kind of gentleness. But she reacted to it with a dimpled smile, once more swinging her skirt at him.

"The Order, drach," she said. And snapped her teeth together like a crocodile. "But it's not the Gateway they want, is it?" She giggled, hands covering her mouth. "No, it's not." That was a relief. They weren't after Gabriel. But they knew about him obviously. Not that it surprised me. "They want the Doombringer."

Um. Crap.

That was me.

"Do you know why they want you, Sydlynn Hayle?" Batsheva bent in half, laughing so hard I could barely make her out. "Because you will betray all of us." She slapped her thighs with both hands, crying and gasping for breath. "You will be the doom of this Universe."

What the hell? No way.

No.

Batsheva's laughter cut off but her evil smile remained. "Your final act will be to ensure the doom of everything you care about."

TWENTY-TWO

Batsheva continued to snicker to herself, doing a little dance around the room in her ball gown as though at a party while the two *lóng* guards watched over her with dark expressions. I chose to ignore her as best I could in favor of the fear she'd planted in my heart.

Could it be true? Was that what the term meant? I'd heard it from Liander Belaisle, from the Black Soul sorcerer, Konstantin. Seen it written in the blocks Pender assembled.

And now, Batsheva.

But it couldn't mean what she said. It couldn't. I would never.

Never.

Moa shifted in her seat. "You understand now our reluctance at first to speak to you."

I shrugged, didn't comment.

"What brought about your change of heart?" At least Max was talkative. He could ask questions for both of us.

"We had thought Sydlynn's departure would mean our safety," Everonus said. Selfish asshat. Who cares about the rest of the Universe as long as their petty lives are saved, right? "But, her return has meant we must, in fact, deal with her."

My head snapped up. "Just try it," I snarled.

Moa held up one hand, looking tired, shining black eyes closing a moment. "We only wish to offer our support and guidance."

"Controls, you mean." I knew where this was going. "You want me to kowtow to your rules."

They didn't comment. They didn't have to. So transparent. But wasn't that what I would have done in their place?

"We must control the moment of choice," Moa said while Nona shifted next to her, looking angry.

"According to you," the old maji woman said. Making me wonder if she was really the Zornov's grandmother after all or someone much, much older. I wouldn't put it past her. Her eyes met mine, spark of power forming there. "There are those of us who believe Fate and destiny are best allowed to follow their paths to the end." She tucked her hands under her thighs, shoulders forward. "The Universe knows what it's doing."

Fate. Zoe Helios. And destiny? Was she talking about

her granddaughter, Trill? Why did I get that impression? I was still angry with Trill for betraying me, for stealing the pieces of Creator. For stabbing me in the back after I'd worked so hard to protect and nurture her. But there was a message in Nona's words and everyone connected to Trill—including my own son—claimed she was on my side.

I hated not knowing. Worst ever. But Nona's tight lips and narrow eyes told me no amount of prodding or demanding would wring answers from her.

"What choice?" Leave it to Max to ask the right questions.

Moa glanced at Nona. "According to a source," the Empress said with a droll dollop of dryness, "there will come a moment when Fate must choose which Universe survives and which is to be destroyed."

Zoe again. A relief. Because surely she'd choose our Universe, wouldn't she? "Then, we have it covered," I said. Doing my best to sound confident even while I wondered why Zoe would talk to this council and not to me.

I had to track her down and ask her.

Batsheva spun close again, smiling her evil smile. "Oh, if only it were up to her alone," she said. "But that's not the case, is it?"

"Zoe Helios is Fate now," I said. "Bellanca and Thanos no longer hold those roles." And hadn't Zoe told me only one Fate existed from that point on?

"In this Universe," Batsheva said.

Craptastic.

"Which means the other Universe has its own Fate," Max murmured, half to himself.

He had to say it out loud, didn't he? I knew it, though. Had figured that out six months ago, had it confirmed by Zoe. I guess I'd wanted to forget along with everything else.

"We have labored for millennia to protect this plane," Everonus said at his most arrogant. "To do so now we must have your cooperation. Surely even you, with your hard headedness and excessive temper, can see that."

He really knew how to make a girl feel special.

"We had Everonus join the WPC as a way to watch over you and Gabriel," Moa said.

"Then why kidnap my son?" I could have smacked the look of derision from the Sidhe's face.

"I didn't," he said. "The Gateway came willingly."

"When you lied to him and told him you were going to help him find me." That temper he mentioned? Heating up again.

"You fool," the Sidhe lord snapped. "The whole point of Gabriel's waking the Gate again was to draw you back to this plane. So we could inform and communicate with you."

Oh. Well, if that was the way of things.

Grump.

"We need you," Nona said, soft and trembling ever so slightly.

"And Trill?" I had to ask as the old maji woman shook her head, knowing I'd not likely get an answer. "Does she work for this council, too?" That would explain her behavior. Help me to stop feeling so awful about her betrayal.

"Trillia works for no one but herself," Nona said.

That was helpful.

"Look," I said, "I appreciate all the doom and gloom stuff, okay? I've lived through this before, in case you've all forgotten."

"Not like this," Everonus protested.

"Right. Because you were there when the entire Universe hung in the balance on the Stronghold plane." I glared at him until he looked away. Point made. "I won't hide and I won't second guess myself." At least not in public and not to them. "I have to believe Creator put me on this path for a reason. And that this Doombringer thing is just a tactic of Dark Brother to make you all doubt me." It had to be true. Didn't it?

"Your arrogance will be our downfall." Batsheva tossed her head.

Oh, I'd be her downfall, all right.

"What about the WPC? And Femke?" If Everonus was messing with my friend, so help me...

"Femke Svennson must continue her course," Moa said, no ifs, ands or buts allowed.

Like hell.

"Give me one good reason," I said.

"Because," the ancient Empress said, "the WPC must remain scattered and at odds in order for us to do our work undetected."

Whatever that work was. "Have you thought, I don't know, working together might be a better option?"

Moa laughed, without humor. "Sydlynn Hayle," she said. "You of all people should know how foolish that suggestion is. That the impulses of the weak and cowardly only interfere with the plans of leaders."

I hated she was right. Lived it enough times I couldn't muster an argument.

"What about Belaisle and Eva Southway?" Maybe they had information I didn't. But Moa's slow headshake answered me and crushed that hope.

"Belaisle, at least, we understand," she said. "He is tied so tightly now to Dark Brother I fear it will be he who opens the way for the Order's soldiers to our Universe." Not if I killed his damned ass first. "But the former Steam Union leader..." Moa sighed. "None of us can pinpoint her purpose."

It wasn't her purpose I was looking for. Just her physical location.

Syd, Max sent. *Tell them about the void.*

No way, I shot back. *They're giving us nothing. Why should we share?*

Because one of us needs to bend, he sent. *And they are too old and set in their ways to do so.*

Oh, and you're not? He was no spring chicken, first of the drach.

He laughed softly in my head. *Ah, but I have your youth to show me the light.*

Smartass drach.

Fine. I grudgingly shared what we learned while the council sat forward with eagerness, hanging on every word. Even Everonus seemed enthralled by Alison's news about the void and its occupants. When I was done, Moa stroked her fingers over her thick, black hair.

"At least we know where the other Universe will end up," she said. "The possibility exists for escape, perhaps." She was thinking worst case scenario, I could see it on her face.

"Unlikely," Everonus said. "Though, if this Alison creature is correct it's likely we won't even know, when the envelopment is complete, that we have lost."

There was an unsettling thought, one I refused to linger on, though it didn't give me much choice. What if all of this was moot? That we'd done this before and failed and everything we were doing now was an echo of what already happened?

Don't go there, my vampire sent, shuddering.

Syd, honestly, my demon grumbled. *You suck.*

Sorry, guys, I sent. *Couldn't help myself.*

"I would know," the sorcerer beckoned me closer, long nails sharp edged, though I refused to budge. "What is this white power you spoke of?"

Oh, crap. Did I let that out by accident? Too late now. I showed her, again with reluctance, heard her hiss as she drew back.

"I know this magic," she said. "Encountered it long ago." Was that sadness in her voice? "Like a distant song I once sang, a long lost taste of perfection." She drifted off, sinking back into her chair, white hair whispering as she moved.

I already knew the origins of the power but kept that part to myself. They didn't trust me to make the right decision, huh? Well, Creator did.

Didn't she?

"One thing you can help me with, if you're willing to act," I said, remembering at last where one of Creator's pieces went. An important piece, if the loss of the Steam Union's members was continuing to progress. "Jean Marc Dumont is now a sorcerer. And has control of the Brotherhood." And white sorcery, damn him. Wherever he got it from.

They muttered together a moment mentally, shielding their words from me. I had just enough courtesy in me not to eavesdrop, though it was damned tempting. When their minds parted, Moa bowed her head to me.

"We shall locate the Brotherhood and their leader for you," she said. So they could do that, huh? Made me wonder what else they were capable of that I'd spent sleepless nights and endless frustration trying to manage on my own. Didn't do much for my temper. "But you must promise us, when the time comes of choosing, you will allow us to advise you."

Not only did I fully expect to be on my own if that ever happened, I doubted Creator would allow interference. So it was an easy answer. "Fair enough," I said.

And wondered if I'd just signed a deal with the dark with those simple words.

We left the elder council to their own devices, returning to the veil, though not going far. I skimmed through the membrane, still on my plane, hurtling us toward Hong Kong as Max spoke in my head.

You're expecting resistance from your former mate. Not a question.

Aren't you? Quaid was the first one to give me a hard time about Gabriel. Well, not the first one. I was pretty eager to beat myself up over using my son to find the pieces of Creator.

Not really, Max said. *The Gateway will decide, his adoptive father's ideas to the contrary notwithstanding.*

True that. Quaid might not like it but Gabriel had the power to leave whenever he wanted. The fact he hadn't yet, that my son had shown this much restraint, had to mean he was waiting for me, too.

Just like the rest of the Universe. For me to get the hell over myself already.

Message received.

As though talking about him summoned him, the moment I set foot in Quaid's quarters my ex appeared in a flare of blue flame. He couldn't have known I was coming, had to be a coincidence, this meeting. So why didn't he seem all that surprised to see me?

I opened my mouth to tell him where he could put his attitude when he shocked the hell out of me.

We need to talk. Quaid's whole posture screamed confrontation, but his tone was soft, almost kind.

Okay then. *About what?*

His hesitation flared with worry, with the image of pregnant Payten and the two kids we'd raised together until just a short time ago. *Are you staying?* He had to come out and ask. *Or are you leaving again?*

I almost told him to go to hell anyway, but he had the right to know. At least, what I knew.

I'm leaving, I sent, not sure if that was accurate as the girls twisted slowly inside me. *Eventually.* That settled them down.

Quaid sighed in my head. *I thought you'd say something*

like that.

Judging me? Like I needed the help.

If I'm going to raise the kids alone, he sent, again with the soft and kind, damn him, though his shoulders twitched, eyes narrow, *I need to know you're okay with Payten being their mom.*

We were having this conversation now why? *The family dynamic talk can wait, don't you think?* I tried to stride past him but my ex-husband cut me off with his bulky body. Not threatening. He knew better. But pleading now with his entire being.

I have to know, Syd. They're my responsibility. Gabriel is.

So this was about my son. I felt myself clenching all over again. *You won't keep him from his destiny.* Now I sounded like Max.

Quaid didn't comment for a moment and then bowed his head. *I'm well aware of that*, he sent, sorrow in his mind, grief even. *I couldn't keep him safe, Syd. When he went missing, I panicked. Called out to you. Before I remembered.*

Damn him. I would *not* cry.

When his dark eyes met mine they were full of resolve. *I can only be the best father I know how*, he sent. *And to do that I realize I have to let go of Gabriel the way I let go of you.* Um, I seemed to recall I did all the letting go, but didn't say anything. *But, when and if you go again... Syd, he has to listen to me. For his own safety.*

My son's power grew daily. Who knew where he'd

end up? And having someone to listen to, to look up to… he had tons of role models in Gram, Mom, and Dad. Even Sass. But he only knew one father.

Okay, I sent. *But I'm not sure why you think I have any control over what Gabriel does.* Because it was becoming apparent neither of us could stand in the way of my son's destiny.

Quaid didn't comment, just nodded and stepped back. Shoulders straightening, he took on his familiar Enforcer confident persona. "Gabriel." He called over his shoulder. The door to my son's room slammed open and he ran out, beaming at me. The recent moments I'd shared with his father seemed to come crashing down around me as Gabriel hurried to my side and hugged me even before Quaid could finish saying, "Your mother is here."

Gabriel looked up into my eyes, smile fading. "Are you okay, Mom?"

I gulped down more tears, hugged him against me. Remembered the feeling of seeing his dad one last time. And nodded into his hair.

"I am now," I whispered. Straightened and cleared my throat as Quaid crossed his arms over his broad chest, Payten peeking out at us from the kitchen. She kept her distance though her worried gaze was on Gabriel. At least she cared about him. That counted for something.

A small, tiny, miniscule something.

"I knew you'd be coming for him now that you're back." Gruff and grim. A show for Gabriel's sake? I almost laughed. Quaid's gaze finally traveled to my arms, over my face. Noting the change in color back to my usual hue? From my continued sharp vision I could only guess my eyes remained the multi-facets of diamonds. But my transformation back to the woman I had been was at least partially complete.

I nodded. "We have work to do." I tucked my son against my side, Gabriel's jaw set and shoulders tight.

"I know." Quaid said. "Gabriel?" My son met his adoptive father's eyes. "Keep your mother safe. And yourself."

The beaming smile of pride that lit the boy's face was abruptly smothered when he lunged forward and hugged Quaid around the waist.

While Payten squeaked a faint protest before hanging her head.

Quaid ignored her reaction and so did I. She could be afraid all she wanted. This was the family she was tying herself to. I gave her a year, tops. My ex distracted me from that nasty thought with his next words. "Syd, we need your help."

Femke. I could say screw the elder council. And I should. Femke was my friend, before everything went to hell. But.

But.

"I can't," I said. "At least, not yet."

Quaid's anger flashed in his chocolate eyes before he looked away, shrugging, hands falling to his sides, sliding into his pockets. "How many times did I pray you'd stop meddling?" So much irony. "Only to wish you'd stop being so damned contrary."

Careful what you wish for.

My gaze settled on my daughter's firmly closed door. I really needed to talk to her directly, to make her understand. To apologize to her and hold her and tell her everything was going to be okay, even if that was a lie. But I didn't have time. None of us did, if Alison was right.

There would be time after this was said and done. I'd make time. And we'd win, we had to. I wouldn't allow anything to happen to this Universe.

It wasn't until I turned to go I realized there was someone missing from the picture, a someone I had yet to see since returning. The absence of the black hound who had been my children's closest companion for a long time now felt off.

"Where is Galleytrot?" I asked the question of Gabriel, but it was Quaid who answered.

"He left," the Enforcer leader said. "Didn't say why." Quaid sounded distracted, and fair enough. But for Galleytrot to leave the kids...

Had to be important, didn't it? Still, he was a big dog,

could take care of himself.

And yet his loss made me think yet again of my daughter. And the fact she had no one here to look out for her. No, Quaid didn't count, not in this state. Nor did the pregnant witch hiding in the kitchen.

I was moving before I could stop myself, marching to her door. And shoving it open with power before she could stop me from coming inside. Heavy handed, you betcha. Ethie had already expressed her distaste for me in no uncertain terms. But there came a time in every Hayle witch's life she had to suck up her feelings and just get on with it.

Wow. I sounded like Sassafras. He'd be so proud.

Ethie glared at me from where she perched in the middle of her bed, arms crossed tightly, scowl so dark it pulled her entire face down. "GET OUT!"

"No," I said. "You get up."

"I HATE YOU!"

Hadn't I used those very words against my own mother? Something to do with an arranged marriage and the handsome man in the next room who used to be my husband.

"Yes, dear," I said. "Now get up and be a Hayle already. We have work to do."

Ethie paused, her anger shutting down as she gaped at me. And, all at once, I felt her real pain even as she spoke. "You need me?"

Sydlynn. Thaddea. Hayle. Was I that dense? Clearly.

"Ethpeal," I said, holding out my hand. "I will always need you." Yup, Sass would be very proud indeed. "Now come and do your duty."

All of her anger seemed to vanish, blue eyes huge as she slipped from the bed and came to my side, fingers sliding over mine. In awe of my words. What did she see when she looked at me? Who did she think I was?

I hadn't been much of a mother lately. I could at least be a leader.

TWENTY-THREE

Wilding Springs never felt so like home. I stepped out into the kitchen with my kids at my side to find Gram and Demetrius waiting for us. Sassafras stood on the table, tail thrashing, and I knew he was going to give me a lecture on leaving him behind. But before he could say a word I scooped him into my arms and bussed him on the top of his head with noisy lips.

"Oh, Sass," I said. "You're the bestest puddy tat EVER."

He snorted. And relaxed in my arms. "You suck," he said.

"So I've been told." I kissed him for real while Gram doled out glasses and frothing, ice cold chocolate milk. Within moments I was seated with Sass beside me lapping his own bowl of creamy goodness while Gabriel quite calmly informed me he'd been searching for other pieces of Creator all along.

Surreal, really. All in a day's work for the Hayle family.

"I'm not sure what to tell you, Mom," he said, serious eyes large and full of more maturity than they should have been for his age. I wanted to tousle his blond hair, to kiss his soft cheeks. Instead, I sat on my hands to keep from doing so, wanting to grant him the gravity of his seriousness for as long as he needed it. A thin, green ribbon peeked out from the cuff of his sleeve before disappearing again. I'd almost forgotten the drach souls that had attached themselves to my kids, souls I'd rescued twice now from the grasp of the Brotherhood. He must have had the rest of them secreted away on his person. While it might have been startlingly freaky to another mother, I found it endearing, like frogs in his pockets. "I've searched and searched but I can't find anything."

My fingers itched to stroke his hair. One glance at my pouting daughter reminded me we weren't just here for Gabriel. "What do you think, Ethie?" She looked up from glaring at her milk, startled. Wary. "Any suggestions?"

She shrugged, looked away. "I tried to help," she said. "But I can't." How much that had to hurt her. Meira would understand, I was sure. It couldn't be easy, being the younger sibling of someone important. How had I missed it, neglected her?

You and your beatings, my vampire sighed. *Get on with it,*

Syd. It's never too late.

I hoped she was right. "I meant it when I said we needed you. Do you understand that?"

Again the noncommittal shrug. But she was listening. I could almost see her ears perking.

"The coven will be yours one day," I said, meeting Gram's careful eyes. What was she thinking?

"Oh," Ethie said, seeming to deflate. "That."

Gram choked, then barked. "Yes," she said, making Ethie jump. "That."

My daughter shrank from her great-grandmother's anger while I glared at Gram. But whatever reaction I'd expected from her, Gram was deep in something else entirely.

"I've had just about enough of your petulance, young lady." Implying this was a long term state of affairs, something outside of my experience. I tried to remember if Ethie seemed unhappy before. Before the Brotherhood attack, before Quaid and I started having problems. Before my life turned upside down again. And couldn't remember. She'd seemed happy, hadn't she? Or, like Quaid, did my daughter hide her unhappiness behind her lovely smile and beautiful eyes?

Was I as deluded with Ethie as I had been with my ex-husband?

"This family," Gram said, poking the table in front of my daughter with one finger, "is the reason we're all here." She waved around the circle of us. "Without this coven," again the jab at the table, "without their support, your mother," I was now the focus of her pointing, "would never have been able to fulfill her destiny." She was absolutely right. All I had to do was think of Ameline and how she turned out in the clutches of the Dumonts. A swelling pride filled my chest, choking me up.

I really had to get a handle on my emotions before I turned into a blubbering basket case for good.

Ethie didn't seem impressed. "It's just the coven," she snapped back. Her blue eyes flickered to me. "Small stuff."

What had I done to my daughter?

Gram's power, the magic of the coven, grasped my daughter firmly in her chair and held her there. Ethie's eyes flew wide, mouth hanging open and it took everything I had not to stop my grandmother from pinning my child in front of her. Everything. Protective Mama Bear roared in my head. The only thing that saved Gram was the fact that, well. She was Gram.

Anyone else would be minus a head by now.

"Young lady," Gram said, voice shaking. "If you're unwilling to accept the power and duty of this family's lineage, I will find another heir to take your place."

She'd do no such thing.

Hush, girl, Gram sent. *I know what I'm doing.*

Manipulative old bat.

How do you think I managed your mother all those years? Gram had amusement in her mental voice. *Now hush, I said.*

Ethie's lower lip trembled as she looked at me, faint defiance there. "Mom won't let you," she said.

"Your mother," Gram said, swelling with the power of the family magic, eyes glowing with blue fire, "is no longer a member of this coven and has no say in what I do."

That reality seemed to come as a complete shock to my daughter. I knew she was smart. But watching the wheels turn in her head fascinated me. So clever, too clever by far, this daughter of mine. She relented quickly, bowing her head to Gram.

"I'm sorry," she said. "Coven leader."

Watch this one, Gram sent, humor gone.

She just needs to feel included, I sent.

Perhaps, Gram sent. Paused. *You're right. Of course.* As though fighting herself, some thought she'd had. *I'll make sure to do just that.*

There is far more of your mother in her than you, Ethpeal, Sass sent, sounding sad. Trust him to eavesdrop.

Gram's reaction came in a violent burst of denial. *Don't you ever say that again, Sassafras. Not in my hearing.*

What the hell was that? *Sass?*

He wouldn't answer, though I did catch the words he spoke directly to Gram. *She feels like Mahalia. Lilibeth at the very least.*

I warn you, cat, Gram growled.

You two, I snarled my own interruption, *will tell me what the hell you're talking about.*

They both fell silent. Before Gram spoke, too quickly and rushed for my liking. *My mother... is the reason this coven is so powerful. The reason I became an Enforcer. And we'll leave it at that.*

Will we? Sass sighed. *I hope that's the end of it.*

I really needed to know what they were talking about. But Gabriel was finishing his milk, pushing back from the table, looking at me with expectation and eagerness.

"I'm ready to try again, Mom," he said. "When you are." He fiddled with his cuff, smiled at me, a secret thing. "I had an idea."

"Let's explore it then," I said, rising with him. While sending a tight message to Gram and Sass. *This conversation isn't over,* I sent. *Watch over Ethie. But I'll be asking questions when I get back. And I expect answers.*

Neither responded. We'd just see about that.

When we reached the basement, Gabriel at my side, I glanced back over my shoulder, happy to see my daughter had followed us, just ahead of Gram, Sass at her feet. The veil parted as we touched down, Max and Jiao joining us again. The drach leader bowed to my son who nodded gravely back.

"Max," Gabriel said, "I haven't been able to find the

pieces on my own. But, I was wondering, do you think they might help me?" Green fluttered at his wrist again before the multicolored rainbow of ribbons burst from his clothing to soar around the drach leader's head in a dance of delight.

He smiled at the old souls with kindness and patience, nodding to them as though they spoke to him before meeting my son's gaze with his diamond eyes. "I believe that will be up to them," he said.

Gabriel held out his hands and the ribbons came to him immediately, like a twisting tornado of happiness, settling in his palms. He stroked them one at a time until they settled. And opened a Gateway.

Frozen tundra lay on the other side, a wash of crisp white under a lavender sky. It made me shiver just looking at it, though harsh temperatures didn't bother me anymore. Gabriel grinned, turning to me with excitement in his face.

"It worked!" The ribbons rose in a spiral, settling on his hair, his shoulders, draping themselves as if exhausted. "They helped me focus what I learned by being part of the veil."

They what? "How?"

Gabriel's little nose scrunched as the ribbons calmed, preening and humming. "They can see different threads of magic," he said. "Far more clearly than we can because they are pure energy." I could tell my son struggled with the explanation, but not the concept. As though trying to fill me in was like he was talking to an infant. It was in equal measure pride stirring and insulting. "Because they were drach they can feel the veil." Gabriel huffed a breath. "Am I making sense?"

I thought of my time as a drach, of the different feeling to the space between planes. How its organic nature felt almost alive. And nodded. Enough sense at least I trusted he knew what he was talking about.

The black ribbon around my wrist purred its approval.

"Only one?" I hated to sound ungrateful but there were still the majority of pieces floating around out there and we were on the losing end of acquisition as far as my tally could track.

"Well done." Max's not-so-subtle comment made me wince. I should have been the one praising my kid. Priorities, Syd. The drach leader didn't wait for me to apologize, instead gesturing at the opening. "Shall we see if what we seek awaits on the other side?"

A soft kick of fear poked me in the belly as I thought of Belaisle and Eva Southway. They'd tracked me in the past when I'd gone hunting the pieces. She'd used my connection to her son, Piers, to follow me and allow Belaisle to snatch the prize out from under me at the last minute. But that connection was long gone, severed even before my departure from this plane, on purpose, in

Zoe's presence and Piers's. With his understanding if not his blessing.

And Gabriel and I managed to retrieve a piece afterward, from a watery world, from the hands of merpeople. Without incident. I could only hope that would again be the case. Regardless, we were all in now.

I was all in.

I turned, waved purposely to my daughter. Who raised her hand, face settled into a brave smile though her lower lip trembled as she waved back. And let us go without protest.

She'd be fine. I'd make sure of it.

I hastily erected a shield of warmth around Gabriel as we passed into the icy world, only to have him smile up at me and push the protection away gently.

"It's okay, Mom," he said. "I don't feel it. Haven't really felt much of anything since I was part of the veil."

That scared the crap out of me. But he seemed unfazed, willing to accept such a momentous truth as par for the Universe saving course. I suppose I had to do the same if I was going to come out of this with my heart and mind intact.

If it wasn't already too late, that was.

Jiao moved on ahead, seeming to float over the icy surface. It wasn't until I tried to walk forward myself I sank into hip deep snow, cracking through the surface crust of thin ice.

Max pulled me to the top while I slipped a shield beneath me, holding me buoyant. Gabriel already had the hang of it, was racing after the *lóng* where she crouched over a chunk of rock sticking out of the snow.

"Here," she said, while Gabriel pounced on the object with a squeal of glee.

"A foot!" He turned to me, waving me closer as Jiao breathed softly over the surface of the stone. The snow melted away in a wash of liquid that quickly reverted back to ice, a cloud of steam dissipating in the wind. Tendrils of frigid air pulled at my ponytail and tried to buffer me off my feet while Gabriel ran his hands over the uncovered foot carved from white stone.

I was thrilled to find another piece so quickly. But it had been my experience in the past the parts of Creator weren't so easy to just stumble over and retrieve. Where were the guardians of the chunk of rock? The people to protect it?

I looked around me at the frozen world and shrugged at last. Long gone, I guess. Frozen under the ice and snow. Still. This seemed far too easy.

Gabriel stepped away as Max's power grasped the foot and pulled it free. Tried to. The moment his magic touched it the ground began to shake. Shaylee acted before I could, trying to steady the trembling earth beneath us, cracking and shifting ice and snow settling. Without our supportive shields we would have sunk deep beneath the surface, I was positive of that.

And thanks to my Sidhe princess's determination and focus was unprepared when Trill appeared next to Gabriel, one hand settling on the foot. And vanished.

Taking the piece with her.

Not this time. I went after her with a roar, latching onto the dissipating tail of her power, weaving my own magic through it like a braid, a leech she would never shake loose. Oh, she tried. She dragged me, heaving and struggling, into the veil, through three different worlds, crashing me physically into the side of a mountain, into the depths of an ocean. I gulped water and emerged coughing in the veil but held on, clothing dripping a long stream of moisture behind me while Trill jerked and bucked against my grip.

Finally crashed us into a forest, falling through sharp boughs and to the brambles below. I panted with exertion, a dog with a bone I would never release as she turned to me, shielded so heavily I couldn't reach her to hurt her.

All I could do was hold on. And try to accept the fact that Trill was stronger than me.

Dear elements, what was she becoming?

"Syd." And then Zoe was there, her dark eyes expressionless, voice multilayered. The voice of Creator. "Let her go, Syd."

I glared, fumed, raged inwardly. Couldn't speak.

Scowled at Trill who shook and stared, hands full of the foot of the statue I was trying to reassemble.

"Syd." Zoe's voice this time. "Please. You have to let her go." She sounded tired.

DAMN IT.

I released Trill, backed off. Immediately regretted it as Liander Belaisle appeared in a puff of black. But wait, here was my chance—

No, Zoe sent while Trill handed off the piece. *No, Syd.*

Rigid, betrayed, I could only glare my hate at Belaisle as he accepted the foot from Trill's shaking hands with flourish before laughing at me.

"How does it feel, Syd?" His cold, yellow eyes gleamed with joy. "To have Creator herself turn against you?"

Bastard.

He disappeared, leaving Zoe and me. And Trill. Who didn't run this time. She instead turned to the Helios oracle who was Fate with grief twisting her face so painfully I almost felt sorry for her.

"Please," she whispered. "Let me tell her."

Zoe shook her head, stoic. "Trill, just go."

The Zornov woman's face settled, anger rising. "You can't make me," she said, defiance in her voice. "If I really want to, you can't stop me."

Zoe sighed. Turned to me. "Do you want to destroy this Universe?"

I shook my head, heart aching. Desperate to understand. To know what to believe, who to trust. They'd both just done the unimaginable. And they were supposed to be on my side.

"Then trust me. Trust Trill. And go."

With no other option, if Zoe was right, I did as she bid. And hoped I'd made the right choice after all.

TWENTY-FOUR

I returned to find Max, Jiao and my son waiting for me with unhappy expressions. It didn't take words for them to get the point.

Another loss, another failure. Another blow. And no, I wasn't going to run away. But, damn it, this was getting old fast.

Max and Jiao left for the Stronghold while I whisked Gabriel into the veil and back to Wilding Springs. Gram and Sass paced the basement, coming to a halt as I exited the dark and bent to kiss my son. He looked up at me, anxious, upset.

"I'm sorry, Mom," he said.

"What happened?" Gram's stiff posture made her look older.

"Trill Zornov happened," I snarled. "And Zoe Helios. And Liander Belaisle." The more I talked, the more people I listed, the madder I got. Had I really let Zoe talk me out of chasing Belaisle? Just letting the foot of Creator go? What the hell was I thinking?

Sass's whiskers drooped. "What are you going to do?"

I could just stand here and fume. Let Zoe's assurances be enough. Or I could stop being complacent and make her tell me what was going on.

The more I thought about it the more it sounded like the best idea ever. I spun away from Gram and the silver Persian, leaving my son behind with his head bowed, guilt in every line of his body. Passed into the veil, knowing no amount of comfort would make him feel better. He had too much of me in him. The only way to help Gabriel recover was to beat some sense into the Fate of the Universe.

Temper, Syd, my vampire sent. *Zoe wouldn't act without good reason.*

I'm getting hellish tired of being left out of this particular loop, I sent while my demon grunted her agreement.

Kick some ass, she snarled.

Shaylee sighed. But had the good sense to stay quiet. I wouldn't have listened to her anyway.

Problem was I had no idea how to track Zoe. Forget about Trill. And could think of only one place the Helios Fate could be shacking up. With one of the only people on my friends and family list I hadn't seen yet.

I had no idea what to expect when I stepped out of

the veil into the wide, central foyer of the Scottish castle Piers Southway and the Steam Union took over when the Brotherhood fled its halls. I already knew my friend was losing his people hand over fist and might not be in the best of moods thanks to that. Hated I couldn't help him without the piece of Creator I was sure Jean Marc Dumont used to convert Steam Union sorcerers to the Brotherhood.

He wasn't exactly waiting for me, but the startled young man who spotted me first wasted no time contacting his leader and, within moments, Piers appeared from a tunnel of blackness. I almost smiled, happy to see him, the corners of my mouth twitching. Then falling downward at the dark, furious scowl he leveled at me, arms crossing over his chest, spill of pale hair hanging to his knees where the ends quivered in time with his angry head jerk.

"Well, well," Piers said in his crisp British accent, with more coldness than I'd ever heard from him. "Look who decided we were worth her time." No, I'd heard that tone before. But not aimed at me.

Reserved for the fury he felt at his traitor mother.

The room flooded with sorcerers, all young it seemed to me, whispering among themselves. Come to gape at the freak, I could only imagine. Made my stomach flip over with anxious anger in response. I caught sight of Apollo and Owen Zornov watching from a doorway, the taller, older brother's face pinched with displeasure. But the younger's brilliant blue eyes were sad, one hand rising to wave at me.

"Piers," I said, returning my attention to the bitterly angry Steam Union leader I'd once considered one of my closest friends. "Can we talk?"

He glanced at his wrist, at a bulky watch, leather band loose around his narrow bones, arching an eyebrow at me. So much disdain in that one gesture. "Sorry," he said. "Can't make the time right now. Important things to do." He spun away from me. "I'm sure you know what that's like." And strode off, hair a whirling banner behind him.

The sorcerers parted, muttered to themselves as they, too, retreated. As quickly as the foyer had filled with the ranks of the Steam Union, it emptied, leaving four people behind.

The woman with the dark hair and eyes, her face pinched with regret, came forward, hesitant but hopeful. "Syd," Clover said, Piers's younger sister bobbing a bit of a curtsy.

That made me wince. "Hi, Clover," I said, offering my hands to her. She grasped them in her own, squeezing tight a moment. I could feel the shiver in her, the way she barely contained her trembling. "Is he okay?"

She shook her head, dark braid bouncing behind her. "He's not," she whispered. Wiped her nose with the cuff of one sleeve. "None of us are."

Funny, there seemed to be lots of sorcerers here. Were the thefts from his ranks less extensive than I'd been told? "You seem to be doing all right?" Came out as a weak question. "All those young, new faces?"

She nodded quickly, tried a little smile. "Recruitment has tripled," she said. "Sorcerers are appearing all over the continent, as though triggered by something. And the Brotherhood seems to be doing nothing to claim them. Leaving us to bring them into the Steam Union."

That was news. "How many new sorcerers are usually discovered in a year?"

She shrugged. "It's hard to know because of the Brotherhood's influence," she said. "They take on far more than we are able to rescue. But I'd say no more than fifty."

"And now?" Was this something I should add to my list of worry about?

"It's insane," Clover whispered. "Over two hundred in just the last three months."

Okay, I was officially freaked. "No idea why?"

Clover wrung her hands before her then rubbed the palms against the front of her tweed skirt. "None," she said. "And Piers is so concerned about the loss of our numbers to the Brotherhood he hasn't taken the time to investigate." She glanced toward the vaulted corridor Piers had used to exit, where three young men watched us. Apollo and Owen held their ground, but it was the sight of my old friend, Simon Clement, standing with them that made me start. Distracted me as Clover went on. "He's obsessed," she said, voice trembling. I turned back to her, to the wide, frightened gaze of her dark eyes. "And no one can make him listen."

"Not even Zoe?" Was she even still here?

Clover turned half away, sorrow on her face. "He made her go," she said, tears dripping to her hands even as she raised her arms to wipe the moisture away. "And she did."

More bad news. "I'm looking for her, Clover," I said. "Do you know where I can find her?" I hated how she vanished into thin air just when I thought I had the Fate pinned down. The gazillion questions I knew she'd never answer had to wait, I guess.

Clover hesitated. "I hoped you were here to help Piers." I guess I deserved the faint accusation in her voice.

"If he won't let me," I said as gently as I could, "what am I supposed to do?"

Her hands fluttered, fell still at her sides. "Zoe didn't tell me where she was going. Good luck finding her." With that Clover left, head down, shoulders bowed. I wanted to reach out to her, stop her, comfort her. But what could I say or do that would make things right?

Nothing. Except find the piece of Creator making Piers crazy. And take that burden from my friend so he would forgive me. If that was even possible.

"He hates you, you know." Simon's voice cut deeper than it should have, so soft and emotionless. Owen hissed at him, shook his head, but the young hacker I'd once adored, who'd left me over a fight about Trill, to come here, it seemed, to Piers and the sorcerers, kept right on slashing at me with his words. "Blames you for abandoning him when he needed you the most." Sounded like Simon agreed with Piers. Maybe felt the same way about his own relationship with me.

I didn't have the heart to remind him he was the one who left Wilding Springs before I did.

Owen closed the distance between us, shooting Simon an angry look over his shoulder while Apollo chewed the inside of his cheek and glared at me. "Piers is as troubled as all the rest of the leaders of this plane," Owen said, with more kindness than Simon or Apollo believed I deserved from their growing irritation at him. "He's losing sorcerers all over the place, even as he recovers those who are waking to their power."

Leaving Piers with a castle full of newbies and the Brotherhood with the most experienced ranks of sorcerers available. Jean Marc Dumont had been on my shit list for a long time now. After joining the Brotherhood with the death of his father, Andre, and the resulting dissolution of the Dumont family magic, Jean Marc's new allegiance led him to the leadership of the sorcerer order. I didn't think anyone could be as nasty or make me want their death more than Liander Belaisle. But this really was the most diabolically clever and evil thing Jean Marc had ever done. And I'd make him pay for it, one way or another.

Owen didn't continue, didn't get a chance. Piers came storming back into the foyer, alone this time, rage clear on his face, his sister trailing behind him with her head still down. Tattled to him, had she? Whatever she'd said he was worked up into a froth so deep I saw his mother in him the moment before he spoke.

And that scared the hell out of me. Not for my own safety but for his state of mind.

"You're still here?" Piers's sorcery thundered a clapping boom through the castle, black power thrumming against the rock and making the floor shake. Shaylee steadied us while my own sorcery sampled his power. So much hurt and anger. I never meant to leave those scars behind.

On the other hand, my demon grumped, *why is it our fault he's falling apart and can't take care of his own crap?*

There was that. But it was deeper, this hurt. Piers had lost his mother, the woman he looked up to, respected, wanted to be like his whole life. Had lost her to her own rage, to her despair. Seen her betray everything he'd ever believed in and thought she believed in. Took her place as head of the Steam Union with the best of intentions.

Only to suffer failure after defeat after betrayal.

I could see where his thoughts had carried him, inhaled the pain of them as if they were my own. Because he and I were that much alike it didn't take much for me to track exactly what he thought of himself at that moment.

He wasn't mad at me, not really. He hated himself.

"I have people searching for Jean Marc," I said, as carefully as I could. "They'll find him. And the piece of Creator."

Piers slashed the air with both hands. "Don't pretend you're doing it for anyone but you," he said. Bitterness washed into his power and to me, crippling in its weight and pressure. How could he live with feeling this way? "If you didn't need that piece for your big finale none of us worthless mortals have anything to do with, you'd still be long gone."

Ouch. Just ouch.

"You were never my friend, were you?" He leaned toward me, angular face pinched, gray eyes sparking with fury. "Someone like you can't have friends. I can't believe I lied to myself about you even being human all this time." Piers gestured at my face. "Drach now, then?"

I'd almost forgotten about my diamond eyes. But I wouldn't apologize for it. Nodded firmly. Considered arguing with him, trying to convince him, but felt the impenetrable wall he'd built around himself, one of emotion and pain.

He wouldn't hear me until he was ready. If he was ever ready.

"You're not welcome here," he said, voice dropping to a low, controlled command. "Go do what you need to do to save the Universe because that's all that means anything to you. But the days of the Steam Union harboring you or helping you are over."

I could have pushed the issue and stayed. But a glance over his shoulder at Owen's pain filled face, at Simon's cynical smirk, the way Clover huddled, weeping silently while Apollo turned his back on me just felt like a lost cause.

The veil swallowed me whole. And I didn't look back.

TWENTY-FIVE

The Stronghold plane welcomed me, drew me in as I settled on the wall, wings furling behind me. I held onto my drach shape for a few moments, feeling the brush of the wind over my scales, inhaling the scent of fresh air and the meadow below, the moisture of a coming rain lingering over me.

I'd flown here on purpose, embracing the drach in me though I'd seemed to have fallen back into the habit of traveling the veil as a woman. My chest expanded, the fires within stoking upward, heating my long throat, sending tendrils of smoke from my nostrils.

Feel better? My vampire's soft voice felt out of place in my drach mind.

No, I sent. I really didn't. For some reason taking this form just made me feel worse. And the Stronghold no longer felt like home.

Max ascended to the top of the wall, Jiao behind him. And my son between them. I puffed out the last of the smoke as I gaped at Gabriel.

"What are you doing here?" He was just as wide eyed, looking up at me with his hazels huge and glistening. "I left you in Wilding Springs."

"I know," my son said, coming to lay one hand on the tip of my snout, stroking his fingers over the hard, bonelike covering protecting my nose. This had to be the first time he'd seen me in my drach form. And though I was tempted to shift, to become the woman he knew, he needed this. We both did. Gabriel had to understand I wasn't just his mother anymore.

Funny, I think he was having an easier time absorbing the changes in me than I was the inherent power in him.

"The ribbons helped me find another piece," he said. "Guarded by some kind of fire magic. But it's there, I'm sure of it." He spoke with more confidence than any boy his age should have. "We're going again right away." Gabriel didn't even glance at Max for approval or ask me even with his tone if that was all right. He commanded us instead. The press of his power fired up the flames in me again, and my anger. I nodded.

"And this time," I snarled, "we're not coming back without what we went to find."

Fast and hot. We'd see if Trill could stand against the fire of a drach on a mission.

"I've only found one more piece," he said as my mind counted, or tried to. How many did that make? Two returned to Creator's statue—the hand and head. Was that really the sum and total we'd accomplished so far? I couldn't think about it. Too depressing. The arm was with Jean Marc and the Brotherhood, if Apollo Zornov was to be believed. Two resided with Belaisle—the foot he'd just taken from me with the help of Zoe and Trill— not dwelling on that or anything— and, possibly, the heart. Or that last, if she'd intended to keep it all along, still with Trill. And four missing—the ear, eyes, brain and soul. There were nine originally scattered. If we counted out the ones being hidden by sorcery, it was possible Belaisle hadn't located the four missing pieces. Seemed most likely to me.

I'd take it.

"And the outstanding four?" Max asked the question I didn't.

Gabriel seemed uncomfortable as the ribbons of drach souls rose from his shoulders, his clothing, then settled again, sighing their agitation. "Even they seem confused about the rest," he said. "Wherever they are, the drach souls can't find them. And neither can I."

We'd worry about their absence later. For now we had a piece to return to Creator.

"I'm going alone," I said, glaring at Max who opened his mouth to protest. "No hesitation, no stopping. In, get the piece, whatever it is, and out."

Jiao cleared her throat. "Try and stop me," she said.

Damn it.

Gabriel stepped back, opened the Gateway. And waited, eyes shining at me. Pride. Was that pride? He had to stop looking at me like that.

I dove for the opening, turning sideways to slip through the extra-large Gate he'd created, feeling Jiao slide through beneath me, long, thin body twining through the air. *Protect Gabriel*, I sent to Max before exhaling into the flaming heat of the plane on the other side.

Fire engulfed the world below, lava crawling over the ground like a living, devouring creature of heat and molten rock. My drach body was impervious to flame but even I felt the crushing pressure of thermals that tried to force me higher.

Jiao skimmed ahead of me, her body wavering in the mirage of rising heat. I kept pace with her, wings low and tight to my ribs, claws tucked firmly beneath me. And only then thought with a jolt of fear about how much trouble I'd been having lately keeping aloft.

Now you mention it, my demon grumbled.

Just focus, Syd, my vampire sent.

Right.

Interesting, Shaylee sent as Jiao turned, serpentine form shifting to the right, toward a dark outcropping I only just noticed myself, lone blackness in a sea of glowing red. *How each of the pieces locations seems to coincide with the elements and other magicks.*

She was right. Water, earth, air, now fire. Was that a clue to the location of the last pieces, or did the presence of the parts of Creator alter and shape the planes on which they resided? I didn't have time to think about it at the moment but filed that thought away for later.

Might be useful.

Jiao slowed, spun around the center of the black space below as I forced myself down to the flat base of dark rock, a tiny island surviving somehow the relentless flow of magma pushing at its borders.

A curved, pale shape lay on the surface, a brain so real looking despite the stone it was made from it might have come from a morgue or a special effects shop. I was so intent on retrieving it I forgot how icky it should have been. Certainly it was a stone brain but it looked alive. Had been, I assumed, at some point. Living tissue of Creator's mind. Instead I focused on protecting it at all costs.

When Jiao hit my side with her slim body, the shock almost carried me down into the lava.

About as much as her betrayal. No, not Jiao, too? Until a roar and a ball of liquid fire flew past my shoulder, just missing my wing membrane and skimming across the *lóng's* back.

I turned with a gasp to the towering, raging form of a creature best left to nightmares. It seemed formed of the magma itself, gaping maw jagged with flame, two pits for eyes deep set with sparks that glowed with the hottest of fire colors, a chilling blue. Its clawed hands formed a ball of lava between them, moving slowly, like newly woken rock, before it hurtled its weapon at the two of us.

I dodged easily this time, doing a quick flyby of its head to distract it. Only to squawk as I was forced to twist my body sideways, barely clearing the tiny distance between our attacker and his rising companion, flowing upward from the rushing lava.

Time to go, I sent to Jiao. She was already diving for the island of stone while three more of the magma creatures rose from the churning river of heat. I shuddered away from a hurtled fireball, roaring in the first creature's face to distract it, just as Jiao's claws wrapped around Creator's brain and she lifted off.

I tried to open the veil immediately but it was too tight of quarters, the shimmering heat rising from our attackers stifling my efforts. And I had no idea what opening a slice would do if it happened in the middle of one of these creatures. Didn't really want to find out.

Jiao was on the move and I chased her, ducking low, so low I could feel even my heat impervious hide begin to crisp as I came within a foot of the surface of the lava. Tucked my wings tight as I slipped between the legs of the first attacker, drawing his fire. The ball of liquid rock he threw missed me, impacting the face of the creature behind him in an explosion of flame and sun hot droplets. The second creature began to topple backward in slow motion, sending gouts of fire high and wide.

One landed on my wing membrane. I couldn't help the scream that emerged in response. Wait a second. This wasn't supposed to happen. I was invincible. But we were past them then, rushing onward, the surface of the molten world below already rising with new creatures, pursuing us. Too late for them, I finally had the room I needed to open the veil. And zoom through, Jiao skipping ahead of me even as a fireball burst through after us, disappearing into the quiet of the veil.

I slammed the cut shut and backwinged to hover, breathing hard, head pounding, my wing aching from the burn. It was already healing, the tiny hole sizzling around the edges. But that fire had to have been magical to damage me. Considering it had come to life, I realized with a shudder of real fear just how much danger we'd been in.

We could have died there.

Jiao slithered back toward me, tendrils around her mouth waving, the normal sheen of her red and green and blue body dull with ash and char. *Fun,* she sent. *Want to do it again?*

I was grateful for the chance to laugh. And shunt

away my fear as I led her through the veil toward the Stronghold, keeping a careful eye on the brain in her claws.

I'd shake and cry and think about it later. For now we had a victory to celebrate. That was, after we returned the piece to Creator. I wasn't taking anything like temporary possession at face value ever again.

TWENTY-SIX

Gabriel held the brain in his hands, stumbling a little from the weight, despite the fact I could feel his power supporting it. The moment we touched down on the wall of the Stronghold, Jiao transformed and gave up the piece to my son, though it was almost the size of his torso. A slim, shivering thread of silver slipped from the interior of the rippled surface and wrapped itself gratefully around Gabriel's wrist even as he beamed at me.

"Finally," he said.

Tell me about it. I guess it was too much to ask that this piece didn't have an attitude problem. Seemed every one we rescued couldn't keep its mouth civil. A male tone to it this time, deep and frustrated. *Do you have any idea how heat like that wreaks havoc on my stone?*

I rolled my eyes and sighed, grateful the ribbon I carried didn't talk. That I knew about.

And blocked out the voice, though from the way Gabriel's lips twitched he continued to listen and, for all I knew, spoke in return the short time it took us to descend into the Stronghold's core.

This time, a small collection of drach followed us as we went down into the center of the structure, Mabel leading them, a silent procession of hopeful drach come to watch my son return Creator's body closer to whole.

My son crawled up into the statue's lap, onto her shoulder. There were times when he'd done this I'd wondered at the irreverence of him scrambling like a little monkey over Creator's statue, winced when he used her right breast for a foothold. Rubbed at my own, though I knew it was silly. Creator wasn't in there anymore. That was the whole point. Still.

The song of the drach rose as the piece connected with the side of Creator's head. Turned almost liquid, finally drawing an "ew" of grossness from me as it softened and slithered into the gaping ear hole. A flare of rainbow light finished the job, the brain now tucked safely back inside Creator's noggin. Gabriel slipped down and away, turning to watch as the silver ribbon that was a drach's soul unwound from his wrist and spun, forming a tall, dark haired male who smiled at Mabel, waved.

She slowly, painfully, waved in return. And then, he vanished.

Soft keening, the song of the drach, rose in answer.

Max's hand fell on my shoulder, his deep voice carrying through his touch, rattling my bones.

"The brother of my heart, if not my bloodline," he said. Best friend? Had to be. And, from the naked grief on Mabel's face now streaked with tears, more than that to her.

Gabriel crossed to my ancestress and hugged her knees. She slowly stroked his hair as he leaned into her.

"He said to tell you he still loves you," my son said.

Mabel nodded. And wept.

Chest tight, I retrieved Gabriel from where he still hugged her, drew him away while the drach circled Mabel and their song supported her. Max just watched, an outsider for the first time since I'd met him, head bowed.

Well, this sucked. Like with everyone else I cared about who was suffering, there was nothing I could do but lead my son away.

Back to the veil. To allow the drach to mourn while I figured out where to go from here. The last missing pieces, the others stolen from me. We were a third of the way to completion of this giant Creator jigsaw puzzle and I'd be damned if I was going to quit now.

The price I'd paid—that everyone I cared about paid, and still were paying—was just too high to fail.

I don't know what impulse carried me, not to Wilding Springs, but toward Harvard and my mother, but that was where we ended up. Maybe it was my need for comfort, some deep seated and childish attempt to have Mom soothe my aching heart. Or maybe it was because I still thought of her as one of the smartest and most confident people I knew. She'd have an answer or a suggestion. Something.

No matter the reason, the moment I stepped foot in her office her mind latched onto mine as though already reaching for me. And, from her panic, Fate might have had a hand in the real reason I was there.

Which meant it might be good for something after all.

Syd! She grasped me firmly with the power of her territory. *Thank the elements. I need your help.* She showed me something that brought a roar of fury from my throat, not a hint of drach music in the sound. Enforcers, blazing blue fire. And Femke in the middle of it. Facing off with my mother.

The North American Witches Council was under attack. Over my dead body.

TWENTY-SEVEN

I burst through the veil once again, hand on Gabriel's shoulder, yelling for Max though I wasn't sure what he'd be able to do for me since he'd already made it clear he wasn't going to interfere in this plane's politics anymore.

To my surprise he answered immediately. *On our way.*

Our way. Not his way.

Oh boy.

I made sure my entrance was grand, tossing Gabriel up and over my drach shoulders as I burst through the veil and into the still air of the council chamber at Harvard. The ceiling was high, I recalled, the space vast. At least to the woman I normally was. But my bulk as a drach filled the emptiness quite nicely, the roar I released a physical thing that forced the witches below to crash to their knees.

All but my mother who held her ground. And Femke Svennson.

The blonde WPC leader looked up with horror in her eyes, mouth gaping while Mom crossed her arms over her chest and nodded once.

"You were saying about displacing me?"

She wouldn't dare. There was no room to land so I backwinged softly with my power holding me aloft, even as the air beside me parted and Max emerged. Mabel. Three other drach on their tails. And Jiao.

I have no idea how they did it, layering themselves over me and beneath me, hovering in silence. Not interfering exactly. Just observing like a floating mass of impending doom.

We will do nothing to alter the course of politics on this plane, Max sent to me. *But I'm curious enough to observe.* His vast mind touched every witch in the room, through me, to buffer the pressure of his power. *As long as there are no objections?*

Mom looked up with a diplomatic smile, all calm and poised as though she hadn't just been facing possible arrest and who knew what else from the clearly insane leader of the WPC. "No objections," she said in a sweet voice before returning her attention to Femke. "Are there, Leader Svennson?"

Varity stood behind Mom, wavering, face clearly showing her exhaustion. But she still had the wherewithal to wink at me.

I'm getting too old for this, she sent.

I'd never believe that.

Everonus glared up at me from where he stood behind Femke who seemed to falter, her head falling forward, a frown of confusion on her face. She looked around as though only then realizing where she was. Unsure of what she was doing there.

Damn the elder council. *YOU*. I boomed the word into the Sidhe lord's mind. *THIS . IS YOUR TAMPERING.*

We told you to leave this to us, he sent, unrepentant.

You did, Max sent. *And though I will not tamper in the politics of the true leaders of this plane, the time of the elder council has clearly reached its end.*

Who decides that, drach? Everonus's disdain was the wrong attitude to use with Max. *You?*

Max roared. Made my little show of pique look like a hissy fit. When the screaming died down and the ceiling of the building stopped shaking, even Mom looked afraid.

TELL MOA IT IS DONE. Max's diamond eyes flared, wings brushing against me as he seemed to swell further, power pushing out and down over the Sidhe lord below, driving Everonus to his knees. *YOUR USEFULNESS IS ENDED.*

Max let him go only when the Sidhe nodded, slow and painful. And just watched as Everonus vanished in a wave of green power.

Gone to tattle, I sent.

Let him. Max sighed, sounding pleased with himself before a soft wave of guilt hit me. *Too much?*

I looked around at the mess below, laughed. *Oh no*, I sent as Femke backed off, dragging her Enforcers with her, fleeing without a word into flares of blue fire. *Just enough, I'm thinking.* I should have been grateful not to see Quaid among her people before she vanished. But it only made me afraid for him. *I have to go after her.* But Max's power held me still.

You must deal with this first. His people were already leaving. Our people. Damn it. *And make a choice, Sydynn Hayle. They are waiting.*

My son's mind touched mine. *Mom*, he sent. *Are you going away again?*

Of course I was. Wasn't I?

Gram appeared below, Sass in her arms. Both looked up at me. Mom, the coven leaders, their panic reduced but their fear renewed. They needed me.

Syd, my vampire sent. *We're not going anywhere.*

Not until this is through, my demon sent.

When it's over, Shaylee offered her suggestion in a sad voice, *we go then. Find a place to be at peace and alone, if that's what we want.*

But for now, I finished, *we can't just abandon them again, can we?*

I guess I knew that all along.

COUNCIL LEADER HAYLE. I could have done this another way, but Max had set a precedent. And if I was going to stay put, to be free to do what I had to do, it was better they feared me. *WHILE I KNOW MY ASSISTANCE WAS NOT REQUIRED, I AM HONORED TO BE WELCOMED.*

Mom nodded to me. *You can stop shouting, sweetheart,* she sent, pert and almost giggly. *We can hear you just fine.* "Doombringer," she said out loud, making me shiver by using that name so calmly when we really didn't know what it meant. "You are always welcome here."

How did she do that? Get all hysterically mushy on the inside but seem so collected on the outside?

Practice, she sent.

Smartass mother.

My time away was necessary. Big lie. And not so much. Let them wonder. I wasn't giving details, not now. Not ever. *But I see that the tasks that have taken me from you have left you without the support you might need from time to time to maintain order.*

That was a nice way of putting we're a freaking mess and you're coming to save us. Sassafras almost made me snort. *Tactful, Syd? You?*

I was going to throttle him if he made me laugh and ruin everything.

It is my intent to return to this plane and make it my

responsibility to ensure the continued safety and balance of all magicks here. Like it or not, this was part of my job. Had to be. Otherwise, why would Creator have made me the way she did?

At last you see it, Jiao whispered in my head.

Thanks for sharing, I sent.

You needed to get there on your own.

The girls inside me seemed as surprised as I was. But it made sense, didn't it?

While I will not do your dirty work for you, I sent to the crowd below, *I will also not allow this place to fall apart any further.* No more pulling punches. *Until this crisis is ended, I will be handling things from here.*

Deposing your mother? Sass's sharp words made me realize what I'd just said.

With the help and guidance of the leaders of this plane, I amended.

Nicely done, sweetheart, Mom sent. *Now stop flapping your wings like that. You're messing up my hairdo.*

Ten minutes later, while witches under Mom's command magically cleaned up the giant mess Max and I made in the council room, I sat on the edge of a chair in my mother's office with my son on one knee and my demon cat on the other.

Mom sank into her seat behind her desk while Gram stared out the window, Varity perched on the edge of the heavy wooden table, tossing a small ball of fire from hand to hand and Dad paced back and forth.

Uncle Frank and Sunny arrived shortly after, Charlotte in their wake. Mom's office, though large, felt suddenly crowded. I wasn't complaining. We all waited in uncomfortable silence for five more minutes, my heart hurting. Mom finally cleared her throat when it was obvious the last invited member wasn't going to show up.

Piers was being true to his word. He wanted nothing to do with me.

Well, screw him. I was going to save his scrawny British ass anyway.

Before Mom had a chance to speak, the air flared with blue fire and the last person I expected to appear blinked his chocolate brown eyes at me before bowing his head to my mother.

"I hope I'm not overstepping," Quaid said. "But I guessed all of you would be meeting. And I wanted in."

Mom welcomed him, rising to her feet to kiss his cheek. "Femke?"

He bowed his head. "I've been a traitor before," he said. "I'll do it again if it means helping her." Was that really how he thought of himself? He'd infiltrated the Dumont family to protect me, to uncover the truth about his own family. To get revenge for the deaths of his parents. That didn't make him a traitor. And yet, in Quaid's eyes, that was clearly the case.

And I thought I was screwed up.

I told them about the elder council, about Moa and Everonus and Nona. Charlotte seemed keenly interested in the fact older versions of werewolves existed, but we would have to leave such things for later.

If we had a later.

When they were all up to speed on everything I knew—from the missing vampire's locations to Trill's betrayal and Zoe's involvement, to the most recent piece's return—I fell silent and waited for them to talk it out.

They didn't. As a group they stared at me, waiting. For what?

"I'll do everything I can," I said. Stuttered to a halt. "I meant that earlier."

"So you're staying then." Gram's voice sounded thick. She cleared her throat. "For how long?"

"Until this is done," I said. Felt my own sorrow while the girls embraced me. I couldn't give them up. Not when I needed them so much. "I won't leave you again. And I'm sorry I did in the first place." Whispered the same to the egos in my head.

Felt their love and embrace in response. And the wall between their egos and the drachness of my soul fall away. No longer needed.

We will see this through together, my demon sent.

And we will never abandon you, Shaylee sent, fierce and

earthy.

If the day comes you ask us to, my vampire finished, *we will gladly go into the darkness to give you peace. But not today.*

I didn't deserve them.

While my egos knew my most intimate secrets, my family was another story. And I just couldn't bring myself to tell them what I'd admitted to Meira. Might make me a coward but even I didn't have that much strength in reserve.

Gram nodded, turned back to me. "And then?"

"I don't even know if we're going to survive this," I said.

"We always do." Uncle Frank's soft quip made me grin despite the bleakness of the situation.

"I have to be honest, here," I said. "We're missing two thirds of the pieces of Creator still, only three of which we think are lost." Maybe. Belaisle could have them, too. But I doubted it somehow. If he did have them, surely he'd have made some kind of move by now. Even holding one in his possession meant access to a giant amount of power. "That means the others are in enemy hands." Funny, I realized only then there was balance in the number. Three with Belaisle or his equivalent and three missing. And three returned. Was this a sign of something or just me grasping at straws? I shook off the numeric oddness and went on. "While a vast force of warriors I know are stronger than me—than the drach," I let that sink in a moment before going on, "wait on the other side of the seal between our two Universes. Something I've been told won't hold them forever. That the Order is coming. And unless I can recover the rest of Creator there will be nothing we can do to stop Dark Brother and his army from taking over everything and making their Universe dominant." Or worse. Destroying ours completely.

I sat there in the quiet, their glum mood matching mine, silence muffled by the still air while outside the office door I could hear witches moving around, talking, living. For how long?

"Enough of that," Gram said, straightening up, blue eyes flashing. "I won't let any of us stray into this pit trap of fear and regret we seem to be wallowing in right now." She jabbed a finger at me. "Tell us what to do next. And we'll do it."

A plan. She wanted a plan? "Until Gabriel and the drach souls can find the other pieces," I said, "missing or in Belaisle's possession," my son's brow furrowed with frustration, "all we can do is hunt Trill and Belaisle. Jean Marc Dumont and the Brotherhood." I might even make that my next priority. "But you have to be prepared. Because I might not be the one you should count on in the end."

Mom shifted in her seat. "Doombringer," she said.

Did she know what I'd been told it meant? How

could she? Mom was smart. Must have guessed.

"There's a chance," I said, "coming back is the worst possible choice I could make. If what I've been told is right I'm meant to betray all of you. This entire Universe. And bring doom in my wake."

"I don't believe that." Sass's claws dug through my jeans into the skin of my leg. "I'll never believe that."

"Neither do I," my son said, eyes shining with absolute confidence, reminding me so much of his father in that moment I choked on a sob. "No matter what happens, Mom, you will never make the wrong choice."

But what if the choice wasn't up to me? If I was only the tool of the choice in the end? I didn't comment, just stroked Gabriel's hair. And reached for Gram.

If the time comes, I sent. *I expect you to make sure I don't get us all killed.*

Girl. She paused. *Oh, girl.*

I'd take that as a yes.

I bowed my head over my son's hair and felt tears burn in the corners of my eyes. And when I opened them again felt my vision shift, this choice at last made, the incredible, crystalline brilliance of my sight gone, reduced. Returned to normal.

Whatever that was.

TWENTY-EIGHT

I stood in the quiet of the Sidhe cavern and listened to the sounds of my kids pattering and chattering their way in and out of the stacks in the archive. So young and fresh and innocent, even now. Able to laugh, to play. I was just grateful they hadn't lost that.

At least, not yet.

Gram had, of course, offered immediately to turn over the house in Wilding Springs. And the power of the coven, to return the family magic to me. The thought of either made me shudder and reject such a thing on a purely instinctual level.

"I can't go back there," I told her quietly, privately huddling with her in front of the big window in Mom's office while the others murmured to each other behind us. "Too much water under that burned bridge."

The family magic shivered, yearned for me. But retreated into Gram again. "I guess I should be insulted it's so eager," she said, wry twist to her mouth. "Ungrateful."

I felt its regret, its instant clinging to her through the thread of connection I shared with her again. Sighed as I reached out to the people in this room and realized the bonds had snuck their way inside me without my knowledge. Even the family power had its way with me, tying me tightly to the coven yet again, as a member if not a leader. That, for better or worse, I was bound so tightly to them all again I might never win free this time.

Gram's blue eyes glittered with tears. "Where will you stay?"

There was only one logical choice though it was going backward as well. I stepped forward to the sound of giggling in the next doorway, looking into the dark room on the right, at the large bed with the living, growing tree canopied over it. Nothing had changed. Not the scent of earth and fabric softener, fresh and alive, not the crumpled white t-shirt lying like a crushed animal on the pillow that had been Liam's. I'd left it there the last time I'd slept here. Wept into it. Just before I married Quaid.

So long ago. A lifetime.

Something large and dark groaned in the corner. I jerked into protective mode, power pulling to me, but the cavern sighed its sorrow as a giant head lifted from the stone and black eyes met mine, a pit of red fire barely awake in their depths.

"Galleytrot," I whispered. "What are you doing here?"

I'd meant to look for him, remembered momentarily the concern I'd felt he was gone from his place of protecting the kids. Even as his large body rose as though in pain from the stone floor, nose so low a tiny dot of moisture darkened the rock as it brushed the surface.

"I've failed him for the last time," he whispered. "It's time for me to go."

"Failed who?" I crossed to him, hands buried deep in his black fur. He moaned his agony, turned from me.

"You know who," the great dog said.

Liam.

I sank to the edge of the bed, sagging myself. "You've never been anything but faithful," I said. "Not since the Moromonds deceived you."

He shook his big head, blinking slowly. He seemed diminished, reduced to me, as though he'd shrunk inside the massive body I took for granted, shining coat dull. "I couldn't keep him safe," Galleytrot said, voice equally dim, "and though I tried, I couldn't protect Gabriel, either."

That's what this was about. Gabriel's kidnapping. "He came here on his own," I said.

I should have known that wouldn't make a difference.

Instead, the big dog sighed and nodded.

Just as the two giggling children who shared my life entered the room.

"Galleytrot!" Ethie squealed his name and lunged for him, hugged him tight. Gabriel seemed to sense something was wrong, approaching more slowly.

"Children," the dog said. "I have something to tell you."

I held my tongue and the tears wanting to fall as my kids fell silent.

"I'm going away," he said. "Back to the Sidhe realm. And I won't be coming back."

You have crappy timing. That was cruel but I sent it anyway. *They already have issues with the people they care about leaving them.*

You should know. Galleytrot's retort wasn't angry. Just sorrowful.

I shut up. Because I felt in him what I'd felt in myself. He was done. And I was the last person who had the right to try to change his mind.

Ethie wept and pleaded as the big dog rose from his haunches, padding on his large paws past her even though she clung to him. There was nothing her little arms could do to hold neither him back nor her power when he called up the magic of the Sidhe to support him. Inexorable, a tiny child's need against a moving mountain, he literally dragged her into the Gate chamber before shaking himself, fur quivering, Ethie finally falling away.

"Syd," Galleytrot said. "If you would." He sat down before the Gate and waited.

"Let me." Gabriel joined the big dog, not touching him, his own head bowed. "This is my fault."

"It is not," Galleytrot said. "I have merely outstayed my usefulness." His nose touched the back of my son's hand. "You don't need me anymore. If you ever did."

"I need you." Ethie's wail ended in a coughing sob. I reached for her, hugged her to me as the big dog sighed one last time.

"Gabriel," he said, voice vibrating with loss.

The Gate glowed with sudden life, green and sparkling. I knew Gabriel could have used his power to simply open the way but it felt right for him to use the Gate of his ancestors.

It responded happily, answering with swift action, swinging wide as though it had been waiting for him. Which, I guess, it had. And, though maybe I should have been able to, I couldn't muster surprise at the sight of Gwynn ap Nudd waiting on the other side as though he'd know what was coming.

"My lord." Galleytrot bowed his head to the former leader of the Wild Hunt.

Gwynn nodded in turn, blond hair catching the light on the other side, sparkling gold over his elaborate tunic. "You're certain, my faithful one?"

"I am, my lord." The big dog rose and shook again.

Gwynn's green eyes met mine then those of my children before he smiled, faint but real. "Do not depart in misery and regret," he said. "Nor with a heavy heart. You have done well and more than any hound. Repaid your debts with your soul and the compassion you once disdained."

Which reminded me I had no idea of Galleytrot's past. And now, maybe, would never know.

Didn't seem all that important.

"If only that were the case," the unhappy dog said.

"I say it is." And then, Gwynn wasn't alone. A second dog stood with him, shaggy and dark, eyes deep set but head more delicate. And I knew that voice though I hadn't heard it in years. Grew up with it.

Erica.

Galleytrot's ears perked before he bowed his head once more. "What good am I to you, my love, like this?"

"Leave that for me to decide." She looked up at Gwynn who nodded. And before my eyes the dog that had been Erica Plower, Mom's former second, the last leader of the North American Witches Council before being banished into this present form, stood and altered.

And became human again. Held out her hands to Galleytrot while I gaped.

She was beautiful, young, fresh. As though none of the terrible things we'd all lived through had happened at all. Maybe I should have been pissed—she'd almost been the cause of the end of all witches in our territory, had betrayed us to the Brotherhood. But none of that mattered now.

"Things are different here," she said. "The Wild is dissolved and we who were damned, even we have our lives to live."

Galleytrot hesitated. Turned to Gwynn. "Do not do this to me, my lord." More pain, layers of it.

"She speaks truth, faithful one," Gwynn said. "Now come. And make peace with yourself at last."

Galleytrot stepped forward, leaving me behind, the kids. Ethie clung to me, Gabriel openly weeping but making no attempt to stop the dog from going. The giant black hound paused just before his nose touched the shimmering green barrier keeping the Sidhe realm from ours, turned to look back. Then passed through, body low and slow as though carrying the weight of the Universe on his shoulders.

The moment his feet touched the grass he was a dog no more but a tall, handsome man. "Jared," I said. Waved one hand as the man I'd first known as Jared Runnel turned to look back at me with wonder on his face.

Erica tucked herself under his arm, smiling, before meeting my eyes. "Tell your mother," she said, "I will love her forever."

I had to bite my lower lip as the Gate closed on them,

sealing them away while my daughter screamed Galleytrot's name and my son closed the way even as he cried.

TWENTY-NINE

I tucked Ethie into bed, the light beside her on the curving, bush like end table dampening on its own as she sighed and half turned over, cheeks pink from crying. At least she'd finally wept herself into exhaustion. Maybe a good sleep would heal her heart enough she could move on.

I'd found the doorway to her new bedroom after the Gate closed, startled by two additions—one on the same side as the room I'd shared with Liam and another next to the archive. The cavern knew, it seemed. Happily made room for us.

I left my daughter to sleep in the pale green bed, peeking my head in across the corridor. Gabriel was passed out, too, lips parted, left foot twitching under the covers as he dreamed. The power of the cavern whispered around me, soothed him back into quiet.

I wanted to believe it was Liam. But I knew better than to go looking. My love was gone this time, for good. And no amount of wishing would change that.

A silver furred mound detached from the end of Gabriel's bed and plopped down on the floor, pacing past me out the door and into Ethie's room. I let Sass go without a word, grateful he'd shown up an hour or so ago, pawing at the shields around the cavern until I let him in. Made sure it wouldn't keep him out again. And breathed a sigh of relief as his furry presence finally eased Ethie's hurt. He'd spent the last little while going back and forth between bedrooms. I had a feeling he was in for a long night.

The soft touch of Enforcer magic hurt more than it should have, but I stepped back from Gabriel's door and went to the entry, welcoming Quaid into the space. He materialized in a flare of blue fire, robeless, black t-shirt and dark wash jeans making him look young again. How familiar, that handsome face, the way his brows pulled together, the chocolate of his eyes, the zing of his power.

But not mine anymore. Never again mine. And I was okay with that.

"The kids." He shifted his feet. "Are they all right?"

"Sleeping," I said. Told him about Galleytrot.

Quaid grimaced. "I should have gone after him."

I didn't bother arguing. It wouldn't have helped.

"Syd." Quaid stopped, breathed. Seemed to deflate

before meeting my eyes. "I'm sorry."

"So am I." I really was.

"I know I'm the reason you left." He ran one hand through his hair. "Or part of it. I never meant to hurt you like that."

"I just wish you'd told me," I said, my greatest regret. "That you were unhappy for so long. I never wanted that for you either."

Quaid sighed, shoulders straightening. "It was supposed to be a fairy tale ending."

I should have been sadder instead of this soft, aching loss. "How's Payten?" The babies.

He nodded his acknowledgment of my kindness in asking. "She's fine," he said. "Worried about the kids."

"Does she give you what you need?" It wasn't fair to ask but I needed to know. "Did she? Before we…?"

"I never cheated on you, Syd." Anger flared, faded. "Never. And I never would have. But the night you divorced me I was so hurt. I blamed you. And Payten was there, waiting for me." He sighed, a gusty sound. "It wasn't supposed to happen this way."

"Because our lives have been textbook, haven't they?" I managed a soft laugh.

He did, too.

"She looks up to me," he said, hesitant and quiet. "Says I'm her hero. Syd, she needs me." I understood. How important that was to him. For the first time ever, I got it.

And nodded. "I'm just glad you're happy," I said.

He closed the distance, hugged me. Gratefully, I hugged him back. Because, damn it, he was my friend. And I didn't want to lose that along with everything else.

"He'd be proud of you," Quaid whispered into my hair. "He loved you more than I ever could have."

It had to have taken him a lot to admit that about Liam. Because of course that's who he meant.

I leaned away, squeezed his hands. Broke the bad news. "Batsheva is alive," I said. "I'm sorry I didn't kill her."

Quaid shrugged. "We'll get around to it," he said. "I have more important things in my life than that old hate."

Good to know we were both growing up. He backed away from me, the hurt in him diminished and I felt myself able to breathe, to relax. And smile.

"I'll keep you posted on Femke," he said. "But Syd, whatever reason you have for not helping her... please. If she was ever your friend."

I nodded firmly. "I made a semi-promise to mind my own business," I said, thinking about the council and the way they'd tried to hurt my mother. Worst. Choice. Ever. "That's over now. I'll do everything I can to make sure Femke recovers." If that were even possible. But one thing was crystal clear. No matter who tried to stop me or get in my way, I wasn't going anywhere.

And anyone who tried to hurt the ones I loved were in for a hell of a ride.

I let him go. Turned, looking down at my pink hands with my human vision. And felt my final visitor of the night step through the veil, waiting patiently for me in the Gate cavern.

With a faint feeling of trepidation and loss, I went to tell Max I wasn't drach anymore.

I'm pretty sure the drach leader already knew. At least, he didn't seem surprised when he saw me. In fact, by the time I reached his side the loss of my new family hit me rather keenly, like a blade severing something important I didn't know I missed.

His gentle smile was as kind as always, as supportive. The Max, who had, briefly, turned bitter and confrontational, had gone again. Which made me think, with some irritation, if his pressure about the "small stuff" was some kind of Fate construct meant to push me over the edge.

Zoe and I had a lot to talk about. Either that or I was in serious need of therapy for my paranoia issues.

"How do you feel?" Kind of him to ask.

I reached inside, for the drach in me. Found her but distant, my wings a dream, the song of the species fading. To the point I knew, even if I tried, I could no longer sing his name to him, or my own for that matter. I didn't expect that to make me so emotional.

Who was I kidding? I used to call Mom a supernatural faucet. She had nothing on my waterworks lately.

"I'll miss flying," I whispered. Was that really the most important thing I wanted to tell him? Silly Syd. He was drach. He understood.

Flying was everything.

"That part of you will always remain," he said. "And be waiting for you when the time comes."

I wasn't used to losing what I'd gained. Every time I added a new ego I only became stronger. This felt entirely different, like backsliding. Absolutely and utterly disappointing.

"I want it back now." I sounded so petulant in my own ears. Like Ethie.

Max chuckled. "You do know," he said, "we were both fools to think you could ever stop being Sydlynn Thaddea Hayle above all else."

The black ribbon, quiet for this little while, flexed and sighed, settling in happier contentment. This should have made me feel better but just made me sad.

My vampire sighed. *Max is right, of course.*

Hate it when he's right, my demon groused.

We'll survive, Shaylee sent. *We always do.*

I would fly again. If it was the last thing I did.

And then, in a move that floored me completely and left me gaping, Max leaned forward and pressed his cool lips to my forehead. *Daughter of my heart*, he sent. *How I've adored having you with me all these days. But even I know I must let you go now to do what must be done.*

Daughter? Choke. I had a dad, of course I did. But Max. Yeah.

I hugged him, arms tight around him, and he embraced me in turn, gently, as though not certain it was a good idea. "I'm scared," I whispered into his robe, feeling his drach power hum through me. "What if the council is right? Batsheva? What if I'm meant to end this Universe?"

Max sighed, the sound rumbling in my ear. "If you are it will be for the very best of reasons and because it is absolutely necessary for you to do so," he said. "Of that I will never, ever doubt." I wished I had his confidence, clung to him a moment longer. "I have known you long enough now, Syd, to be assured whatever choice you make it will be the only one that serves the greatest good."

That wasn't exactly reassuring. Because there were a gazillion scenarios out there I couldn't foresee. "Even if it means everyone I love dies?"

Max pushed me gently away, hands on my shoulders. "Do you really believe Creator would go to so much effort to make you, to nurture and form you, to strengthen you, just to send you to a fate that would destroy you?"

Did I really have to answer that?

Max left me, a slow, gentle wave of one hand preceding his departure. I hugged myself in the return of the quiet of the cavern. Considered going to bed. But I was too wound up just yet. I turned, watched Sass pad across the corridor one more time, returning to Gabriel, the midnight sentinel of happy dreams. And rejected the idea of sleep.

Instead, I drifted to the door of the archive and peeked inside. This had been Liam's true domain, the place he always seemed happiest. According to legend— and I never doubted Liam's information was true—the Sidhe archive possessed every book ever written in the history of the Universe. In every language, from every race. How the magic accomplished it, I had no idea. But, I'd tested it a few times when Liam was still alive, asked for random tomes and found them readily available, as if the cavern was eager to prove itself to me. And to him.

There was a lovely comfort in entering the archive, the long, narrow walkways disappearing back into endless darkness, only the front portion near the door lit with perma light. Liam's desk stood just inside, a heavy oak thing carved with Sidhe symbols and people, trees and flowing water that looked almost real. I ran my fingers over the carvings, across the back of the velvet cushioned chair that I typically used, across from Liam's larger, more elaborate seat. Continued to circle until I could pull back the padded chair, sink into its soft surface. Bring my knees to my chest, heels hooked on the edge of the cushion, close my eyes. Breathe in Liam's scent still lingering on the upholstery.

I told myself I wasn't going to. But I couldn't resist searching for him despite what I already knew. That his soul, the part he'd left behind, had burned out in the search and connection with Alison. Did I really need to pile on more sadness? As I allowed my magic to hunt for him, to connect with the cavern, I felt myself calm, heal a little.

He was gone. But this place, his home, was my home now. And even if I'd never see him again, at least my heart lived where his had lived.

I opened my eyes, found myself smiling. Looked down at the shining silver cover of his closed and quiet laptop. It sat here for years, waiting for him to return. I was shocked to realize the tiny light on the front glowed green. That the computer had power.

Well, the cavern was magic after all. Liam was never able to explain to me why he was able to get Wi-Fi here, or much of anything else that worked in this place. Like cell phones. Crazy. But I wasn't about to argue with magic like that.

My fingers stroked the surface and, in a swift motion, I opened the lid, not sure what I expected to find.

Froze as the wallpaper came to life, backlit and glowing.

The handsome young man with the strawberry blond hair hugged the beautiful twenty-something woman, her dark hair piled in curls around her, white dress hugging her slim body. He was laughing, mouth open, hazel eyes alight, as was she, looking up at him as though he was the center of her whole world. In the background, the sun set over the house in Wilding Springs.

Our wedding day.

My hands trembled as I closed the lid. I could do this. I could.

I just needed a minute to cry.

Sass showed up just in time to purr me into gentle heaves of grief as I clung to him and wept for what could have been.

THIRTY

One day at a time. Wasn't that the right motto?

It was hard, not just because I struggled with my own issues, but to see my kids having a hard time, too. They both seemed content to stay with me—even Ethie, though I made sure she spent every day with Gram and the coven. It would be her responsibility one day and I wanted to be sure she understood that as clearly as I hadn't at her age.

But it was different for Gabriel. I could feel his frustration at his constant failure to uncover the pieces of Creator. There were still three stray pieces missing from what I could tell. The ear, the eyes and the soul were outstanding and Gabriel couldn't track any of them. The three we did know about—the arm, heart and foot—were in hands not our own. Belaisle's sorcery was clearly hiding the known piece he had in his possession, Jean Marc's as lost in the dark as he and the Brotherhood. Which made me worry Belaisle, or other of my enemies, had the rest in their grimy paws, too.

And Trill? Well, I wasn't holding my breath my son would find the heart she took until she wanted to return it. If she hadn't given it to Belaisle already.

No one blamed Gabriel. Which, of course, knowing my son and how much like me he was as much as his father, only made things worse.

I just had to trust what Max said, that Creator would make sure the pieces were found. That Fate would guide me. If only Zoe Helios would show up and reassure me that was the case, I wouldn't have felt so anxious.

My attempts to contact Piers continued to be rebuffed but I'd reached the point where I refused to give up on anyone. He'd either come around eventually on his own or I'd become such an annoyance he'd have to deal with me. I caught myself grinning a time or two into the quiet of the cavern as I shot the Steam Union leader a cheery good morning through the veil before leaving him alone to stew.

I wasn't trying to be mean, really. But he was going to talk to me if it killed him.

Sunny and Uncle Frank still had their hands full with vampires, though the former queen confessed to me the influx had slowed and, in fact, their numbers were slowly shrinking again. Fear was high but hope remained she could save them. I only wished I could remove the pressure from her shoulders such dependence was causing.

At least she had Uncle Frank to lean on.

Sunny never voiced her fear out loud but it crossed my mind many times, so it had to be doing so in hers: what happened when all the vampires were gone to the void? And why them and the spirit magic?

Just once I would have loved more answers than questions. For variety.

I could only hope the same diminishing was happening to Dark Brother's army. While I had zero illusions about our ability to defeat the Order, at least if their numbers were knocked down to, say, close to the ranks of the remaining drach, we might at least hold them off for a little while.

I'd give myself an ulcer with all those what ifs.

Instead, I focused on what I could change. Or, at least, influence. My plan to sneak the Kennecott healer twins into a delegation of werewolves visiting the World Paranormal Council headquarters won me nothing. Both Lula and Phon reported back regretfully they could find nothing physically wrong with Femke, though neither had been able to get close enough to her to confirm that.

I could have forced the issue, gone and scooped the WPC leader up and dragged her somewhere I could give her a good shaking and going over, but Mom suggested caution. Quaid's reports Femke seemed even more withdrawn and the disappearance of Everonus from the council gave me bouts of nervousness and relief in equal measure.

I'd hit that problem head on as soon as I decided what impending disaster fit where on my game plan.

As for my daughter, I was proud of her. She seemed to be taking her responsibility as coven heir seriously. Though Gram told me in confidence she was now worried the girl had gone too far the other way, Sassafras was pleased with Ethie's commitment so I trusted him to keep an eye on her.

Payten had been keeping her distance in wake of the renewed warmth between Quaid and me. I actually found I enjoyed having him as a friend without the pressure of the magic that once controlled our feelings for each other. His new wife, however, seemed to sense I wasn't quite as open about her shacking up with my ex the way she did.

Made me wonder what kind of mom she would be to my kids. And gave me a horrible moment that almost made me puke.

Oh. My. Swearword. I'd have to co-parent with the woman.

Shudder.

All of my attempts to reach Alison and Sebastian again failed. Not that I expected success but a little give and take on the whole Fate thing doling out dribs and drabs of info would have been nice.

The black ribbon protested every time I tried, doing its best to keep me safe. And while I still had no idea why a drach soul from the other Universe would want to protect Doombringer, it wasn't leaving my wrist without major surgery or death. And since I only ever sensed support and kindness from it I had to believe it had my best interest at heart.

Or was some kind of planted spy from Dark Brother merely lulling me into false confidence about our little relationship.

Paranoid? You betcha.

At least my sister was mostly over being mad at me. When I contacted her to fill her in on everything that happened, she ended the conversation with a lisping rendition of my nickname as a farewell. Her giggling did my heart good, even if I was pretty sure that joke was going to get old fast.

Mom stood her ground against the other councils, though I was on standby, knowing things would have to come to a confrontational head at some point. It wasn't Femke who was the issue, but the other territory leaders. It pissed them off to no end their own witches were now demanding equality.

Progress in the witching world? Go figure.

The only problem with this kind of progress was the

way it was being handled. I knew from talking to Quaid and Charlotte there was a great deal of unrest in the covens of other territories, propaganda making rounds for the status quo while the world teetered on the brink of a witch rebellion. And while I was all for change... really? They had to do this now?

Sigh.

At least Charlotte, as werequeen, and Sunny, who finally came forward and claimed her place as queen of all vampires—I could just hear Moa's cursing at her temerity—were stable voices on the WPC, some of whom were demanding Femke march on their own people to keep them in line.

From time to time I thought of Tallah and wondered what her plans were. But I just couldn't bring myself to care what the selfish coven leader was up to. As long as she didn't interfere with what I was doing, she could have her privacy.

For now.

Zoe Helios, on the other hand, I actively pursued, as much as Trill and Belialse. Wouldn't you know, the Fate of this Universe was conspicuously absent? The longer she avoided me, the madder I got. Well, fine then. If she wanted to be like that. Not even Fate would get in my way.

Didn't do much to ease my worries about the whole Doombringer situation. I woke some nights in a cold sweat without a clear vision of the nightmare I'd just endured, only knowing I'd been on the brink of making a choice and couldn't, stuck in limbo forever, unable to decide.

I think once I actually reached the point of choice it would be easy. I was already over the way it haunted me all the time. So impatient.

My vampire was fond of reminding me of that fact.

More riddles, the puzzle of Trill Zornov. Did she betray me or, with Zoe stepping in to stop me, did that mean Trill really was on my side and I'd been getting in the way of Creator's plan? Seriously, if the mother of the Universe wanted me to take care of her business, she had to give me something I could work with already.

Every time I put finding Liander Belaisle and Eva Southway at the top of my growing to-do list, something else came up. So much so, I second guessed the choice every time I considered it, then growled to my alter egos about my hesitation. This whole wondering if Fate was making things happen around me was really starting to piss me off.

What I really needed, what would actually be helpful, was a way to track Belaisle and Jean Marc. Maybe through the pieces, maybe through their sorcery. Something. Anything.

Creator. Throw me a bone.

Jean Marc's discovery and elimination would help me

kill two birds. By saving the Steam Union, and, if I could figure out how he was switching sorcerous allegiances, by finally eradicating the Brotherhood forever.

That would be the sweetest revenge against Belaisle of all.

I missed seeing Max all the time, the hum of the drach song that I didn't realize permeated everything they did until it wasn't there anymore. Of course, I could see them any time I wanted just by going to the Stronghold, and did. But it wasn't the same.

Jiao had half moved in with me and the kids, seemed to adore them as much as they loved her. I never expected my quiet and serious *lóng* friend to have any kind of maternal instinct, but apparently her attachment to her sister and brother translated into caring about my kids. Though I noticed more and more frequently it wasn't Ethie or Gabriel she spent her time with, but the human form of Sassafras she bent heads with over books from the archive.

I refused to speculate. Still, when Jiao laughed and Sass laughed with her, my heart smiled.

The nights I didn't have nightmares, I dreamed of flying. And woke at times with tears on my pillow. I'd tried to take drach shape, in private, not wanting Max to know if I failed. Which I did, over and over again. To the point I stopped trying.

I missed my wings.

But I'd promised my sister, and myself, and, in the silence of the night, Liam and Creator and everyone I loved, I wouldn't run again. That I would see this through, do my best, as always, stumbling and falling and picking myself up only to carry on. Until it was done and I could be free.

And go for good. Because I knew, as I'd known for a long time, I'd outlive the ones I loved. So maybe my drach form was a gift after all from Creator. A way to escape the loss of my mortal ties when the time came.

I slept every night in the bed I'd shared so briefly with Liam, hugging his pillow to me. Whether a trick of my mind or the cavern's need to remember him, too, it always smelled of him, of fresh earth and fabric softener, and even when I woke in tears or in terror, a few deep breaths while holding that pillow and I could fall back into a deep and peaceful sleep.

Even gone and lost to me, he continued to take care of me.

Now, if only I could get past sitting at his desk, staring at the two of us on his laptop wallpaper. Fighting the need to cry all over again.

Baby steps.

Like what you read? Find out more at
pattilarsen.com

Here's a look at the first chapter of
Book Six of the Hayle Coven Destinies

THE ORDER

ONE

Their laughter made me smile, the first time I'd felt like smiling in a long time, it seemed. Infectious, delicious, the exuberant excitement of a brother and sister at play without a care in the world.

If only. Though, for now it seemed it was easy for my son to forget his role in the end of the Universe as we knew it. The Gateway, whatever that would ultimately mean for him and the rest of us, my son spent far too much time sad and quiet, doing his best to keep his chin up, his shoulders back. So much weight for a boy, a weight I knew well and could do little to help him carry. I had my own burdens.

The last few days, though, felt different. Our takeover of the Gate cavern—a place I thought long lost to us with the death of my darling Liam—had given my children a refuge from the world, a space that welcomed us with intelligence and love. Shielded us from the outside in ways I could only be grateful for and refused to question. I now knew why this place remained despite Liam's loss. He'd stayed behind, left his soul here for us, in case we would need him again.

I dabbed at a tear in the corner of my eye and held still as Gabriel peeked around the edge of the book case in the Gate archive room, cheeks bright and flushed, hazel eyes sparking green. His tousled, blond curls glinted with red in the low light, reminding me with poignant hurt just how much I'd lost the day Fate took my husband away.

I envied them, Gabriel and Ethie, as his sister dashed from the darkness of a shadowed enclosure, leaping for her brother like a tiger ready to take down her prey. Gabriel snorted a giggle and spun, running back the way he'd come, into the endless distance that was the stacks of the archive. I listened to the two of them howl their glee, my daughter's frowning face no longer a thundercloud of judgment and hurt. At least at the moment. Her anger at me would return, I had no doubt.

I'd earned it.

For now, I simply sat with Liam's computer in my lap, staring after them with my lips aching from the unaccustomed expression, wishing he was here to see.

And unable to let go of the possibility maybe—why

was I torturing myself exactly?—just maybe, he might be able to. Magic was funny stuff, wasn't it? And hadn't I just discovered his soul had remained behind here, or a piece of it, anyway. In the archive where he learned he was Gatekeeper to the Sidhe realm. Hadn't that dear, precious soul connected me to Alison in the void, granting me precious answers I needed? In effect, saving me as he'd always tried so hard to do?

Wasn't it my turn to do the same for him?

Why had it taken me this long to realize Liam was exactly who I needed after all? I shivered at the thought of him knowing how Quaid and I turned out, though my darling Sidhe Gatekeeper would never judge me. Things would have been so different, wouldn't they, if Liam had lived? No Gateway, for one. The Universe intact. Dark Brother without a way to cross from his side to this one, the threat of his powerful soldiers, The Order, vanished with the hurt and loss and death of the past... how long?

Dear elements, had it only been eight months since Zoe Helios crash landed in my back yard and signaled the end of my happily ever after?

I looked down at Liam's computer in my lap, slowly lifted the lid. This was torture, exquisite and demanding. I should have changed the image on the screensaver, should have erased it so I could focus on the task at hand instead of staring for endless amounts of time at the smiling, beautiful couple holding each other, barely twenty two and fresh and, though they had gone through a great deal, so in love. Was I ever that young?

I traced one finger down Liam's cheek, smiling back at him, a soft splash of moisture landing and spreading over the keyboard. I wiped it hastily away, dashed at the tears on my cheeks, unbidden as always when it came to Liam. I'd fought so hard to keep inside all the hurt I'd gathered to me over the years. Being here, knowing how close he was to me, how near he had been... the frustration that I'd lost him again was almost unbearable.

I slammed shut the computer and set it aside, rising to the sound of my children's giggles in the distance. While it might have been an unhealthy obsession, Liam had waited long enough. If there was any way to bring him out of the Gate space where his soul had resided, I would find it. Selfish, of course. Not to save him, or not just to save him, but to have him by my side during the darkest time of my life.

I needed him, plain and simple. And the children would benefit from his presence, too, wouldn't they? We all would. And anyone who told me he wasn't enough— strong enough, powerful enough—could go to hell and stay there.

Never mind Gram told me the piece of him he'd left behind was burned up, gone. I'd believed her at the time. But being here the past few days, living in this space that felt so much like him, I was beginning to doubt her. And allowed maybe more hope than was healthy for my already shattered heart.

Whatever the truth, good or bad, I'd find it. Liam deserved the best from me.

My feet carried me out of the archive and into the passage, down the hall to the Gate room itself. Knees bending of their own accord, I sank to the ground, looking up at the stunning carved form of the route between my world and the Sidhe realm. How simple it seemed to me now, though at the time of its discovery I was in awe of the power of the Gate. But over a decade of regular travel through the veil between worlds— including time spent as a drach—had left this place unremarkable in some ways.

And incredibly precious in others.

If what Gram said was true, that Liam was gone at last, so be it. I just couldn't bring myself to believe it. After all, the fact he'd stayed at all, remained stuck here for all this time, was a miracle. And I believed in miracles, these days. I had to. They were the only things keeping me from crumpling to the floor and weeping in desperate loss.

There was no doubt in my mind I had bigger things to worry about than this. Giant, huge, Universe ending things. The practical part of me demanded I stand up, exit the Gate cavern's protective space and get the hell back to it already before the entirety of creation imploded on itself.

But.

This was Liam we were talking about. And true love had to come first.

I refused to regret Quaid or my marriage to him. We'd created Ethie, after all, our gorgeous if stubborn and distinctly Hayle daughter. And despite our differences I still had fond memories of the quiet time we'd managed, that short and delightfully dull eight years between one disaster and the next. But it was clearer to me now than ever before the magic my mother and Batsheva Moromond embedded in us as infants was the only thing that held us together all that time. Severing it as I did left me empty and sad, but relieved, too.

Free. I liked freedom. I had so little of it.

Liam's loss gnawed at me as I let my mind wander. Not for the first time I reached out with my power, seeking him again. His touch was the most familiar thing in the world, should have been easy to locate for my not-inconsiderable magic. I had the strength of the Universe behind me it seemed at times and yet, tears returning as frustration won, I clenched my teeth against the frustration of my inability to find one lost, dear soul. Refusing to believe, at last, Gram had been right.

Refusing.

I exhaled at last, angry, sorrowful, turning my face from the Gate. My gaze dropped, eyes falling to the black ribbon wound around my wrist. It twitched, sympathetic, the end stirring to stroke my skin.

"Help me," I whispered to it. "Please, I ask so little. Help me find him."

It tried, I'll give it that. It joined its power to mine, enough the suspicion I had about its origins added an extra layer of surety. Its power felt different, more like sorcery than drach magic. Max's supposition it came from the Dark Universe seemed to be correct, though it had never once threatened or tried to harm me. To the contrary. It had saved me a few times so far, including two ill-conceived attempts to reach the vampires in the void space between the edges of the veil.

The slender, pulsing ribbon of the drach soul I wore tried its best yet again, as it had since the moment Andre Dumont's dying vengeance against his former ally landed this treasure in my possession. I wondered at times what Liander Belaisle, the former leader of the Brotherhood and now pawn of Dark Brother in our Universe, would have accomplished with the ribbon in his grasp. I'd never know. He'd have to pry it from my cold, dead wrist.

Despite its attempt, and mine, our joined power twining through and around the magic of the Gate, diving deeply into the magic that created the barrier between my world and the Sidhe, we found nothing. Not a scrap, a hint, a breath of Liam. At last the ribbon settled on my skin and sighed.

I stroked it gently, sadly. "Thank you."

It twitched in its own frustration before falling still.

Another failure. But I wasn't giving up. Not on Liam, not ever again. There was a way and I would find it. Because he would never have given up on me.

I didn't have time to further beat myself to an internal pulp of regret and guilt. Not when the air of the chamber whispered behind me and a familiar power touched mine.

Anger rose against her as I felt my jaw tighten on its own in response to her arrival. The last time I'd seen her, she'd betrayed me. I didn't get up, didn't even look at her as Fate waited for my attention.

"Zoe," I said, voice rough. "I was wondering when you'd show up."

ABOUT THE AUTHOR

Everything you need to know about me is in this one statement: I've wanted to be a writer since I was a little girl, and now I'm doing it. How cool is that, being able to follow your dream and make it reality? I've tried everything from university to college, graduating the second with a journalism diploma (I sucked at telling real stories), am part of an all-girl improv troupe (if you've never tried it, I highly recommend making things up as you go along as often as possible). I've even been in a Celtic girl band (some of our stuff is on YouTube!) and was an independent film maker. My life has been one creative thing after another—all leading me here, to writing books for a living.

Now with multiple series in happy publication, I live on beautiful and magical Prince Edward Island (I know you've heard of Anne of Green Gables) with my very patient husband and multitude of pets.

I love-love-love hearing from you! You can reach me (and I promise I'll message back) at patti@pattilarsen.com. And if you're eager for your next dose of Patti Larsen books (usually about one release a month) come join my mailing list! All the best up and coming, giveaways, contests and, of course, my observations on the world (aren't you just dying to know what I think about everything?) all in one place: http://smarturl.it/PattiLarsenEmail.

Last—but not least!—I hope you enjoyed what you read! Your happiness is my happiness. And I'd love to hear just what you thought. A review where you found this book would mean the world to me—reviews feed writers more than you will ever know. So, loved it (or not so much), **your honest review would make my day**. Thank you!